Days Of Perdition

V Plague Book Six

DIRK PATTON

Dirk Patton

Text Copyright © 2015 by Dirk Patton

Copyright © 2015 by Dirk Patton

Published by Voodoo Dog Publishing, LLC

2824 N Power Road

Suite #113-256

Mesa, AZ 85215

Printed in the United States of America

First Printing, 2015

ISBN-13: 978-1511505024

ISBN-10: 1511505028

Dirk Patton

Days Of Perdition
Table of Contents

Author's Note

Thank you for purchasing Days Of Perdition, Book 6 in the V Plague series. If you haven't read the first five books you need to stop reading now and pick them up, otherwise you will be lost as this book is intended to continue the story in a serialized format. I intentionally did nothing to explain comments and events that reference book 1 through 5. Regardless, you have my heartfelt thanks for reading my work and I hope you're enjoying the adventure as much as I am. As always, a good review on Amazon is greatly appreciated.

Days Of Perdition

Always on the run

A destiny

It's the rising sun

I was born

A shotgun in my hands

Behind the gun

I'll make my final stand

Bad Company - Five Finger Death Punch

1

Katie Chase cursed, jamming the transmission of her husband's truck into reverse. As usual when she drove the mammoth beast he loved so much, she had pulled too far into the garage and slightly angled. She missed her little Mercedes, but John had left for Atlanta on a business trip early that morning and had driven her car because his truck was too tall to fit in the parking garage at the airport. She normally drove him when he flew so she didn't have to give up her car, plus she liked that last goodbye kiss at the curb, but today she'd had a full schedule and no time for the more than hour long round trip.

Finally getting into the right spot, Katie turned off the rumbling engine, grabbed her purse and yoga matt and jumped down from the driver's seat. She had just finished an intense hour and a half yoga session followed by coffee with a friend and was running behind schedule. They'd dawdled too long. She still had to run five miles then spend half an hour kicking and punching the combat dummy set up on the far side of the garage.

Days Of Perdition

The treadmill was as boring as ever, but the time passed quickly with The Real Housewives of New Jersey playing on the TV. Taking a short break, Katie rehydrated then threw herself into attacking the man sized BOB or Body Opponent Bag. It was hot in the garage and by the end of her half hour workout she was dripping with sweat. Toweling off, she grabbed more Coconut water, shivered under the air conditioning in the house and headed for the back yard.

Stepping out, the heat hit her like a physical presence. It was summertime in Arizona. She glanced at the thermometer. 113. It was only 1:30 in the afternoon, the hottest time of day still four hours away. Finishing her drink, Katie sat down on the shaded patio and checked the calendar on her phone. John's flight would be landing within half an hour.

He always texted to let her know he'd landed safely. Wanting to be ready to text him right back, she peeled off all of her sweat soaked clothes and dove nude into the sparkling blue pool. Half an hour later, refreshed from her swim, Katie grabbed her phone when it dinged to indicate she'd received a text message.

"In ATL. Cops everywhere. Odd. Love U!"
It was from John. Katie smiled and texted back, then gathered up her clothes and headed inside.

Stepping out of the shower half an hour later, she dried off and paused to examine her body in a full-length mirror. Turning side to side she was pleased with what she saw and knew her husband certainly was. Despite years of marriage, John still acted like a teenager, always trying to sneak a peek and the damn man had the fastest hands she'd ever seen. She missed him already, and with a smile pulled on a lightweight sundress. She left her long, thick hair wet, knowing the Arizona summer air would suck the water out of it in no time.

The remainder of the afternoon went by quickly. Katie went and had her nails done, came home and paid a few bills, shopped online for a bit, then prepared a lite dinner for herself. At 6:00 PM she gave up on waiting for John to call. It was 9:00 PM in Atlanta and she was surprised but not concerned that she hadn't heard anything from him. She dialed his number, but the call went immediately to his voice mail. Hanging up without leaving a message she paused, considering the idea she'd just had. With a smile she ran into the closet, let the dress drop to the floor around her feet and once she had the pose she liked, snapped a pic of her naked body reflecting in the mirror. A moment later she texted the image to her husband, pulled the dress back on and returned to the living room.

With a sigh, Katie turned the TV on and clicked through channels until she found something to watch. It wasn't football and no one was shooting anyone, so she knew John would hate it. She tried his number a couple more times, but now she couldn't even get his voicemail. The call just failed each time.

Shortly after 8:30 she groaned when the show she was watching was interrupted. A "Breaking News" banner appeared diagonally across the screen and a deep male voice intoned that the network was interrupting the normally scheduled program with an urgent newsbreak.

Five minutes after a harried news anchor began describing the nuclear detonations in New York, DC and LA, she snatched up her phone and tried to call John again. Call failed. She tried twice more with the same results, finally giving up and nearly flinging the phone across the room in frustration.

Katie sat glued to the TV, wanting more information than what the talking head kept repeating. Intellectually she knew the network didn't have any additional news to share, but emotionally she was furious that all she really knew was that nuclear bombs had been set off in three major American cities.

"Stupid!" She said to herself when she remembered the satellite phone John kept for emergencies.

Jumping to her feet she dashed into his office to the gun safe that took up half of one wall. She came to a stop when she looked at the keypad, unable to remember the combination. Thinking for a minute she ran back to the sofa where'd she left her iPhone and snatched it up. John had made her put the combination in the Notes app on the phone, despite her assurances that she'd remember the combination and her doubts that she'd ever need to open the safe on her own.

Thankful that he had insisted, she punched in the number, the locking bolt clicking loudly when it released. Spinning the wheel she tugged the heavy door open and looked inside. A row of four assault rifles was centered, three shotguns to the left and two large caliber bolt action rifles with long distance scopes to the right. Two shelves held a variety of handguns. Below that on the floor of the safe were neatly arranged cases of ammunition and another shelf with stacks of loaded magazines.

The inside of the door had several pockets and a thin, black cord disappeared out of one of these into the back of the safe where it was plugged in to an internal electrical outlet. Pulling open the Velcro cover, Katie retrieved a small satellite phone and hit the power button. While she waited for it to power up her eyes ran over the weapons.

She may have settled into a suburban lifestyle, appearing to be nothing more than a spoiled housewife whose biggest concerns were working out and shopping, but Katie was hardly what she appeared. Nearly fifteen years as a case officer for the CIA had hardened and sharpened her. That may have been in her past, but once your eyes are opened the way that job had opened hers, you can never look at the world the same way again.

Reaching into the safe, Katie grabbed one of John's shotguns and quickly fed seven shells of buckshot into it. Carrying the weapon in both hands, she ran to the master bedroom and after laying it on the foot of the bed she pulled the dress over her head and tossed it onto the floor. She quickly pulled clothes out of a drawer, dressing in a pair of heavy cargo pants and a tank top with a black T-shirt over it. Dashing into the bathroom she took a moment to put her hair up in a ponytail then ran into her closet.

In the back of the closet, behind boxes full of stylish high-heeled shoes, she found what she was looking for. A pair of desert tan combat boots that John had given her a couple of birthdays ago. She had been less than enthralled with the gift, but he'd made up for it by taking her dress shopping after dinner at her favorite restaurant.

She'd only worn the boots when she'd gone out into the desert with him, but they were sturdy, supportive and had steel caps protecting her toes. Pulling them on, she laced them up and paused a moment to remember the right way to tie them so they stayed tied. Dressed, she grabbed a small backpack and ran to the bedroom where she threw in some clean underwear and a change of clothes.

Shotgun in hand and pack over her shoulder, Katie quickly returned to the safe. She threaded a holster and a magazine carrier onto her belt and grabbed John's favorite pistol. It was a

large frame .45 caliber and five loaded magazines `
were neatly stacked next to it. Slapping one of
those into the weapon, she racked the slide to
chamber a round, set the safety on and holstered
the heavy gun. Two more loaded mags went into
the carrier on her belt, the last two tossed into her
pack along with a box of fifty shotgun shells.

Placing the pack between the door to the
garage and the front door, Katie racked the
shotgun to load a round and leaned it up against
the wall. Feeling marginally more secure, she
made sure the keys for the big Ford were in her
pocket before picking up the sat phone again. She
had just turned on the screen, peering at it to see if
the phone had locked onto a satellite signal when
the doorbell rang.

Katie jumped and almost dropped the
phone, barely suppressing a small scream. Taking a
deep breath she forced herself to calm down.
Training at the CIA's Farm at Camp Peary in Virginia
had been a long time ago. Work in the field where
keeping her thoughts, feelings and emotions in
check could mean the difference between life and
death was something she had put behind her, but
by the time the bell rang a second time she had
calmed her breathing and heart rate.

John had been known to answer the door with a weapon in his hand if they weren't expecting visitors. Even though they lived in an upscale community with large, iron gates restricting access, he constantly reminded her that the gates only kept out people with good intentions. Part of her felt a little foolish as she drew the pistol and clicked the safety off, her index finger resting along the outside of the trigger guard.

But the practical side that had served her so well for many years was coming out. Katie had seen firsthand how swiftly society could disintegrate in response to a disaster, whether natural or man-made in origin. She'd done a tour in Bosnia and a few other hotspots around the world during her time with the Agency, and knew that neighbor could and would turn on neighbor. Stepping to the door she looked through the spy hole, relieved when she recognized her friends from two doors down.

Holstering the pistol, Katie unbolted and opened the door. The older couple standing there smiled at her and she quickly ushered them in before closing and bolting the door behind them.

"We know John's out of town and we wanted to check on you, dear." Janice Wilson said, concern creasing her still beautiful face as she looked Katie up and down.

"I'm fine," Katie said, leading the way deeper into the house where all of them paused to stare at the horrific images playing on the TV. After a few minutes the husband, Mike Wilson, broke the silence.

"You look better prepared than we are," he said, pointedly glancing at the pistol on Katie's hip and the shotgun resting by the front door.

"Well, you know John." Katie said with a forced smile. She wasn't one who liked to show her emotions to other people. John was different. He was her husband, but she had no interest in this disintegrating into a crying jag with Janice.

"Have you heard from him?" Janice asked, taking a seat on a bar stool at the kitchen island.

"I got a text when he arrived in Atlanta this afternoon, but nothing since. I was just going to try to get through with a satellite phone." She held the phone up for them to see.

While they watched, Katie checked the signal lock again, muttering to herself when it still said 'searching'. Walking out into the back yard she moved out from under the roof that covered the patio and stood by the edge of the pool, nothing between the phone and the sky above. The phone quickly locked onto a signal and she dialed John's number.

Her heart skipped a beat when it started ringing, but it only rang once then she received an "all circuits are busy – please try your call again later" message. She tried three more times with the same results, shaking her head when Mike and Janice walked out and stood next to her on the pool deck.

Mike looked calm, or as calm as anyone could, but Janice appeared to be heading down the path to hysteria. Her husband circled his arm around her shoulders and pulled her close, gently rubbing her shoulder. Suddenly Katie just wanted them to leave. She had her own worries, and didn't need to be burdened with anyone else's.

"Do you have anything to drink?" Mike asked. "I think we could all use a stiff shot and see what we can find out about what's going on."

Katie looked at him, considering asking them to leave, but despite his outward demeanor she could tell that Mike was only keeping it together for Janice's benefit. Compassion won out and she led the way inside and pulled a bottle of vodka out of the freezer.

2

Katie poured three shots that were all downed quickly. The ice-cold alcohol was smooth at first, but blossomed into a pleasant fire when it hit her stomach. She wanted a second shot, but was more concerned with keeping her head clear. Her guests weren't so pragmatic. When Katie didn't pour another round Mike picked up the bottle and refilled his and his wife's glasses. The second shots disappeared as quickly as the first and he was reaching for a third when Katie put her hand on his.

"Maybe that's enough for now, Mike." She said. "We need to stay sharp."

Janice pushed their hands out of the way and poured herself a third, which she swallowed in a single gulp, refilling her glass before Katie could take the bottle away and return it to the freezer.

"OK, that's really enough." She said, her tone firm. "I don't need either of you getting drunk."

Mike nodded and they moved to the couches arranged in the large room where the TV was located.

The news was looping footage from military drones showing the devastation of New York City. The anchor had caught his stride and was narrating non-stop, managing to not give out any new information while at the same time not repeating himself. Then they cut away to a video that had been uploaded from LA. It had obviously been shot with a cell phone and showed two mushroom clouds climbing into the evening sky.

The video lasted for nearly a minute and the three of them were riveted to the screen. When the video ended the network restarted it, the anchor continuing to babble about the horrific attacks. He said he wouldn't speculate on who was responsible, then immediately opined that the attacks were most likely the work of a radical Islamist terrorist group.

Katie shook her head at the man's ignorance. This wasn't terrorism. This was a state sponsored attack. An act of war. She well knew how dangerous the terrorists were, but the thought of any group being able to get there hands on what was being reported as a minimum of ten nuclear weapons, and use them in such a precise and coordinated manner was ludicrous. This was most likely North Korea or Iran. It had to be some country with leaders that were so out of touch with reality that they thought they could successfully attack the US and get away with it.

The images on the screen changed again, switching to a reporter in Chicago, drawing Katie's attention back to the TV.

"...thousands of people have been affected by whatever was released from the small plane, perhaps tens of thousands." The reporter was a blonde woman, standing on a street corner in downtown Chicago. In the background dozens of bodies were clearly visible lying on the pavement, the sidewalk or in one case draped across the hood of a car. The respirator the reporter was wearing muffled the woman's voice, and she would have looked ridiculous if not for the terror that was plain in her eyes.

She started talking again, babbling on about a plane and something having been released into the air. As she was speaking, several of the bodies in the background began moving. The cameraman must have alerted her. She turned to look, then started walking towards them, the camera following. A man climbed to his feet on the far side of the street, staggering like he was either drunk or hurt. Moments later two women stood up, looking around and spotting the reporter that was coming towards them.

Katie, Mike and Janice stared in shock as the two women screamed and charged directly at the reporter. The woman froze, unsure what was happening, and was tackled to the street a moment before the camera operator was either taken down or dropped the camera and ran. The reporter was still half in the shot as the two females tore her apart, her screams abruptly being cut off when one of them locked her teeth onto the woman's throat and tore it out.

"What the fuck was that?" Mike shouted, leaping to his feet.

Katie had stood up also, fear pulsing through her body. The screen changed to images of what looked like riots in Detroit, Dallas, Miami and Atlanta. When Atlanta came on the screen, Katie stopped breathing.

Downtown Atlanta was a nightmare. The streets were full of running women and stumbling men. Finally the footage from Atlanta ended and they were looking at thousands of people tearing others apart with their bare hands in Seattle.

"What's going on?" Mike asked again. Katie looked at him but couldn't respond, turning her attention back to the TV as it cut to Atlanta again.

Fires were burning in several large buildings in the downtown area. A local TV station actually had a helicopter in the air, and it was zeroed in on the fast moving flames. As they watched, fire leapt a narrow alley, igniting the building next to one that was already burning furiously.

Katie dashed back outside and as soon as the sat phone had signal she hit redial. John's phone didn't even ring. All she heard was an error message telling her the network was temporarily unavailable. Hitting the end button to silence the repeating message, fear for John gripped her heart and it took every ounce of her self-control to hold back the tears that were threatening to start.

She'd never made a trip to Atlanta with her husband. She knew he was in one of the cities that was in the metropolitan Atlanta area, but had no idea which one or how far it was from downtown. Why the hell hadn't she paid more attention?

Looking up through the glass door, she could see Mike and Janice still glued to the TV. What was she going to do? What could she do? Katie wandered over to where John stashed his cigarettes, for the first time in ten years wanting one to help her think. John thought he was hiding them from her. He was cute like that, she thought, and couldn't help but smile. Retrieving the pack and some matches she lit one and slowly lowered herself onto a padded patio chair.

Was the Phoenix area safe? That was the first question. How many and which cities had been attacked with the nerve gas? So far, from the news, she knew that Chicago, Detroit, Miami, Atlanta and Seattle had fallen. But where else? This was a well coordinated, professionally planned and executed strike on America. There would be more cities. But how many more?

And what about John? Katie well knew what he was capable of, having witnessed it for herself live and in person the night they'd met. But Atlanta was what, 2,000 miles away? How could she ever hope he'd be able to make his way home? The thought of trying to get to Atlanta passed through her head, but was completely dismissed as foolish. Even if she made it, which was very unlikely, the possibility of finding John was basically zero.

Drawing deep on the cigarette, she checked on the Wilsons. They were still on the couch, staring at more horror unfolding on the screen. Mike Wilson was a pilot and he had his own plane! How the hell had she forgotten that? Jabbing the butt into a small ashtray John also kept hidden, Katie leapt to her feet and charged into the house.

"Mike, you still have a plane. Right?" She asked.

"Yeah. Why?" He turned to look at her and she could see the terror in his face from watching the TV.

"Can it make it to Atlanta?" She asked.

"It could. But you really can't be thinking about going there. The fire is spreading and they're saying the whole city will be burning by morning." Katie could hear the panic in his voice.

She rushed into the kitchen and grabbed the vodka out of the freezer, pouring two small shots and carrying them to the couch where Mike and Janice were sitting. Both of them grabbed the glasses like the liquid was their salvation, tipping them up and downing the drinks. Mike coughed once, wiped his mouth and looked at Katie.

"There have to be plenty of airfields in the area that are clear of the fire." Katie said, realizing how foolish it sounded as soon as she said it. Even if they could make it into the area, where did she start looking? For that matter, John wasn't going to just sit still and wait for her to come find him. She knew better than to think that. Damn it, what did she do?

3

The Wilsons seemed settled in and Katie decided not to ask them to leave. Together, they sat and watched the news unfolding from around the country as more and more cities began to fall to the nerve gas attacks. By 11:00 PM, Arizona time, the news stations had set up a reporting format similar to what they used on national election nights to tally the number and location of attacks. At a little after 11:30 the anchor said the President would be giving a speech to the nation from aboard Air Force One, but as time wore on they never cut away from the frightening reports from around the country.

Katie made at least twenty more attempts to reach John with the satellite phone, none successful. Looking up numbers he'd given her for co-workers and friends, she tried each of them, but none of the calls were going through. At 12:30 she thought about food. She wasn't hungry. She suddenly realized that the damage to America's infrastructure was so significant that deliveries to grocery stores were probably a thing of the past.

Standing in the middle of the kitchen she looked around then opened the pantry and surveyed its contents. Not much on hand, and similar results when she checked the refrigerator. She and John were in the habit of only shopping for a couple of days of food at a time. They primarily only ate fresh foods, preferring organics, and as a result there was no stock of canned or frozen foods in their home to fall back on.

"We need to go get food. Now." She said to the Wilsons, distracting them from a report out of Memphis that showed a sea of people surging forward to attack a hospital.

"If you're hungry we've got plenty of food at our place." Janice said, looking confused.

"That's not what I mean," Katie said. "Look at what's going on. There's not going to be any more deliveries of food for some time to come. We need to stock up before it's too late. I'm going to the Safeway. They're open 24 hours. You should come with me. We can fill up the truck."

"She's right," Mike said, standing up. Janice remained seated on the sofa, looking frightened.

"Janice, Mike and I will go. You stay here and see if the President comes on." Katie was actually relieved to have an excuse to leave the woman at home. She and Mike could move faster without her.

"If you think that's best, dear." Janice sounded relieved.

Katie led the way to the garage, grabbing the shotgun on the way through the door. She and Mike climbed into the truck, Katie starting the engine a moment before pushing the button to raise the door. She backed out of the garage and down the long driveway, accelerating towards the gates that guarded access to their neighborhood.

The grocery store was only a few miles away and they drove in silence. There weren't any other vehicles on the road, which was slightly comforting for Katie. "But this is only a few hours old," she thought to herself.

Safeway was on the corner of a major intersection, the lot brightly lit when Katie steered into it. It was rare that she or John had been shopping this late and she was mildly surprised that there were only half a dozen cars in the parking lot. She didn't know if this was normal or not, parking with a few empty spaces between her and the closest vehicle. The last time she'd been to the store after midnight was two years ago when John was sick with the flu and she'd run out to pick up some medicine for him.

She and Mike stepped out and for a brief moment Katie thought about bringing the shotgun with her, but decided that wasn't a good idea at this point. Things should still be fairly normal, so she locked the weapon in the cab of the truck. She did have the holstered .45 and had no qualms about walking around with it.

As they approached the automatic glass doors, both of them paused to read a large hand lettered sign that announced that credit card processing was down and the store was only accepting cash.

"There's an ATM inside," Mike said. "Maybe it's still working."

They stepped forward, the doors sliding open at their approach. To their left were the checkout lanes. Three men with several shopping carts piled to overflowing were arguing with the cashier. The clerk was telling them that he had no way to accept a credit card, and they had to pay in cash. A man that was most likely the night manager was walking swiftly towards the commotion at the register.

Mike started toward the ATM, which was close to the confrontation, but Katie placed a hand on his arm to stop him. The men with the full carts weren't backing off, and she didn't like the vibe she was getting from their body language. Instead she headed to the right, Mike in tow, fading into the produce area of the store. They had just stepped behind a large table loaded with apples and pears when several gunshots sounded from the front of the store.

Drawing her pistol, Katie pushed Mike towards the back of the building, urging him into a run. She didn't know if the men had noticed them come in or not, or if they would even worry about witnesses to their crime, but she didn't want to stand around and find out. Ahead she could see a set of stainless steel swinging doors that led to the stock area and she charged through, Mike on her heels.

Two teenagers, a boy and a girl dressed in jeans and Safeway T-shirts, were just inside the door. Katie ran into the boy when she slammed through the doors, knocking him to the floor. She stumbled but was able to recover. The girl stood looking at her, eyes wide with fear as she stared at the pistol. The boy wound up on his back, scrambling away from the crazy woman with the gun.

"Don't hurt us!" He cried as he kept scooting away. Mike stepped around Katie and reached out for the boy.

"Quiet! Some men just shot your cashier and we're hiding from them." He said.

Katie scanned the area and not seeing anyone else moved to the swinging doors and peered through the small glass windows. One of the men she'd seen arguing at the register was standing in the produce section, a chrome revolver in his hand, looking around. He spotted the doors she was hiding behind and started walking in her direction.

"Who else is in the store?" Katie asked the frightened girl.

"Why?" She asked.

"Because the men that shot your cashier and manager are walking around out there looking for witnesses."

"Oh my God!" The girl said. A moment later she started crying.

"Just the four of us," the boy said from the floor. "Julie and I clean and take product out for Bob and Tim to stock. They're really dead?"

"Yes they are, and one of the killers is coming. Is there a back way out of here?" Katie asked.

The boy swallowed nervously, then climbed to his feet. "This way," he said, grabbing Julie's arm and pulling her along as he led the way to the rear wall where a man door was located next to a large rolling door.

A push bar ran across the middle of the door, a large paddle attached to it with a red warning sticker stating an alarm would sound if pressed. The boy fished a key out of his pocket and used it to unlock a spring-loaded deadbolt, letting them open the door without having to use the bar. They moved through quickly, Katie softly closing the door behind them.

They were on the store's loading dock. A ramp next to them allowed semi trailers to be backed up to the rolling door. A large mercury vapor light was set high in the wall over their heads, brightly illuminating the whole area. Katie led the way off the dock and past a pair of stinking dumpsters, then into the dark at the end of the store.

Hugging the wall they moved to the front edge of the building. They stood in darkness, Katie and Mike looking around the corner into the well-lit parking lot. Two of the men were loading food into two different vehicles. The third man wasn't in sight. They had just finished emptying the shopping carts when the third came running out of the front of the store, several cartons of cigarettes under one arm and big bottle of liquor in his hand.

The man with the booze shoved the carts away to roll across the parking lot where one slammed into the passenger door of John's truck. Katie wished John was here to kick the man's ass, but settled for being happy when all three of them jumped into their vehicles and sped away. Taking a deep breath she holstered the pistol and grabbed Mike's arm.

"Let's go," she said. "The store's empty."

"What? We have to call the police! They just murdered two people." He sounded like he was in shock.

"Fine. If you can find a working phone, you call them." Katie said. "This is just the beginning. We need to get what we came for and get out of here."

Katie turned and looked at the two teenagers. Julie was still crying, the boy holding her as she sobbed. "You two should go home. Now. Go be with your families."

The boy looked at her and nodded, leading Julie out into the parking lot and helping her get into a lowered Honda Civic. He got behind the wheel and it started with a high-pitched snarl of exhaust, then he roared away with a squealing of tires.

"The police would want to talk to them," Mike said, following Katie to the front of the store where she grabbed two carts. She paused and turned to look at him.

"Mike, you've seen what's happening. The police aren't going to come. How many of them do you think have already gone home to protect their families? We can't count on them, or anyone other than ourselves. You just have to trust that I know what I'm talking about. Now, we need to load up some carts and get the hell out of here before more people show up and decide to take away what's ours."

Katie pushed the two carts through the automatic doors at a trot, heading for the aisle with canned foods first. A few moments later she heard the doors open again, followed by the wobbly squeal of shopping cart wheels as Mike followed her back into the store.

When they returned to the house Janice was still seated on the sofa, but the bottle of vodka was sitting on the table in front of her. Katie eyed it and noted the level of the alcohol was significantly lower than the last time she'd put it away. Picking the bottle up she made sure the cap was tight and returned it to the freezer. Janice was visibly drunk, staring at the TV with watery eyes, slurring her words as she talked to her husband.

"We should go to Mexico until this all blows over." She said. "We could stay with the Allens in Cabo for a while."

Mike looked at her, thinking about it for a moment before turning to Katie. "You should come with us. It's a six hour flight in my plane. We can leave a note for John."

"I can't leave," Katie shook her head. "Not yet. If there's anyone that can make it home, it's him. But you two should go if you have a place to stay. I'm afraid it's going to get really bad here."

Katie didn't really want to be alone, but she sure wasn't interested in having to be responsible for the Wilsons. She knew Janice liked to drink, and it was looking like that was going to be a problem. A problem she didn't need.

Mike stood in thought, looking around at the TV as footage of Atlanta burning played on the screen. He looked at Katie and nodded his head, leaning down and taking his wife's hands and pulling her to her feet.

"We're going to go get ready to go. We'll be leaving in about fifteen minutes if you change your mind."

Katie stepped forward and hugged each of them, wishing them luck, then walked them to the front door and securely bolted it when they exited. With a sigh of relief she went to the garage and started carrying armloads of canned goods into the house. She worked for some time, sorting out the food she'd looted from the grocery store.

Two cases of bottled water were brought into the house, but she left four more in the truck. She also left a couple of week's worth of food, not wanting to contemplate having to make a quick departure, but knowing she needed to be prepared. Food distributed between the house and the truck, she went back to the gun safe and pulled the door open.

Already knowing which rifle she wanted, Katie grabbed it out of the safe, slapped in a loaded magazine and pulled the charging handle to put a round into the chamber. She rummaged in a closet until she found a larger pack, stuffing it full of loaded magazines. Unable to think of anything else to do she returned to the TV, settling on the sofa with the rifle lying across her lap.

The news was once again playing a loop of the drone footage of the devastation in New York. She cared about New York, cared about the millions of people who were dead or dying, but she wanted them to switch back to the coverage of Atlanta. She had only been watching for a couple of minutes when the screen went blank, then displayed the banner for the Emergency Broadcast System accompanied by a high pitched, dual tone alert.

Grabbing the remote, Katie changed the channel but all she could find was the same EBS alert. With rising panic she snatched up her iPad to check for news of anything on social media, but the Internet connection was down. She was cut off from any source of information.

4

The morning after the attacks, TV and radio broadcasts hadn't come back on and Katie continued to have no luck in reaching John or any of her friends or family on the satellite phone. She even dug out some numbers from her past and dialed former friends and colleagues that she was reasonably sure were still with the CIA. None of those calls went through either. Buried deep in her jewelry box was a scrap of paper with an international phone number written on it in faded ink.

Taking a deep breath she punched the number in so it was held in memory then replaced the scrap of paper and walked out by the pool to connect with a satellite. When the phone showed it had signal she pressed the SEND button and held it to her ear. There were a couple of clicks then after what felt like a long time she heard a ring. On the sixth ring the call connected, but no one said anything.

"Steve?" She asked tentatively. There was silence for a moment, then a suspicious male voice.

"Who is this?"

"Thank God! It's Katie," she answered, nervous yet relieved to actually reach another person. There was silence on the other end of the phone; just a faint hiss was all that let her know the connection was still open.

"Are you there?" Katie asked after the quiet became unbearable.

Steve Johnson had been a fellow case officer at the CIA, and Katie's former fiancé. They'd been engaged for less than a month when she met John. She and John had fallen in love at first sight, and there hadn't been any going back. She'd broken it off with Steve but he hadn't handled it well. Not that she could blame him. Even after all these years she still felt bad about it, but her heart hadn't given her a choice.

"I'm here. Just surprised to hear from you." His voice was sullen, but at least he hadn't hung up on her. "Are you OK? Where are you?"

"I'm fine. Safe for the moment. I'm at home in Arizona. Are you still with... uhm, our former employer?"

"Our former employer," he laughed. "Yes, and you can say it. C fucking IA. I'm still assigned to a surveillance post in Western Australia.

Keeping an eye on this part of the world, but I don't think that matters much any more."

Katie gripped the phone tighter and took a deep breath. What had happened to Steve? He had always been a happy person, intense about his work, but with a wicked sense of humor and a quick wit. That was what had attracted her to him in the first place. In many ways he was the polar opposite of John, in others they were just alike.

"Why are you calling, Katie? Still married to the hero?"

Steve had been calling John that since he'd found out whom she'd left him for. She had had a high enough clearance level to gain access to John's Army file, but somehow had managed to resist the temptation to check him out. Steve, however, hadn't been able to let it go, and it was the final straw for the CIA when the Army called wanting to know why one of their case officers was reviewing Army Special Forces files. Steve had been demoted, received a formal letter of reprimand and reassigned to a two-man station in the middle of the Western Australia desert.

"That's why I'm calling, Steve. I know I don't have any right to ask, but I'm asking for your help. John is in Atlanta and I haven't been able to reach him. All TV, radio, Internet, phones... everything is down. It's getting scary here and I don't know what to do. Do I stay here and wait for him? Do I try to make it to Atlanta?" Katie didn't like the note of desperation that crept into her voice as she spoke, but there wasn't anything she could do to stop it.

"If everything is down, how are you calling me?" Steve asked, the note of suspicion clear in his voice.

"We had a satellite phone stashed away." Katie said, giving him time to think about her plea for information.

"I've got your number," Steve finally spoke. "Let me see what I can find out and I'll call you back."

"Thank you, Steve." Katie said, flooded with relief. "How long do you think it will take you?"

"As long as it takes." He said curtly before breaking the connection.

Katie slowly exhaled a deep breath, feeling sorry for the man and also feeling a little guilty.

She'd broken his heart when she left him for John. She knew that. But she also knew that she'd made the right decision.

Going back into the house Katie walked through the master bedroom and into the closet. The closet was large with multiple, very long rods for hanging clothes and built-ins for shoe and clothing storage. All but one of the rods was full of her clothes, only two of the slots for shoes holding anything that belonged to John.

She smiled, thinking how he never complained about not having any room in the closet, then reached for one of his jackets and pulled it to her face. There was still a trace of his aftershave and she tried to fight the tears but they got the best of her. Going into the bathroom, she dried her eyes and decided she had to get out of the house for a little while.

A couple of minutes later, heavily armed with pistol, shotgun and rifle, Katie backed out of the driveway and drove through the gates to the main road. Her house was on the far edge of town, only a few miles from National Forest land, and as she expected there wasn't any traffic when she turned to head into the city. She had decided she would go check on a friend who lived a few miles away.

Passing several other gated neighborhoods, she drove slowly and looked carefully at each of them. Not seeing anything concerning, she continued on, slowing as she approached the entrance ramp for the 202 freeway. Two cars were crashed into each other, abandoned, blocking part of the northbound ramp. Letting the truck idle forward, she slowly got a better view of the sprawling city that filled the valley in front of her.

Fires were burning in multiple locations, tall plumes of thick, black smoke rising into the blue sky. The truck's windows were up with the air conditioning on high, and she lowered the driver's window and turned the fan speed to low so she could hear. Sporadic gunfire sounded, somewhere in the distance. There was the hiss of tires from a steady stream of traffic on the freeway, heading north, but the southbound lanes were eerily empty.

Leaving the window down, Katie gently accelerated across the overpass and towards the intersection with the Safeway. She began to see cars moving as people rushed about, most of them ignoring the speed limit and traffic lights. The sound of gunfire grew in volume and intensity as she approached the intersection, then she got a look at the grocery store.

The parking lot was jammed full of angry people, all of them facing a small group of well-armed men who were guarding the entrance. One of the men was firing a rifle in the air, trying to deter the crowd from coming any closer. Katie didn't know if the men guarding the store were actually protecting it, or if they had seized the building and were intent on keeping all of the food for themselves. Either way, she said a small prayer of thanks that she'd gotten in and out with supplies when she had.

Pushing on, she sadly noted that her assessment of depending on the police had been accurate. There was zero police presence, and the mob scene was repeated at another grocery store she drove past. A few vehicles whizzed by her, traveling in the same direction at a high rate of speed. One of them with two men in the front slowed to look her over. Driving with her left hand she drew the pistol with her right, but fortunately they decided to go on about their business, suddenly accelerating away.

"What the hell am I doing?" Katie said to herself.

Her friend was a single woman, divorced actually, but the boyfriend du jour had just moved in with her so Katie knew she wasn't alone. Checking her mirrors, she stepped on the brakes and cranked the big truck through a U turn. Time to go back home before something bad happened.

She had only driven half a mile back to the east when she looked in the mirror and saw a car rapidly approaching from behind. It looked like the same Buick with the two men that had slowed next to her, but she couldn't tell for sure. Resisting the impulse to accelerate, Katie held her speed steady with an eye on the rearview as the car quickly caught up.

A few moments later it swerved to the side, the driver braking to match her speed and put it in position alongside the truck. The passenger leaned out his window and shouted.

"Hey! You look like you could use some help. Pull over so we can talk to you!" He was pointing to the right side of the road.

"I'm fine. Just on my way to pick up my husband." Katie shouted back, hands starting to shake as adrenaline dumped into her system.

"We can help you find him. Just pull over and we'll help you." The man shouted back.

The Buick drifted closer to the truck and looking down from the cab Katie could see a shotgun resting across the man's lap. That didn't mean anything. She was armed too and didn't have any bad intentions. Just because they had guns didn't mean they were bad guys. But she wasn't naïve, and wasn't about to trust them.

"He's just up the road. Him and his brothers. Thanks anyway." She shouted back, knowing her pitiful ruse would most likely not deter them.

She wanted to step on the gas. Go faster. Run away from the men, but there were a couple of big problems with that idea. On pavement there was no way the truck could outrun or out maneuver the much nimbler car. And assuming the men were willing to hang back and follow her, she wasn't about to lead them to her house.

Katie was watching from the corner of her eye and the man made the decision for her when

Dirk Patton

he raised the shotgun and stuck it out his window.
Yanking the steering wheel to the left she smashed
the truck into the side of the Buick. The man
barely got his weapon and arms back in the vehicle
before the side of the Ford struck the car hard
enough to shatter glass and send it spinning across
the oncoming lanes.

The truck weighed roughly twice as much as
the car and Katie had delivered a solid blow. The
car's driver fought the wheel, trying to get them
back under control, but he ran out of road before
he could stop their slide. The Buick came to a stop
in a rock filled water retention basin a few feet off
the side of the street. The rear tires spun uselessly
when he tried to accelerate back onto the
pavement.

Katie was shaking all over, but managed to
control herself and floored the accelerator. The
engine roared as the truck sped up. She hadn't
covered much ground when she heard two booms
from behind her. Not letting off the gas she looked
in the mirror and saw the man who had been
talking to her standing outside the disabled car. He
had fired two blasts from his shotgun, but as far as
she could tell neither had found their mark.

Staying on the throttle Katie shot through a couple of intersections, then forced herself to slow when she realized she'd pushed the truck to over a hundred miles an hour. Slowing to a more sedate speed she looked at the Safeway as she passed, a grim expression settling on her face when she saw several bodies lying in the parking lot. The men were still guarding the front of the store. The crowd in the parking lot had withdrawn behind their vehicles. Even at a glance she could see lots of long guns and didn't want to be anywhere in the area when the real battle started.

She made it home without any further incident, impatiently waiting for first the gate then the garage door to open. Katie didn't step out of the truck until the door was fully closed behind her. She started to survey the damage to the truck, but the dim bulb in the door opener didn't provide enough light. Turning on a bank of overhead fluorescents, she caught her breath.

The sheet metal on the driver's side of the Ford was dented and scraped for most of the length of the vehicle where she'd rammed into the Buick. Walking down the side she stopped and shivered when she saw the damage from two shotgun blasts. The man hadn't missed, and she hadn't been far enough away.

On the left rear fender an area larger than a dinner plate had close to twenty holes punched through the metal. A matching spot was also on the tailgate, directly in line with the driver's seat. If he'd aimed a little higher... Katie started to think, then stopped herself from going there. She had made it back safely, that was what mattered.

Turning the lights off, she walked into the house, poured a stiff shot of vodka and sat down on the couch to see if there was any news being broadcast on the TV.

The time passed slowly, Katie struggling to deal with the tedious boredom. The power was still on so she tried running on the treadmill, but was distracted and after half an hour shut it off. Not only wasn't she in the frame of mind for exercise, she was concerned about not being able to hear anything other than the whine of the belt and her pounding feet. She didn't have any information that conditions had gotten worse, but she didn't see how they could have improved.

A couple of days passed and Steve hadn't called her back. The sat phone didn't have signal and wouldn't ring in the house, so she was in the habit of going outside every half an hour to check for voice mail. Every time she was outside she dialed John's number, but never received anything other than a recorded message that the network was unavailable.

More times than not while outside, she'd hear gunfire. Sometimes it was distant, others it sounded fairly close. The pistol never left her hip and she'd taken to carrying the rifle outside with her, hanging from a one-point sling around her shoulders.

Late in the afternoon she couldn't wait any longer to hear from Steve. Walking out into the heat, she gave the phone time to connect to a satellite then dialed his number. After several rings he answered, sounding groggy from sleep. She'd forgotten the time difference between Arizona and Australia.

They talked for a few minutes, Steve sounding slightly warmer than the first time she'd spoken to him. He had finally found a way late the previous evening to gain access to satellite imagery and filled her in on what he'd seen. He started with Atlanta; her heart sinking when she heard the majority of the city had burned.

He took her around the country, describing the devastation he was seeing and the herds of infected that were starting to form.

"What does the Phoenix area look like?" Katie asked, holding her breath.

"Lots of fires," he said after a few minutes of looking for the right feed and zooming in. "Lots of fighting. There's a steady stream of traffic heading north on the Interstate, but it's barely moving. Where are you in the area? Wait. Never mind. I can pull your GPS location from the phone's signal."

Katie could hear rapid fire typing for a couple of minutes, then just the sound of Steve breathing as he waited for the adjusted feed to display on his screen.

"OK, got you. Is that you standing by a swimming pool?" Katie involuntarily looked skyward, as if she could see the orbiting camera that was capturing her image at the moment.

"That's you," Steve said a moment later. "Just as beautiful as ever."

"Steve…" Katie started to admonish him.

"Sorry," he said. "It's just that I thought I'd never see you or hear from you again. It's really good to be talking to you."

Katie took a breath, biting off her impulse to remind him she was married. He was obviously still not over her, and didn't sound to be in the most stable state of mind. She needed his help and alienating him wasn't the way to go.

"It's good to talk to you, too." She finally said. "Now, tell me what's going on around me. Please."

"OK, the neighborhood you're in is quiet. I don't see any movement or any damage. The gates are still up and intact. Open desert to the east and northeast of you. A couple of trucks driving on the highway that runs up into the mountains to your northeast. Fires to the south of you, but the closest one is five miles away."

Katie turned to look to the south, seeing three plumes of black smoke climbing into the air. "I see the smoke from the fires to the south."

"North of you is more neighborhoods. They all look gated. One of them has had the gates torn out, but I don't see any movement or any other damage. West is... west is a problem. The freeway a few miles to your west is jammed with cars. No vehicles moving, but people are walking along the shoulder and in the median, heading north. What's north?"

"The mountains," Katie answered. "It's summer here. Hot as hell. People are trying to get out of the city and that's the only direction that isn't more desert."

"Makes sense. All right, on west of the freeway it looks like a war zone. We've got burned out buildings and vehicles all over the place. Lots of movement on the ground. Medium sized groups and they're all armed."

"Does it look like any of them are coming this direction?" Katie asked.

"No. They're occupied with fighting each other. Looks like lots of stores and that's where the biggest concentrations of people are." Steve said.

Katie stood silent, processing the information she had just gotten. None of it surprised her. There were five large grocery stores all within a couple of miles of each other and that's what everyone was fighting over. Her fear was that when the stores were stripped bare the mobs were going to start spreading out and forcing their way into homes to take any food the people in them might have.

"What?" Katie asked. Steve had been talking but she hadn't been listening, lost in her own thoughts.

"I said I've been doing some research and I have an idea how to get you out of there." He repeated.

"Steve, I really appreciate all you're doing, but I can't leave. What if John shows up and I'm not here." Katie said.

"Listen to me. This isn't about me or him, this is about getting you to safety. We both know things are only going to get worse, and in a hurry. The country is shattered. Do you really believe he'll make it all the way from Atlanta to Phoenix? That's what? 1,800 miles at least?"

Katie stifled a deep sigh, not wanting Steve to hear her frustration. She knew he was right about the odds, but she also knew her husband. There weren't many like him.

"What's your idea?" She asked, more to placate him than anything.

"Do you know where Gateway airport is?" He asked.

"Yes," Katie said. The airport was a former Air Force bomber base that had been closed due to budget cuts and taken over by the city to supplement the main civil airport in Phoenix. It was about 15 miles due south of where she stood.

"That's the Arizona hub for FedEx. I'm looking at them on satellite right now and they've got half a dozen long range cargo planes sitting on the tarmac. Long range enough to make it here to Western Australia. You remember our contract with them? I've already checked and I can still access their systems and create a flight with you on the manifest. All you have to do is make it to the airport." Steve's voice sounded hopeful. Cautious, but hopeful that she would say yes.

"I have to think about it," Katie finally said, knowing her answer would be no.

"OK, but don't think too long. This will only work as long as there's a pilot available." For the first time since Katie had called him, Steve sounded upbeat.

"I'll think about it," Katie said again. "I'll call you back in a couple of hours to check on the fighting in the area."

"I'll be waiting," Steve said, keeping the connection open until Katie finally pressed the END button.

6

Katie talked to Steve several times over the next few days. Her concern grew as he described what he was seeing on the satellite. What had been small groups at first were now forming into larger crowds. Each one had successfully taken one of the grocery stores, and for the moment things had reached a degree of equilibrium.

More plumes of smoke were visible all around her home, and the sporadic gunfire she heard was coming closer each day. Then, just after noon on the sixth day the power went out. Katie had been expecting it and was more than a little surprised that it had stayed on as long as it had without anyone from the utility maintaining the grid.

Within an hour the temperature inside the house climbed from a comfortable 75 degrees to a stuffy 85. She knew it would only keep climbing as it was well over 110 outside with another eight hours before sunset. She dumped all of the ice from the freezer into a cooler before it could start melting, but there wasn't much else she could do.

Going outside with one of the last bottles of cold water, Katie sat down and lit another of John's stash of cigarettes. Six days since the attacks. She had no idea where John was, or if he was even still alive. Steve had described to her the massive herds of infected moving around in the southeastern part of the country. Had John gotten out ahead of them?

Katie knew that if he'd had the chance to get out, he'd have been able to fight his way clear of about anything. But had he had a chance? He could have fallen victim to the dispersal of the nerve gas. He could have become trapped by one of the massive herds Steve talked about. Any number of things could have happened to him. She was finally ready to acknowledge that it was time for her to do something other than wait for him to show up.

But what? Flee to Australia as Steve wanted her to do? Then what? If she made it was she ready to live her life out without ever knowing what happened to her husband? Maybe she should head to the mountains. The temperatures wouldn't be dangerously hot and she could leave John a note letting him know where she was.

Deciding that was the best course of action, Katie stubbed the cigarette out and stepped into the sun to call Steve. He answered on the first ring, sounding happy to hear from her then disappointed when he learned her final decision was that she wasn't coming to Australia.

"Whatever you do, you need to do it soon." He said in a subdued voice. "There's a large group formed up just to the west of you and they're starting to move into the residential neighborhoods to loot the houses. You don't want to be home when they show up."

"How bad is it?" Katie asked.

"Bad. They're doing things... well, you've seen this happen before. I don't need to tell you what they're doing, especially to people that try to fight back."

"No, I don't want to know." She said. "How does the highway northeast of me going into the mountains look?" Katie wanted to rush inside and make her final preparations to depart, but she couldn't move under cover until she was through speaking with Steve.

"Hold on," he said. Katie could hear him breathing into the phone as he typed for a few moments. Then, "It's wide open at the moment. A few abandoned vehicles along the way, but they're to the side and not blocking the road. There's some traffic moving, but you're far enough out of the city that it seems to have been overlooked."

"Thank you, Steve. I have to start moving now. I'll call you once I'm on the road."

"Do that, and be careful." He said. "I love you."

Steve ended the call quickly, almost before what he'd said had registered with Katie. She paused for a second then dashed into the house. A small pack with some clean clothes was ready to go by the garage door. Grabbing one of John's large packs, Katie filled it with every rifle magazine that was in the safe. A first aid kit went in on top of the magazines and she topped it off with another pistol and several loaded pistol magazines.

Setting this aside she sat down at John's desk and pulled a spiral notepad and pen out of the center drawer. Thinking for a moment, she started writing.

Waited six days. Things were getting bad in the area and I had to leave. I'm going to the place in the mountains where we got drunk and I got mad at you when I thought you were looking at that girl's ass. You have to remember that, and you have to come find me. I'll stay there as long as I can. If I have to move again I'll find a way to leave word for you. Please come find me. I love you! Me

Katie always signed any card or note she wrote to John as Me. She didn't know how it started or why, it just did. Now, that unique quirk would guarantee he would know it was from her. In the modern, digital age she doubted he'd recognize her handwriting any more than she would his. Neither of them actually wrote very often. Tearing the paper off the pad she ran to the large mirror in the entryway and taped it to the middle of the glass.

Rushing, she carried the pack of magazines out to the truck, putting it alongside her bag of clothes in the back seat. Back in the house she grabbed a case of ammunition out of the bottom of the safe and took that to the truck, coming back inside for the cooler full of ice. When this was loaded she grabbed an axe from the garage, tossing it in the bed of the truck along with her looted cans of food.

Seeing the food reminded her to run back inside and get a can opener, a small metal cooking pot and a few basic utensils. When all of this was stowed in the truck she paused to look over her supplies for a moment. Satisfied she was as ready as she would ever be, Katie climbed up behind the wheel and pushed the button to raise the garage door.

The door didn't move. With a curse she remembered the power was out. Jumping back down she looked up at the door opener, but there wasn't enough light near the ceiling for her to tell how to release the mechanism and manually open the door. Realizing she needed a flashlight, Katie ran back into the house and yanked open the closet doors in John's office. Snatching a small LED flashlight off a shelf, she also scooped up a pack of spare batteries and ran back to the truck.

Katie didn't know how to release the door, but she did know it could be released. She'd seen · John do it once when the power went out during a violent thunderstorm. Clicking the flashlight on she played the bright beam across the motor, seeing nothing that looked promising. Examining the track she spied a short rope with a red handle on the end hanging down from what looked like a locking lever. That had to be it.

Climbing up on top of the rear tire, she swung a leg onto the bed cover of the truck to gain enough height to reach the red handle. Pulling, she felt it move a couple of inches, a loud click coming from the lever to which the rope was attached. Jumping down she squeezed between the truck's rear bumper and the door, bending her knees to get low enough to reach the grab handle that was at ground level.

The door moved freely, rolling open in its track as Katie straightened up with her hand wrapped around the handle. She placed her hands on the bottom edge of the door and lifted with a surge, the door rolling the rest of the way and coming to a stop fully open.

Her attention had been on the door and she was surprised when she looked down the driveway and saw two young men standing in the road staring back at her. Both were carrying rifles and wearing backpacks. Katie only had the pistol with her, the rifle and shotgun in the cab of the truck. She froze in place, hand only inches from the holstered weapon, but she had no illusions about being able to draw it quickly and fight with it. That was John's thing, not hers.

Not that she couldn't shoot. She was actually a pretty good shot. On the pistol range with the weapon already in her hand and plenty of time to aim. John had tried to teach her how to quickly draw a handgun and engage a target, but she hadn't been interested. She'd foolishly thought to herself that she didn't need to know how to be a gun fighter with him around.

The two men were frozen also, eyes locked on hers. They both looked surprised to see her, and at least for the moment weren't exhibiting any aggressive behavior.

"I'm leaving," Katie finally shouted to them. "You're welcome to anything in the house. There's food and water inside."

They glanced at each other but didn't answer. After a couple of moments Katie started edging sideways along the back of the truck. She was almost to the corner where she was prepared to turn and make a break for the cab when one of them spoke.

"Wait. Please. Take us with you." Neither of them had raised their weapons, rather had lowered the muzzles even more when the one shouted to her.

Katie paused. Every instinct told her to not trust them. She was a woman by herself, and even though they were young, both were considerably larger than her. If they were close they wouldn't need their weapons to overpower her and take whatever they wanted. Sure, she knew how to fight, but she was also realistic about her chances against two much larger opponents.

As she stood there considering her options and trying to think of a way to turn them down without inciting them into doing something rash, there was a loud, rending crash from down the street. The direction of the gates that secured her neighborhood. The echoes were still bouncing around the neighborhood when she heard a roaring engine approaching.

7

The two men in the street turned to look in the direction of the crash and Katie seized the opportunity to dash deeper into the dark garage. Jerking the door open to the truck, she jumped up on the running board and climbed behind the wheel, pulling the door closed behind her. Turning in the seat she watched out the back window as the men started running.

They headed down the street, away from her house, ducking into the Wilson's driveway before she lost sight of them. The occupant of the vehicle that had crashed the gate must have seen them because a moment later a red Dodge pickup roared past her house and screeched to a stop in front of the Wilson's. Four men hopped out of the bed of the truck, two more exiting the passenger side of the cab, all of them armed and in hot pursuit.

Katie could see the silhouette of the driver's head still behind the wheel of the idling truck. She knew if she backed out of her garage he'd spot her before she made it to the street. But staying where she was wasn't looking like a good option. These guys had to be part of a group that was looting houses, and they had already shown they had no hesitation to attack anyone that wasn't part of their gang.

It was better to go before the others got back. Making her decision, Katie started the Ford, shifted into reverse and floored the gas. The truck shot backwards out of the garage and she nearly lost control when it bounced into the street. Getting it stopped she frantically shifted into drive and pressed the throttle to the floor. The rear tires screamed and smoked for a second, then she shot forward, steering around the curve that led to the gates.

The driver of the Dodge was honking his horn, no doubt calling his friends back so they could pursue her. She didn't think he'd been able to tell she was a woman, and felt some relief about that, though how that helped her at the moment she didn't know. Maybe they wouldn't be as determined to catch her. She hoped, but had no illusions about what happened to women when a society starts disintegrating.

Rounding the curve she caught her breath when she saw another pickup blocking the opening where the entrance gate had been rammed off its mounts. Tightening her grip on the wheel she aimed for the closed exit, keeping her foot firmly on the floor. She had covered half the distance to where the truck was sitting when its occupants noticed her. Racing towards the barricade, she noticed two men stand up in the bed of the pickup a moment before the Ford's bumper slammed into the heavy, iron gate.

The collision was bone jarring, but the momentum of the big Ford battered the gate off its hinges, sending it cartwheeling down the road to bounce off a tree trunk before coming to rest on a neatly tended lawn. Gunfire erupted from the bed of the pickup that had been guarding the entrance, but Katie couldn't tell if they actually hit anything or not. All she knew was no bullets struck her, and if any hit the truck they didn't hit anything vital.

Braking hard, she made a left onto the main road, the Ford threatening to tip up on its outside set of wheels. Fighting it back under control she stayed on the gas and in less than a quarter of a mile had to brake again for a right turn. She spared a glance in the rearview, not seeing any pursuit. Yet.

On the major road that fed into the area, Katie pushed the Ford as hard as she dared, the speedometer needle sweeping up to 100, then beyond. She checked her mirrors and still saw no sign of pursuit, but didn't back off on her speed. Right now the best thing she could do was to quickly put as much distance between herself and the looters as possible.

A couple of miles later she slowed to turn left onto the small, two-lane highway that ran northeast to what she hoped would be safety in the mountains. Negotiating the turn she checked over her shoulder, breathing a cautious sigh of relief when she still didn't see any sign of the men who'd crashed her neighborhood. Feeling slightly more secure, she lowered her speed to 70, though she would have liked to go faster.

70 was fast enough in the truck, though, as she had to brake hard and swerve around a burned out car that suddenly appeared when she rounded a curve in the road. Now she slowed to 60, knowing she missed running into the wreck by only a couple of feet. She wanted speed, but John had built up the Ford for bouncing and bulling its way off road, not high speed driving on pavement.

Katie calmed down after a few miles of not seeing any other vehicles in her mirrors. She'd had to avoid two more abandoned cars, but at the lower speed was able to do so without any adrenaline inducing dramatics. She had already passed the sign welcoming her to Tonto National Forest and soon crested a minor pass in the foothills, dropping back down to the Salt River valley.

A few miles ahead she could see where the road she was on intersected with a larger highway that ran past Saguaro Lake, then on up to the Mogollon Rim. The Rim is the southern edge of the Colorado Plateau and runs 200 miles across Arizona. On The Rim, thick forests of Ponderosa Pine grow and the weather is cool in the summer and cold in the winter. South of The Rim is where the Arizona desert begins, several thousand feet of altitude lower with blistering summers and mild winters.

Turning onto the larger highway, Katie began seeing other vehicles fleeing the Phoenix metro area. Cars, trucks and SUVs crammed full of families and supplies. There weren't a lot of them, but enough that for a moment things almost seemed normal. Until she rounded a long, climbing curve and traffic came to an abrupt stop.

In front of her she could see a long line of vehicles, red brake lights glowing, stretching out of sight around the next curve in the road. Soon a heavily loaded Chevy Tahoe came to a stop only a couple of feet from the back of the Ford and she was glad she had left plenty of space between her bumper and the car in front of her.

She checked the mirror; grateful to see the Tahoe was occupied by two women and a lone man. The car to her front looked like a man and woman, and she scanned ahead looking for any vehicles whose occupants might pose a threat. Not seeing anything she relaxed slightly, watching in the rearview as another car came to a stop behind the Tahoe. Sunlight was reflecting off its windshield and she couldn't see inside.

They sat for close to half an hour, occasionally moving forward a few feet before stopping again for several minutes at a time. The highway was two lanes and the entire time Katie had been sitting there hadn't been a single vehicle pass her heading south. Was there an accident ahead that was blocking the whole road? With nothing else to do, she considered her options.

She could move over into the open southbound lane and drive north, but if that was a good option why weren't the people ahead of her already doing that? Turn around and go back south? She had room to make the turn, but if she did that, where would she go? Because of the rugged and steep terrain where the desert butted up against the Mogollon Rim there were only a very few ways to drive north from Phoenix.

Mentally smacking herself, Katie powered up the satellite phone and dialed Steve. His phone rang ten times before going to voicemail. With a sinking feeling at the thought of losing her lifeline, she disconnected without leaving a message and dialed again. This time he answered on the fourth ring.

"Sorry, I was in the bathroom." He said when he answered.

"You scared me," Katie said. "I was afraid you'd abandoned me."

"Like you did me?" Steve shot back in a haughty tone of voice.

Katie took a deep breath and counted to ten before speaking. "Steve, I've apologized for that more times than I can count. I thought we'd moved past it and you were going to help me."

He was quiet for a long time, only his faint breathing audible. "You're right. You have. It just still hurts. I'm pulling up your location. Did you get out of your house?"

Katie told him about barely escaping ahead of the looters, then asked him to look and tell her what had traffic stopped. He mumbled to himself as he worked, Katie struggling to maintain her patience.

"You're about three miles from a road block," he finally said.

"Road block? Who's blocking the road?"

"I'm zooming. Hold on." She heard some clicks and more mumbling. "There's a big dump truck pulled across the road and at least thirty armed men. They're pulling people out of vehicles and taking supplies."

"Shit. Is anyone fighting back?" Katie asked.

"Doesn't look like it. They're all in some kind of uniform, but I can't tell what it is. Hang on, let me look at the vehicles they have parked behind the dump truck."

Katie wanted to scream. She'd seen this behavior in war torn countries the world over, but had never thought she'd experience it here at home.

"OK, there are Tribal Police vehicles parked behind the truck, but if these guys are real Indians I'll eat my hat. Probably stolen from an equipment yard, and they're using the uniforms to bluff people." Steve finally said.

"Great. More assholes. All right, what about behind me. Is it clear for ten miles?" Katie had another option in mind.

"Hold on," Steve said, the sound of a keyboard clacking coming clearly over the sat phone.

"You're good," he eventually answered. "There's more traffic coming up behind you heading north, but it's mostly single vehicles. Nothing that would obviously be a problem. What are you thinking?"

"There's a Forest Service fire road that cuts through some rugged terrain, but goes all the way to Payson. I've been on it before. I know this truck can make it, it's just going to be a long, rough drive." Katie answered, checking her mirrors.

Cranking the wheel all the way to the left, Katie pulled across the southbound lane, driving off the pavement on the far side of the road to complete her U-turn and head back towards town. The people that were stuck in line behind her stared, wondering what she was doing. She thought about warning them of what was waiting ahead, but was afraid to approach any of the vehicles.

About twenty vehicles had stacked up behind her and she quickly passed them as she accelerated south. As she drove she met half a dozen heavily loaded vehicles heading north, but kept her eyes focused on the road ahead after checking to make sure none of them turned around to follow her. Just over eight miles later she found what she was looking for.

A small, dirt pullout on the left side of the road with a heavy steel gate guarding access to a trail leading up into the mountains. A large combination padlock secured the gate, the whole arrangement solidly set into concrete footings. Pulling to a stop with the front bumper close to the gate, Katie leaned across the cab and dug through the glove compartment.

The Forest Service allowed people to use the fire roads to get into backcountry that wasn't accessible by any other method. All you had to do was fill out a form and they'd issue a free permit that was good for six months and also had a list of date ranges and gate codes printed on it. The lock's combo was changed monthly and Katie hoped John had a recent permit.

Finding the right piece of paper, she scanned the dates, happily finding the current range. Reciting the combo to herself, she checked the area around the truck and seeing all was clear hopped out and ran to the lock. The number wheels were stiff from exposure to the weather, but once she got the right combo dialed in the lock popped open. It took her less than a minute to swing the gate open, drive through, hop back out, close and re-lock it.

8

The fire road was rough. Calling it a road was being generous. It was actually nothing more than a path across the desert leading up the edge of the Mogollon Rim to mountain country. The vegetation had been scraped away and just the largest of rocks removed. It was only navigable with a stout four-wheel drive vehicle with high ground clearance.

John had built up his truck for just this kind of terrain, installing tall off-road tires, specialty suspension components and replacing Ford's factory skid plates with heavy, iron plates to protect the underside of the vehicle. Regardless, Katie knew from experience that if she went too fast or didn't control the truck properly that she could damage it. Not that being stranded out here wasn't looking to be preferable to being stranded in town, but she didn't want to wind up on foot.

Speed wasn't her friend on the trail. Her foot spent more time on the brake, controlling descents into dry washes than it did on the gas. She drove for an hour before coming to a stop at the bottom of the first of many steep climbs as the road pushed deeper into the wilderness. Leaving the engine idling, she was paranoid about turning it off and it failing to start when she was ready to go, she stepped out to find a place to relieve herself.

Needs taken care of she, she drank some water while surveying the area. While she was stopped she decided to check in with Steve. Pulling out the phone she dialed his number, waiting impatiently for him to answer.

"I'm watching you in real time," he said when he picked up.

"Great. Ever think I might want some privacy to use the bathroom?" Katie asked, shading her eyes as she looked to the north and the steep climb in front of her.

"Relax, I couldn't see anything." He chuckled. "You've only covered a little over five miles, if you weren't aware."

Katie was surprised. She hadn't thought to check the odometer when she drove through the gate, and hadn't realized just how slow she was moving. She'd probably be making better time on horseback, she mused.

"Then there should be about 65 miles to go. Right?" She asked.

"68. I've got it mapped out on the computer. Looks like you've got some pretty serious climbs ahead, as well as a couple of canyons to get through. The good news is the road looks open all the way to Payson."

"That sounds like there's some bad news." Katie said, turning to check the road behind her, looking for dust trails that would indicate someone was following. She was pleased to see nothing moving other than birds flitting from bush to bush.

"There is. Payson is overrun with refugees. People in tents, RVs, campers; some just sleeping on the ground. Hard to tell from satellite, but it looks like the wild west. I'm seeing groups of armed men circulating through the camps. It looks like they're taking supplies from people. In the time I've been watching I've seen at least a half a dozen shootings and more fights. Don't see any cops but there's a few guys on horseback trying to maintain order." Katie stood quietly, thinking about what he'd just said.

"How much gas do you have?" Steve asked after she didn't say anything for nearly a minute.

"Just over half a tank," Katie answered after leaning into the cab and checking the gauge. "That'll get me to Payson, but not much farther. This thing uses a lot of fuel in four wheel drive."

"OK, you'd better get moving. You've got less than two hours of daylight left and you probably shouldn't try to move at night. You'll have to use your lights and that will make you stand out like a beacon."

"Good advice," Katie said, realizing she hadn't even thought about what she would do when it got dark. "OK, I'm going to get moving. I'll call you when I stop for the night. Can you look and see if there's anywhere you think I can get gas when I make it to Payson?"

"I'll see what I can find. Be careful. I'll talk to you soon." There was a click and he was gone. At least he hadn't told her he loved her again.

With a grim expression, Katie climbed back into the cab, locking the doors before starting forward. The road in front of her ran level for a hundred yards then made a sharp right as it started climbing up the side of a tall hill. It was narrow, the driver's side of the big truck right against a vertical wall of dirt and rock, the passenger side tires no more than a foot from a drop that progressively got worse the higher she climbed.

Keeping her speed low, Katie gripped the wheel with sweaty palms as she steered as far away from the edge as possible. A couple of times the large exterior mirror right outside her window scraped on rocks protruding from the wall, but she didn't care. She wasn't going to drive one inch closer to what had grown to a several hundred foot drop straight down.

Finally she topped out, the road going back to the left as it crested. Stopping, she looked ahead at a series of progressively taller mountains marching away into the distance. Turning to look over her shoulder she was dismayed to see nothing but a thick layer of smoke blanketing the valley where Phoenix was located.

The sun was low in the western sky, the smoke in the air producing a breathtaking sunset, but she had no appreciation for it. Turning her back on the city she drove forward carefully, bouncing over large stones embedded in the road and steering around a couple of tree stumps that had been left behind when the trail was cleared. Reaching the far edge of the crest she stopped when the road disappeared over the edge, descending into a shallow canyon.

Leaving the truck running, Katie stepped out and walked to the edge. The road wound its way down a couple of hundred feet, switching back on itself several times before bottoming out and climbing the next mountain. The surrounding mountains shaded the canyon ahead of her and it was already dusk at the bottom. She didn't think she could make it to the bottom before she lost the sun and had to turn on her headlights.

Thinking about it, Katie decided to spend the night on the high ground. She looked around for a place to park the truck that would be hidden from the trail in case anyone came by during the night. It took a few minutes, but she felt lucky when she found a spot halfway back to the other edge of the crest. Behind the wheel again she backed up slowly until she reached a relatively flat spot in the terrain that led away from the road. Driving a hundred yards she made a sharp left and came to a stop behind a thick stand of stunted pine trees.

Saying a prayer, she shut the engine off and walked back to the road. Turning, she tried to spot the truck but it was well concealed. She was halfway back to it when she looked down at where she was walking and saw the very visible tracks left by the aggressive treads of the off-road tires. She was losing light in a hurry and cast around until she found a fallen tree branch still heavy with pine needles. Working quickly she erased the tracks into the trees as best she could, but there was nothing she could do about the tracks climbing the hill, crossing the crest and ending at the drop into the next canyon.

Anyone following her trail would notice that she hadn't continued on. She racked her brain, but couldn't come up with a solution to that problem. Not pleased with the situation, but realizing there was nothing else she could do, Katie dialed Steve again as the sun dipped below the horizon.

"I'm stopped," she said when he answered.

"I'm still watching. That was smart wiping out your tracks." He sounded proud of her.

"Hopefully it wasn't necessary," she said. "Any movement on the road?"

"Nothing so far, and it's good you got on it. A truck tried to run the roadblock you were stuck behind and the fake cops started shooting. Lots of bodies and they've had reinforcements show up."

Katie took a deep breath; glad she'd known of another way into the mountains. She was just starting to say something to Steve when a screech owl cut lose from the top of a tree not far from where she was standing. The birds make a horrible sound that if you don't know what it is will scare the crap out of you. Even knowing what they sounded like, Katie let out an involuntary scream of her own, the owl answering her a few moments later.

Steve went into a panic, shouting into the phone. When she was able to speak again Katie told him what had happened and got a little irritated when he started laughing.

"Yeah, let's see how well you do out in the middle of nowhere." She said petulantly. "I was a field officer, but the field wasn't the woods. Now, if you're through making fun of me did you find any place I can get gas when I get to Payson?"

"Maybe. The power is still on and there are a couple of gas stations that are open. It looks like the owners are taking barter only. I guess money isn't worth much any more. And at the edge of the largest camp there's a tanker truck that's been pulled in. It's the largest gang that has it and they're trading gas for supplies. You're either going to have to trade something, or find a vehicle you can siphon gas out of." He said.

They talked for a few more minutes then ended the call with a promise from Steve that he'd watch over her on satellite while she slept. If he saw any vehicles or people approaching her position he'd alert her with a call to her sat phone. Plugging the handset into a car charger, Katie dug out a can of soup, ate it cold, then crawled into the back seat of the truck. Locking the doors she made sure her phone's ringer was turned on in case Steve called, then lay down on the floor of the truck, shotgun cradled in front of her in case she needed it.

9

The night passed without incident. Katie surprised herself that she was able to sleep despite being half frightened out of her mind. She woke with a start when the satellite phone rang, grabbing it and stabbing the green button to accept the call. It was Steve, not with a warning of approaching danger, but a wake up call.

The sun was just clearing the mountains to the east and Katie grumbled at him and talked for a couple of minutes even though she wasn't in the mood. Ending the call she sat up and looked around, then climbed out of the truck and walked into the thick cover of the stand of trees so she could use the bathroom without Steve watching.

A quick breakfast of canned peaches and a bottle of water and she was ready to go. The truck started easily, despite her fears that when she turned the key nothing would happen. She started down into the canyon, riding the brakes as she bounced down the side of the mountain. At the bottom, the road had been partially washed out by a rainstorm, a deep ditch carved out of the hard earth.

Dirk Patton

Controlling the truck's speed, Katie let the front tires drop gently into the ditch then had to give it a little gas to keep rolling forward. Quickly braking, she slowed the momentum as the rear tires reached the edge of the drop. Slowly she inched forward, the rear tires rolling over the edge and the back of the truck dropping.

The drop was arrested with a hard impact, the truck coming to a sudden stop. She sat for a moment, but when everything seemed OK she pressed on the accelerator. The engine picked up, but the truck didn't move. Pressing harder on the gas, Katie cursed when the front tires began spinning, throwing up a cloud of dirt and small rocks. She lifted her foot, the tires immediately stopping their spin.

Popping the door open she stepped out and looked at the back. The rear tires were barely touching the ground and had dug out two shallow furrows when she'd tried to accelerate. The ditch was deeper than the clearance from the rear bumper to the ground. She was hung up, the truck resting on the back bumper, the rear tires held hanging down and unable to gain traction. It wasn't going anywhere.

Katie suppressed a scream of frustration, but lashed out with her steel-toed boot and kicked a sizable dent into the truck's sheet metal. She stopped and stared at the dent, beginning to giggle when she thought about how mad John would be if he were there to see what she'd done. Looking at how the truck was stuck she recognized her mistake. She should have steered the Ford at an angle across the depression. She still might have bottomed the bumper out, but it would have only been one corner and she would have been able to pull free. She wasn't surprised when the phone rang.

"What's wrong?" Steve asked.

"The bumper's hung up," she said, moderating her tone. It wasn't his fault and she still worried he was going to turn petulant and stop helping her.

"Do you have a jack? Lift it up enough to drive forward so it clears whatever it's hung on." Katie was surprised at the helpful suggestion. She'd never thought of Steve as someone who could solve problems like this. He used to be great at puzzles and seeing patterns and trends. That had made him very good at his job, but she hadn't expected him to be of any use other than as her eye in the sky.

Dropping the phone on the driver's seat without breaking the connection Katie ran to the back of the truck, rolled open the bed cover and lowered the tailgate. She started moving bags of canned food and her other supplies, finally spotting the hi-lift jack John kept in the bed. Pulling it towards the back, she had to reposition it so she could lift it. The jack was over fifty pounds and four feet tall, reminding her of a bigger version of the old style jacks that used to come in large, American built cars.

With the jack out she looked it over and saw how it was meant to attach to the truck. Unfortunately, it was designed to hook onto the back of the bumper and the bumper was firmly stuck on the top edge of the wash. She pushed it away in frustration, letting it fall to the dirt, but thought better of her action and muscled it back into the truck.

The tool back in place, she spotted a small folding shovel clipped to the inside wall of the truck's bed. Grabbing it, she extended the spade and started attacking the ground around and under the rear bumper. Ten minutes later she had hardly made any progress. The soil was almost as hard as the large rocks that were firmly lodged in it. The shovel was just too small and light for the task.

Flinging it into the back of the truck, Katie wiped sweat off her face and walked to the cab to pick up the phone.

"Why won't the jack work?" Steve asked as soon as she spoke. Katie explained the problem to him.

"Try the other jack," he said.

"What other jack?"

"There should be a smaller, scissor style jack that came with the truck from the manufacturer. You should be able to get it underneath and lift at the axel." He said patiently.

Katie stood staring at the truck. "Where would it be? I've never seen one."

"Look behind the back seat. If not there, try under the back seat. There has to be one unless John took it out, but there's no reason he would have done that." Steve said.

Katie opened the rear driver's side door and had to shift some more supplies so she could search for the jack. She didn't see one, but kept looking. After several minutes she forced open a large, plastic panel and there was a sturdy scissor jack clamped securely in place. She'd had to put the phone down to pry open panels and when she snatched it up to talk to Steve she could hear him shouting her name even before she lifted the handset to her ear.

"I'm here," She said. "What's wrong?"

"You've got two Jeeps coming up behind you. At least two occupants in each one, but the tops are up so I can't get a good look or see if there's any more people in them."

"How close?" Katie raised her head to look up at the crest where she'd spent the night, afraid she would see the front end of a vehicle nosing over and starting down the fire road toward where she was stuck.

"They're making the climb you made before you stopped for the night. That has slowed them a little, but if they keep coming you've got maybe twenty minutes before they can see you."

"Shit! OK, stay on the phone. I'm going to see what I can do with the jack."

Katie tossed the phone on the front seat and reached for the jack, pausing when she realized she needed to plug the handset into the charger so it didn't die while she was working. The last thing she wanted was to be completely alone out here.

Satellite phone batteries charging, she yanked the jack out of the clips holding it in place and dashed to the narrow space between the rear tire and the edge of the wash. Shoving the heavy tool through ahead of her, she crawled through on her belly, looking at the truck's suspension. Settling for the left side bracket where the shocks were bolted on, she squirmed the jack around on the ground until she felt it was stable.

Unfolding the crank she turned it, the threaded rod pulling half the scissor towards her, which pushed the top closer to the bottom of the bracket. Cranking as fast as she could, the handle stopped moving when the top of the jack met the resistance of the weight of the truck. Cursing, Katie shifted herself around so she could exert more force. The crank began turning again, but slower than she would have liked.

The foot of the jack began to compress into the dirt, but only sank in a couple of inches before the truck began to move. Suppressing a cry of excitement, Katie turned the rod as hard as she could, willing the mechanism to move faster. Not watching the rod, she was surprised when it suddenly came to a stop, her hand slipping off. She had reached the limit of the jack.

Looking at what she'd accomplished, Katie cursed. The jack had been designed to lift a truck sitting on pavement just high enough to change a flat tire. A tire much shorter than the big off-road tires John had put on the Ford. She had succeeded in lifting the left rear side of the truck no more than four inches, and as far as she could tell the bumper was still firmly embedded in the ground.

Scrabbling backwards, she stood up and grabbed the phone. "I've raised it as far as it will go, but the bumper didn't move," she said into the phone. "Where are the Jeeps?"

"Five minutes from the crest on the far side," he said.

"Goddamn it, what do I do?" She asked, not really expecting an answer so much as voicing her frustration.

"Do you have a tool kit?"

"What? Why?"

"A tool kit? Do you have one?" He asked again.

"Hold on," Katie pulled the charging cord out of the phone so she could stay connected with Steve as she went to the back of the truck.

Climbing up the side of the wash she then stepped up onto the tailgate and frantically threw supplies out of her way. John was someone who was rarely caught unprepared, especially if he'd had an opportunity to plan for something. Two heavy canvas bags were stashed at the front of the bed, and the first one she unzipped was full of greasy tools.

"Yes, there are tools. Why?" She couldn't help looking up at the crest to make sure she hadn't already been spotted.

"Get back under the truck. The bumper shouldn't have more than four bolts holding it to the frame. If you can undo them, you're free!" Steve was excited and speaking fast. "Just be careful. There's going to be a lot of pressure on the bumper and you don't know which way it will go when you release it."

Katie was already moving, shoving the phone into her pocket and lifting the bag with both hands, dropping it over the side of the truck. Jumping down she crawled back under the truck, dragging the bag with her. It only took a moment for her to find the bolts Steve was talking about, and he was right about there only being four of them.

Digging through the tool bag she started trying sockets until finding one that was the right size, then spent another few precious minutes finding the right ratchet to match. She had to pause and think about which way would loosen, finally falling back on the helpful rhyme of 'righty tighty, lefty loosey'.

Ratchet set properly, she grabbed the steel handle and pulled with all her strength, sweat popping out from the exertion, but the bolt didn't budge. She stopped for a moment and took a couple of deep breaths, then tried again without any better luck. Wanting to scream in frustration she forced herself to calm down and fished the phone out of her pocket.

"I can't move them. They're too tight!" She said.

"Is there a breaker bar in the tool bag? It's going to have a connection on the end like the ratchet, but it will be long and heavy. If not that, then a long pipe that can slip over the ratchet so you've got more leverage."

Katie set the phone down and frantically dug through the duffel, coming up with a two foot long iron pipe that slipped over the ratchet's handle. She wrapped her hands around the end of the pipe, took a deep breath and pulled as hard as she could. With a squeal of metal on metal the bolt gave a little. She rotated the ratchet handle a couple of clicks and pulled again, the bolt turning more, its resistance finally ending.

Jerking the pipe out of the way she used the ratchet to quickly remove the bolt and let it drop to the ground. Repeating the process she removed the next one, then realized how much time she was using and snatched the phone out of the dirt.

"Two bolts done. Where are the Jeeps?" She asked.

"They're on top of the mountain, about a minute from the edge on your side. Keep working. They can't come down that trail fast. They're going to see you, but you've got time if you work fast."

Dropping the phone again Katie attacked the remaining two bolts. When the fourth one broke free she caught her breath as the bumper shifted and the back of the truck dropped several inches. Hoping that was all that would happen, she carefully began turning the last bolt, squirming away from the bumper as it came free. The truck dropped another inch then stopped, the bumper crushed under the rear edge of the bed. She quickly lowered the scissor jack and yanked it out of the way.

There was a bundle of electrical wires running into the bumper, but she didn't have time to worry about it. Scrambling from underneath the truck she tossed the phone into the cab, dropped the tools into the duffel and swung it up into the bed of the truck. Moments later she had the bed cover rolled back into place and slammed the tailgate.

Katie dashed to the open door, pausing before climbing in and looking up at the trail crest, several hundred feet above her. No vehicles were visible, but she was sure she could see two figures standing at the edge. Ignoring them, she climbed into the driver's seat, closed the door and securely belted herself in. The first time John had taken her off-road she'd thought he was joking when he told her to keep her seatbelt on. Until the going got rough and her head hit the ceiling, then she wished she had listened to him.

Stepping on the gas the truck started rolling. There was the protest of crunching metal from the rear, then more noise as the wiring held and began dragging the bumper. It didn't take long for it to snag on a rock, the wires ripping free and dragging on the ground as Katie bounced across the floor of the canyon.

10

Katie pushed on, the trail climbing successive ridgelines as she moved north. It was rough going, deep ruts and large rocks constantly challenging her driving skills and the truck's capabilities. Keeping a wary eye on the gas gauge she wasn't happy with how much fuel was being burned to cover such a short distance. Cresting another ridge, she stopped and leaving the engine idling stepped out to relieve herself. She made sure to move under a large pine tree with thick boughs so Steve couldn't watch on the satellite.

Business attended to, Katie called Steve as she stepped to the back of the truck and looked to the south. The view was breathtaking, forested hills with canyons carved between them dropping away to the valley where Phoenix sat. By now she was a couple of thousand feet above the valley floor, and could look down on the thick haze of smoke that hung over the city.

"Where are the guys in the Jeeps?" She asked when Steve picked up.

"Just cresting the ridge to your south," he answered. "They're moving a little slower than you. Hard to tell on satellite, but I think one of the Jeeps isn't really set up for any serious off-road travel and the driver is having to take it really easy."

Finally some good news.

"How much farther do I have?" Katie asked, digging a fresh bottle of water out of the back of the truck.

"The computer shows forty one miles, but it's just drawing a line and not taking into account the terrain. You've probably got close to fifty actual miles to go. At your pace you won't be there before dark."

Katie didn't like hearing that answer. Not with two vehicles only a few miles behind her. The last thing she wanted to do was stop for the night and let them catch up. She also didn't like the idea of traveling at night. The road was difficult enough to navigate with the sun shining brightly and it would be three times harder with only the truck's lights. Deciding she'd better cover as much ground as she could while it was daylight, Katie told Steve she'd call him later and resumed her trek.

The north side of the ridge she had stopped on was the steepest descent she had ever driven, the heavy truck constantly threatening to start slipping sideways. She had no idea just how steep it really was, but was glad for the seatbelt that kept her from sliding forward off the seat. The angle had been sharp, but it was only fifteen minutes before the trail bottomed out into a shallow canyon.

Crossing the level terrain, Katie brought the truck to a stop when she came to the edge of a small stream. The water was no more than thirty feet across, but it was running swiftly and she couldn't tell how deep it was. Living in the desert it was an almost daily occurrence during monsoon season that someone would try and drive across a flooded wash and wind up stranded and on the news being winched up from the roof of their flooded vehicle by a helicopter.

It was so common, in fact, that Arizona had passed what was called the "stupid motorist" law. If you drove into a flooded wash and had to be rescued, you would have to reimburse the cost of your rescue. Katie knew it wouldn't take much depth in the fast moving current to push the truck downstream and was hesitant to risk the crossing.

Climbing down, she walked to the edge of the water, but still couldn't gauge its depth. She briefly considered wading out to test it, but dismissed the idea. The streambed would be full of round, slippery rocks and it wouldn't take much for her feet to be washed out from under her. Katie stared at the stream for almost a minute, trying to think what John would do.

With a smile at the thought of her husband she ran to the back of the truck and dug out a length of sturdy rope. Securing one end of it to the truck's front bumper, she wrapped the other around her waist and carefully stepped into the stream.

The water was shockingly cold when it seeped into her leather boots, but she gritted her teeth and pushed on. Five feet from the edge the water was just over the tops of her boots. The push of the current was strong and Katie was having a hard time maintaining her footing, but she pushed on. At the halfway mark the water was to the bottom of her knees and every step she took she was forced further downstream. She started to go back, but realized the water could still be deeper before the far edge.

Pushing on, Katie moved slowly and deliberately, careful to stay balanced and not let her weight suddenly shift and send her plunging into the stream. She walked until she was five feet from the far shore, the depth of the water having receded back to the tops of her boots. Satisfied with her exploration, she slowly turned and began making her way back to the truck.

Wading out of the stream she quickly untied the rope and threw it back into the truck without taking the time to coil it. Shivering from the time she'd had her feet and lower legs in the icy water she stood next to the Ford and compared its clearance to where the deepest water had reached to the bottom of her knees. The lowest part of the truck's body was level with the middle of her knees. Nothing other than the tires would be in the stream for the water to push on.

Feeling more confident, Katie climbed back into the cab and shifted into drive. Switching to four wheel low, she let the truck idle forward into the water. It moved easily, the current pushing against the wheels and splashing water into the air where it created a small rainbow. Approaching the middle of the crossing, the truck began slipping sideways from the force of the water against the tires, but Katie steered against the current and gave the engine more gas.

The tires slipped some, the truck shifting sideways more, but Katie kept the momentum on and moments later drove onto dry land. Stopping long enough to shift back into four wheel high, she continued on and was soon climbing the next ridge. She reached the top, crossed the crest and descended into the next canyon without any further drama.

The trail was just starting to rise for the next climb when the sat phone rang on the seat next to her. Stopping before leaving the canyon floor, Katie answered the phone; afraid Steve was calling with another warning.

"One of the Jeeps didn't make it across the stream," he said. "Current took it a hundred yards down the canyon and it's wedged against a boulder. Don't think you need to worry about them anymore. They can't all fit in one Jeep."

"That is good news," Katie breathed a sigh of relief. "Is the Jeep that made it across still following?"

"No, he's stopped. Looks like families in each Jeep. Right now there's adults and a couple of kids on foot."

This caught Katie by surprise. She hadn't even considered any possibility other than the Jeeps were loaded down with men who were best avoided.

"What are they doing now?" She asked after a moment.

"Just standing there looking at the wrecked Jeep."

"Will they be able to get it out?" She asked.

"Wouldn't do them any good. It's nose down and the whole engine is under water. No way with today's electronics that thing will ever run again without a long visit to a repair shop." Steve answered.

Katie thanked him for the update and ended the call. Stepping on the gas she started up the incline for the next ridge, the tallest so far, but only went a few feet before stopping. She sat thinking for a moment, then with a sigh put the truck in reverse and backed up until she came to a wide enough spot in the trail to turn around. A minute later the phone rang again.

"What are you doing?" Steve asked, sounding irritated that she had reversed course.

"I can't leave them out here." Katie answered. "Not if they've got kids with them. They're stranded and there will probably be more people along that might not have the best of intentions."

"Are you crazy? Just because they have kids with them doesn't mean they won't shoot you and take your truck. Turn around and keep going and let them worry about themselves."

Katie knew that Steve was most likely right. She also knew that John would probably give her the same advice. But she had to live with herself and if she drove away and didn't at least try to help these people, the idea of leaving children stranded in the wilderness would haunt her. Telling Steve her mind was made up she ended the call.

11

The Jeeps had been carrying two families, one with parents and three children, the other parents and two children. Katie had experienced some tense moments as she approached them. The people had heard her coming well before she got there and the two fathers had hidden their wives and kids behind a jumble of large boulders. One of them had stayed nearby while the other stood waiting for her, blocking the trail.

He was armed with a semi-automatic assault rifle, and as she approached him Katie scrutinized how he was handling the weapon. The muzzle was in front of him, pointed at the ground as she came to a stop fifty yards from where he stood. Taking a deep breath, Katie shifted into park and opened her door, careful to stay behind it as she stepped down from the cab. When the man made no threatening move she moved out into the open, seeing him visibly relax and let the muzzle drop a few inches when he realized she was a woman.

"Not a fighter," she said to herself, knowing anyone with any degree of combat experience would never relax just because it was a woman that stepped out of the truck.

"I came back to help you," Katie shouted, still staying close enough to dive into the truck if need be. She had her own rifle ready to go if she had to defend herself. After a few moments he glanced over his shoulder then began walking towards her.

She knew there wasn't anyone else in the area. Steve had been keeping an eye on them while she drove, and it was just the two men with their wives and children. The man approached slowly, eyes focused on Katie. He wasn't expecting problems and never bothered to check the surrounding area. She was mildly surprised he'd made it this far.

"How did you know we had a problem?" He had stopped ten yards in front of the truck.

"I was watching from the top of the next ridge," Katie lied. She wasn't ready to advertise the advantage she had with Steve keeping an eye on her from above. "Was anyone hurt?"

"No, they made it out OK. But the Jeep's a total loss. I'm Brian Childress, by the way."

Katie stood staring at him for a long moment, getting the measure of the man. Finally satisfied that he was what he appeared to be, a man trying to protect his family and get them to safety, she stepped around the open door and held her hand out.

"Katie Chase." She introduced herself.

Brian waved the rest of his group forward and made the introductions. His wife Cathy was a small woman, and it was immediately obvious that she made the decisions for the family. They were the ones driving the Jeep that had made it across the stream. Their vehicle had been lifted and outfitted properly for the rugged terrain. The second Jeep, when she got a better look at it, was a cheaper model that wasn't good for much other than driving on slippery pavement. She refrained from asking them how they thought it would cross the stream.

The group was also heading for Payson where Cathy's sister lived on a small ranch just outside of town. They didn't know if she was OK or not, but they all thought the small town was far enough away from Phoenix that it had to be preferable to the chaos sweeping through the large city's streets. From what Steve had told her about the conditions in Payson, Katie was worried about being able to stay there and wait for John to find her. She had no idea where else she could go, other than away from Phoenix.

They spent a few minutes talking, then Katie shuffled supplies around in the Ford to make room for the family that had lost the Jeep. Everyone had lots of questions for her, all of them amazed that she was out here on her own, but she put them off as they busied themselves moving supplies from the disabled Jeep into her truck. The sun was heading for the horizon and she wanted to get to the top of the next ridge before dark.

The parents were Ken and Patty, their kids John and Samantha. Once everyone was loaded, Katie got the truck turned around and rolling, concentrating on her driving. Brian followed with his family in their Jeep, staying close enough to keep her in sight but far enough back to leave room for maneuvering if anything unexpected happened.

"Do you know Cathy's sister?" Katie asked as the truck lurched over a large rock.

"We do. We're all school teachers." Patty answered from the back seat. "We used to all work together in Gilbert but Trish, Cathy's sister, got divorced and wanted to get away from the city so she took a job with the school district up in Payson."

Katie nodded her head, happy with the answer. Other than her it wouldn't be a bunch of strangers showing up asking for a place to stay.

The sun was almost touching the horizon when they crested the ridge. Katie drove a couple of hundred yards until she found a mostly level area where they could spend the night. There was still plenty of light up where they were, but the canyons on either side of them were already in shadow and quickly getting darker.

As soon as they parked, the two men set about gathering wood for a campfire while the women kept a close eye on the children who were energetic after a long day cooped up in vehicles. Katie almost told them to not light the fire, but decided to check with Steve first. If there was no one around to see it, the night would be passed much more comfortably with a fire to heat their food and keep them warm.

Katie took the sat phone and moved away from the camp before dialing. She had a short conversation with Steve, cutting off his renewed objections about her having gone back to help the group. He had assured her in a sullen voice that there weren't any other people within twenty miles of her current location. She was relieved to get off the phone.

The night passed quietly, Katie sleeping in the truck while the two families settled in around the fire. The sun was up early, waking them and after a lite breakfast they got back on the trail. It was early afternoon when they reached pavement, the sudden lack of bouncing over ruts and rocks disconcerting at first.

Payson was mobbed with refugees and everyone looked frightened. There was a noticeable absence of police or National Guard, but as they drove closer to town Katie frequently spotted heavily armed men on horseback. They sat on their mounts at the side of the road, not moving, keeping a close eye on everyone that passed. She suspected they were locals who had taken it on themselves to maintain order in their small town.

There were thousands of cars crammed into the center of town, tens of thousands of people on foot. Some wandered aimlessly, others strode purposely on some important errand. It was hard to navigate the crush of humanity, but Katie managed to remain patient as she worked her way towards the back of a long line waiting to fuel up at a gas station.

She had passed several stations that were empty, large signs at the edge of the road letting people know they were out of gas. The one station that was still open had two large tanker trucks sitting in its parking lot. Katie hoped they weren't about to run dry as the gauge in the Ford said she had less than an eighth of a tank left.

"I hope there's still some gas when we get there," Ken said, craning his neck to try and get a better look at the station in the distance.

Patty nodded, looking worried but not saying anything. It was close to five minutes later after they had just moved forward a couple of car lengths when the sound of a disturbance came from behind them. Katie looked in the large outside mirror, checking on Brian and his family. They were fine, also looking in their mirrors.

Three vehicles behind Brian's Jeep, two men were standing in the road screaming at each other as one of them gestured at the rear of his pickup. A woman got out of the vehicle farthest back and tried to calm things down by grabbing one of the men's arm to lead him away, but he shrugged her off and renewed his verbal assault on the other man.

"What's happening?" Patty asked from the back seat.

"Looks like someone probably tapped the bumper of the truck in front of them. Hardly worth getting worked up about, but people are scared and emotions are going to spill over." Katie said.

As she finished speaking the first punch was thrown. Then the men were hitting and kicking each other, the smaller one pushing the larger one against the side of his truck and raining blows to his stomach. Katie was startled when movement caught her eye and a horse and rider flashed past her window. It was one of the men she'd seen watching over the refugees. She watched in the mirror as the rider kept the horse at a full gallop, ramming the large animal's chest and front legs directly into the two men that were fighting.

The men were sent sprawling and the horseman reined in his mount. By the time the first man started to climb back to his feet the rider had swung down to the pavement and taking two big strides he hammered the man's head with the butt of his rifle. The man fell back to the ground, unconscious, the second man staying on the ground and raising his hands in surrender when the rider turned in his direction.

Two more horsemen rode up as Katie watched, these staying mounted and pointing rifles at the men on the ground. The first rider said something to the man who was still conscious and he quickly scrambled to his feet and disappeared into his vehicle. The woman who had tried to intervene dashed to the unconscious man and dragged him to their vehicle. She couldn't get him inside and the rider waved her aside, lifted the man by his belt and shirt collar and tossed him into the back seat of the car.

Commotion over, the man swung back up into the saddle and nodded to the other two riders who turned their horses around and slowly walked them away. The first man stayed right where he had mounted the horse, keeping watch over the two fighters to make sure things remained calm. Katie didn't know who these guys were, but was glad to see them maintaining a degree of law and order even if it was frontier justice style.

12

An hour and a half later Katie stopped the truck next to a gas pump. Half a dozen of the horsemen, weapons plainly displayed, guarded the station. A teenaged boy stood with the pump nozzle in his hand, waiting as an older woman walked up to Katie's window, looking the truck over as she approached.

"Big thing uses a lot of gas, huh?" She asked. Katie nodded and held up some cash.

"That don't do you no good, sweetie. Food, booze or cigarettes. That's what's worth somethin' now. What you got?" The woman asked, trying to see into the bed of the truck, but the cover was rolled shut and hiding Katie's supplies.

"Food, I guess," Katie said, unhappy that she hadn't prepared for this.

"OK. Rate is five pounds of canned food per gallon of gas, and you've got to show me the cans before we start pumping." The woman stared into Katie's eyes.

Katie looked back at her, thinking that filling up the Ford's big tank would cut significantly into

Dirk Patton

her stock of food. The truck had a 36 gallon tank and was nearly empty. But if she didn't get gas, she was stuck in Payson, and despite the self-appointed peacekeepers she didn't like the idea of not being able to leave if things got bad.

Making a decision she wasn't happy with she turned the engine off and stepped down from the cab. Walking the woman to the back of the truck she lowered the tailgate and let her see inside the bed. Bent at the waist she peered inside for a moment before straightening up and telling the teenager to fill the tank.

While the boy pumped gas, the woman had Katie start handing her cans of food that she piled into the hanging bowl of a scale that looked like it had been taken from the produce section of a grocery store. They kept pace with the readout on the pump, the handle clicking off at just over 34 gallons. A few more cans added and she checked the piece of paper she was using to keep track.

"One hundred and seventy pounds. You're good, sweetie." The woman said, handing two cans of beef stew back to Katie.

Katie tossed them in with the nearly depleted cache of food in the truck, slammed the tailgate and climbed back into the cab. Pulling forward a few feet she waited as Brian went through the same routine, filling the Jeep's smaller tank. Re-fueled, he pulled up next to her and Cathy leaned out her open window.

"Follow us," she said. "My sister's place is just a few miles away."

Katie nodded and fell in behind the Jeep. They only moved slightly faster going away from the station than they had approaching it. The small town's narrow streets were crushed with traffic, both vehicle and pedestrian. People were frightened, and the fear was palpable, but so was something else. It took Katie a while to recognize it, but her tension ratcheted up a few notches when she did.

Desperation. Now she could see it in the faces of many of the other drivers, but especially in those that were on foot. Fear is one thing, but most people can deal with being afraid. Being desperate is something else entirely. The feeling of complete helplessness will spur some people to sit down and give up, but it will cause others to do things to survive that they wouldn't normally even consider. Then there's the ten percent of the population that just doesn't give a shit and will take advantage of any situation.

It took less than twenty minutes for them to make the drive to Cathy's sister's small ranch. A large, yellow school bus sat in front of the house, children running and playing in the yard as a handful of women watched over them. Introductions were made and stories exchanged, Katie joining the families in a lite meal.

Early evening came quickly and Katie decided to go to the hotel where she had told John in the note she'd left for him that she would be waiting. She didn't plan to stay there, but wanted to leave word with the owners where she was so John could find her if he showed up. Her optimism that he would find her was running short, but she'd learned many years ago to not count him out. He was the most stubborn and determined man she'd ever known.

The hotel was only about five miles away, between the center of town and the ranch where Katie was staying. It had been built in the 1950s and was nothing more than a couple of dozen rustic cabins scattered amongst the pine trees. When the current owners had purchased the property in the late 90s they had completely remodeled the interior of each cabin, and while the place looked vintage from the outside, the interiors were sleek and upscale with every modern amenity.

When she turned onto the short, dirt road that lead to the hotel, Katie was surprised to see people camping amongst the trees. Every available foot of ground was occupied, vehicles parked along the side of the narrow track. When the trees opened up for the hotel's grounds she had to stop as the entire area was packed full of refugees. People wandered about, retrieving water and taking care of other needs.

Pulling to a stop, she climbed out of the truck and looked around as she hit the button to lock the doors. Several campsites were occupied by groups of men, all of them staring at her as she stood there. Slipping the truck's keys into her pocket she adjusted the holstered pistol on her hip and headed for the building marked as registration.

The door to the office was locked when she tried the handle, but she knocked and after a minute an older man wearing jeans and a flannel shirt appeared, staring at her through the glass door. She could see a revolver holstered on his hip and he carried a short-barreled shotgun in his right hand.

"We've got no room, but you can camp under the trees if you want." He shouted through the door.

"That's not what I want," Katie shouted back. "Can you please open the door so I don't have to yell?"

The man looked at her a moment, eyes flicking to the weapon on her belt, then up and over her shoulders to make sure she was alone. Time stretched out, but he finally reached forward and flipped a locking lever and pulled the door open a few inches.

"What do you want?" He asked, a firm grip on the handle.

"I had to leave Phoenix before my husband got home. I left him a note telling him I'd be here. We've stayed here before and he'll know the place. I'm staying at a ranch outside of town and I'd just like to leave a note with you so he can find me if he shows up. Please? That's all I want." Katie made sure to keep her hand away from her pistol and gave the man a smile when she finished talking.

"Oh let her in already, Russ." A woman Katie hadn't seen stepped up next to him and pushed him aside to pull the door open. "Come on in, honey."

Katie smiled at her and walked into the office, Russ pushing the door closed and locking it behind her.

"If I can just borrow a piece of paper and a pen, I'll write a quick note and be out of your hair." Katie said.

The woman stepped behind a polished counter and retrieved a notepad and pencil from a drawer, laying them on the registration desk for Katie to use. Her husband stayed at the door watching something going on outside the building. Katie quickly wrote out a note to John letting him know where to find her, folded the piece of paper in half and handed it to the woman.

"His name is John Chase. I'm his wife, Katie. He's a big guy. Over six foot, strong, shaved head. Well, it was shaved. He may not have had a razor to keep it that way. Thank you so much."

"You're welcome, honey. Good luck to you and be careful out there. There's some real bad guys coming up from the city. We hear women screaming every night." Katie was surprised when the woman stepped forward and hugged her.

Russ opened the door and she slipped back outside into the quickly darkening evening. Campfires dotted the area, the smell of food cooking making her stomach rumble even though she'd eaten just a couple of hours ago.

Walking quickly, Katie reached the truck and popped the locks with the remote in her pocket. She didn't see or hear the man that was following her until she opened the driver's door and it was suddenly blocked from opening far enough for her to get in.

"What's your hurry?" He asked, smiling out of an unshaven face. "Would you like some food? Maybe a drink. Got plenty of both."

The man wasn't large, but still larger and stronger than she was. Katie took a slow step back to open some space between them and darted her eyes around the area to see if he was alone. She felt a little better when she didn't see anyone else. The man was armed with a pistol and a large hunting knife, both strapped to his belt, but his hands weren't anywhere near either weapon.

"I'm just waiting for my husband," Katie said, hoping the thought of a male's impending arrival would deter the man from whatever he had in mind.

"I don't think that's true," he said. "I seen you drive up alone. Now, I'll ask again nicely. Why don't you come have a drink with me?" He pushed the Ford's door closed and started to take a step forward.

Katie smiled at him, which caused him to hesitate, and holding his eyes with hers she kicked straight up with her right foot. The steel toed boot connected solidly with the man's balls, his breath whistling out in a faint, high-pitched hiss as he instantly folded and fell to the ground where he rolled into a knot.

Not waiting to see if he had any friends in the area, Katie yanked the door open and jumped into the truck. Getting the engine started she slammed it into drive and hit the gas, spitting dirt as she whipped the truck around, narrowly missing the man on the ground.

13

The group spent the next few weeks at the ranch. Friends of Cathy's sister drifted in and out, all of them with horror stories of what conditions were like to the south in Phoenix. A large garden and pigs and chickens kept everyone fed. Meals were supplemented with deer and elk taken from the forested mountains surrounding their refuge.

Katie was slowly losing faith that she would ever see John again. She knew the country had been devastated, and Atlanta was a long ways away. A four hour flight before the apocalypse, but now it might as well be on the other side of the planet. Close to 2,000 miles, how could she expect him to fight his way to their home, find her note, then follow her to Payson. She knew that if there was anyone that could pull it off it was him, but as the days began to run together her hope faded.

Daily conversations with Steve kept her, and the group, updated on what was happening around the country as well as the more immediate area in the desert southwest. She was horrified to learn of the nuclear bombs used in Nashville to kill millions of infected. She hadn't seen an infected, yet, and would be happy if she never did.

It was a day much like all the others, Katie on the phone with Steve as she watched a group of children playing. They were about to wrap up their conversation when he suddenly told her to hold on. She could hear him breathing over the open connection, a keyboard and mouse clicking in the background.

"Katie, there's a large group that just pulled into Payson. Heavily armed and organized. Looks like at least a hundred men." He finally said.

"What are they doing?" She asked, turning her back on the kids and focusing on his voice.

"They've already shot several of the Peacekeepers and a couple of civilians. Hold on, let me watch them for a few minutes." He said.

Katie stood in the shade of a pine tree, impatient, but holding her tongue. She could still hear sounds over the phone; the low hum of the equipment in the listening post, the occasional mouse click and the squeak of Steve's chair every time he shifted his weight.

"You should probably get out of there soon," he finally said. "They're spreading out and looting. They're also taking women. If anyone tries to stand up to them they're shooting them. They've got heavy weapons. Either got into a police SWAT or more likely a National Guard armory. No one other than the Army is going to be able to stand up to them."

"Are they coming this way?" She asked.

"Not yet. There's plenty in town to keep them occupied, but I wouldn't count on them to not come looking to see what else there is in the area." Katie ran a hand through her thick hair, frustrated and afraid of what a group of men like that would do.

"If we leave, where do we go?" She asked after almost a minute of silence.

"East," Steve immediately answered. "I've been watching what's going on in the country, looking for a safe haven for you in case you had to move. There's a large buildup of military in Oklahoma City at Tinker Air Force Base. The city is still relatively normal and in the control of the authorities. If you head due east from where you are and cut across the Indian Reservations into

New Mexico, then across the Texas pan handle that will get you into Oklahoma without encountering any problems I can see on satellite. No infected if you stay away from northern New Mexico. No gangs to speak of. That's your best option."

"Have you kept an eye on my house like I asked?" Katie had hoped that if John did make it to Arizona that Steve would be able to see him and let her know he was close. Steve had been a little weird for the past few days and she was hesitant to ask him, but had to know before she could even think about heading out on the road.

"You're whole neighborhood burned four days ago." He answered hesitantly.

"My house?" Katie's breath caught in her throat.

"Yes, your house too. I'm sorry." He said.

Katie couldn't stop the tears from welling up in her eyes and rolling down her face. The house was gone, and so was her note to John. He'd never be able to find her, even if he was still alive and looking for her. She thanked Steve and broke the connection. Getting her emotions under control she went to find the other adults and fill them in on the outlaws that had just arrived in town.

14

It had been a frustrating morning. Infuriating might be a better way to describe it. Having found my truck parked on Tinker Air Force Base amongst the sea of vehicles that had been driven there by refugees, I was forced to deal with more demanding priorities than immediately looking for Katie. There were thousands of infected still wandering around the base that had poured through the intentional breach in the perimeter fence. It was noon before Colonel Crawford, who had taken command of the overall response to the incursion, declared the emergency under control.

Igor and Irina, who had assisted with clearing out the infected, were now in a guarded conference room in the base administration building. I mostly trusted them, but my trust didn't extend to the Air Force, so they were being treated like visiting foreign military VIPs. Certainly not prisoners, but not left alone to do as they wished either. I had made sure they were being treated well. Food and water had been provided as well as medical attention for Irina's leg that was still freshly wounded from a firefight in Los Alamos.

Rachel, Dog, Martinez and myself sat in another room with Colonel Crawford, Captain Blanchard and General Triplett, the commander of Tinker. Various other Air Force staffers were in attendance, taking notes and video taping the debriefing. Kathleen Clark, the new President of the United States and Admiral Packard, CINCPACFLT and the ranking US military officer, were listening in, their images displayed on a large screen mounted to the front wall of the room. Normally each of us would have been debriefed separately, and certainly without POTUS in attendance, but times were hardly normal.

I had been speaking for the better part of an hour, relaying the details of our mission to deliver the three nuclear bombs to the Russians. The only way they'd gotten me to sit still this long was by tasking a Security Forces Major with trying to locate Katie. I was antsy as hell, angry that I had to sit on my ass while my wife was out there somewhere. My mood was apparently evident in my tone as there were several times when Rachel had reached under the table and placed her hand on my leg in an attempt to calm me down.

When I reached the point where the Marines had arrived and plucked us out of the desert, I stopped my narrative. Admiral Packard flipped through several pages of notes he had taken; pausing to read when he found the page he was looking for.

"Major, I'd like some clarification." He said, still looking down at his notepad. "You said Mr. Cummings stated that the President had opened a dialogue with the Russian president and was not in support of the coup being attempted by the GRU?"

"That is correct, Admiral." I said, flicking my eyes to the half of the screen displaying the President.

"And you stated that, in your opinion, the rendezvous was a ruse by the Russians to get our remaining three devices out into the open and capture Captain Vostov. Correct?" He looked up over the top edge of his reading glasses at the camera, staring at me out of the high definition screen.

"Yes, sir. That is correct. They were in place ahead of us. If all they'd wanted was to arrest Captain Vostov they could have done so before she departed Kirtland. They wanted the nukes off the table, sir. Didn't want us with any type of strike weapon."

"And it seems that part of their mission succeeded. You detonated two of them, the third one destroyed in one of the explosions. Correct?" This from President Clark.

"Yes, ma'am." I said, seething internally that I was wasting time repeatedly going over the same facts when all I wanted was to be searching for Katie.

"Colonel?" Her gaze shifted to Crawford.

"Initial interrogation of Captain Vostov confirms the facts Major Chase has provided. We've lost all three devices. Mr. Cummings was killed in a missile strike on the Russians who ambushed the meet." Crawford answered.

Packard looked around the room before leaning back in his chair and exhaling a deep breath.

"Madam President," he said. "We still have signal intercept capability and I'd like to play an audio file for you that was intercepted yesterday."

"What's on the recording, Admiral?" She asked, her face neutral.

"It's a satellite phone call made by Mr. Cummings from Tinker Air Force Base prior to the team's departure for Texas, ma'am." The President stared into the camera on her end for several long moments before shaking her head.

"That won't be necessary, Admiral. I need to think about these developments. I'll be in touch." A moment later her image disappeared from the screen.

"Well if this isn't just a cluster fuck of monumental proportions." He said. "Colonel, we need to speak. Privately. Call me in ten minutes."

What the Admiral probably wanted to discuss was the fact that both himself and Colonel Crawford had been working with the renegade GRU to support the overthrow of Russian President Barinov. They now had a President who seemed to be willing to betray them. Crawford read between the lines and nodded at a look from Packard. I suspected there was something more going on behind the scenes, but right now all I really cared about was finding my wife.

The debrief wrapped up quickly from that point. Admiral Packard shut down the videoconference from his end, one of the Air Force staffers powering down the equipment in the room. I had just asked Crawford to excuse me and was starting to stand when an Air Force Major knocked and hustled into the room. He was carrying a laptop and stepped up to the end of the table.

"Sir," he addressed General Triplett. "We have video of the individual responsible for the breach in the perimeter fence."

"Who was it?" Triplett asked, looking surprised.

"One of ours, sir. Captain Lee Roach."

I was almost out the door when I heard the name, freezing in my tracks so suddenly that Rachel bumped into my back. Turning back into the room I met Crawford's eyes and he nodded at my just vacated chair, telling me to sit down and listen. I glanced at Rachel who looked as shocked as I felt. We hadn't talked about it, but I suspected she assumed he had died in the Mississippi River, just as I did.

Slowly we took our seats as the Security Forces Major connected his laptop to a video cable attached to the display at the front of the room. As his computer finished booting up he began speaking.

"This is actually a much more complicated matter than just the sabotage of the perimeter fence." He began. "Captain Lee William Roach appeared at the main gate three days ago with a woman he claimed was his wife."

The laptop was up and running now and the Major clicked a series of icons. Momentarily we were looking at a still image of Roach and a girl I didn't recognize taken from video recorded at the main gate to Tinker. A large Security Forces Sergeant was escorting them out of a civilian pickup and Roach was still dressed in his underwear and a tactical vest, as he'd been when he went into the river.

"He claimed that he and his wife had escaped Tennessee ahead of the secondary outbreak and arrival of the herds. We performed as full of a background investigation as possible with the limited resources that are still operational. There were no red flags found and after validating his identity and service record he was cleared and assigned as refugee liaison officer."

The Major continued to talk, telling the story of a missing Tech Sergeant at the base's water treatment plant and a missing Security Forces Airman. He had pieced together video footage from various security cameras around the base and I watched as Roach first threw his wife over a fence to be eaten by infected, then killed a witness.

From a different view he attacked a female Airman and placed her body in the back of his Humvee before driving out of the frame in her vehicle, presumably to hide it as he returned shortly and left in his. Another jump in the video and we watched from a high angle as Roach hooked a chain to the perimeter fence and used a Hummer to tear it open.

The Major kept narrating what we were watching, the video following Roach as he drove across the base after breaching the fence. It jumped from camera to camera as he moved, the angle and perspective continually changing. He went to a large brick building, hurrying inside, a moment later panicked people visible running across the screen.

"This is when we believe he called in an alert that the fence was breached." The Major said, hitting the pause button.

"Why breach the fence, then call it in?" Asked General Triplett. "Is he trying to be a hero? Set up a crisis and be the one to sound the alarm?"

"No sir, I think it was to create a distraction. Watch." The Major responded.

A few short minutes after Roach ran into the building he reappeared with a woman who appeared to be carrying a pair of boots in her hand. The long, red hair and the way she moved caught my eye and I leaned forward to peer at the screen, fingers turning white as I gripped the edge of the table, but the camera had been high in the air and too far away to make out any details.

The image jumped a few times as the pieced together video followed Roach's Humvee to the flight line where a young pilot stood next to a Pave Hawk waiting for him. The camera angle and position was better and as soon as the Hummer's passenger door opened I stood and stepped close to the screen to watch. Watched as Katie ran for the Pave Hawk, Roach by her side.

I stopped breathing when I saw him raise what at first I thought was a pistol and point it at the back of her head as she started to climb into the aircraft's side door. Relief flooded through me when I realized it was only a Taser. I stood helplessly watching as my wife was tossed into the helicopter that then took off, disappearing from view.

"Major?" It was Crawford speaking to me. I was now standing directly in front of the screen, back to the room and couldn't respond. A moment later I felt a hand on my arm and turned my head to look at Rachel. I was in a daze. I was frightened, angry, and unable to form a coherent thought for a few moments.

"Major, are you alright?" Colonel Crawford again.

I slowly turned to face the room. Everyone was on their feet staring at me. Rachel was next to me, hand on my arm, and when I looked at her I could tell she knew.

"My wife." I said in a low voice.

"Your wife, son?" General Triplett asked, confusion creasing his features.

"My wife, sir." I said in a stronger voice as the fury in my gut began churning its way up. "That was my wife that was taken by that son of a bitch!"

15

The room was silent as everyone looked from me back up to the screen at the frozen image of Roach lifting a disabled Katie into the Pave Hawk.

"Major, where did that helicopter go?" Colonel Crawford broke the silence.

"We don't know, sir. This was an unauthorized flight, so in effect the aircraft was stolen. We're trying to identify the pilot, but we don't have an image that's good enough for facial recognition software to give us a match. There are investigators tracking down every pilot on base at the moment.

"I've checked with Air and they didn't track the helo on radar, so it apparently flew low to avoid detection and had the IFF beacon turned off. We're in the process of trying to force activate the IFF remotely, but that's a long shot at best." IFF stands for Identify Friend or Foe and is how aircraft let radar operators know they are friendly. Every civilian and military aircraft has one, but they can be turned off if the pilot wants to hide.

"Captain," Crawford turned to Blanchard. "See if we've got any sat imagery of the area from the time that aircraft took off."

"Yes, sir." Blanchard said, bending over his laptop.

I was in a daze. My heart ached and anger pulsed through me like a sonar ping, but I didn't know what to do. I didn't know where to start looking for Katie. Waves of helplessness washed over me like a physical force, feeding the white-hot ball of anger boiling inside.

Rachel took my arm and guided me back to a chair as one of General Triplett's aides entered the room. He stepped up to the General and whispered in his ear. A moment later Triplett stood and strode out of the room. Crawford watched him leave with hooded eyes, then excused himself to presumably go have a private conversation with Admiral Packard. I sat at the table, hands balled into fists, staring at Captain Blanchard.

"I'm downloading the image files now, sir. It will take a few minutes." He said, feeling the weight of my stare.

I nodded as he stood and walked out of the room after letting me know he was just going to the latrine and would be back before the files finished downloading. Rachel wrapped her arms around me and kissed the side of my head, then followed Blanchard out into the hall.

There were a few Air Force staffers still in the room, and finding themselves alone with me they quickly started packing up and preparing to leave. I idly noticed them all stand at the same time and come to attention. No matter how angry you are, if you're in the military and see a bunch of people snap to attention, you look around to see why.

General Triplett stood just inside the doorway, three large Security Forces Airmen to his left. I could see half a dozen more crowded in the hallway. I slowly stood, pushing my chair away with the backs of my legs and turned to face the General.

"I'm sorry, Major. By order of the President of the United States you are under arrest for the murder of Brent Cummings and Treason for conspiring to assassinate a foreign head of state."

I stood staring at him, dumbfounded. Then I thought about what I knew. President Clark had betrayed our plans to Barinov. Perhaps Cummings had made the actual call that the Admiral had referred to, but he had done it on her orders. Now, she was going to shut down any resistance to her plan to lie down and spread her legs for the Russians.

The lead Security Forces Master Sergeant stepped forward, hand on the butt of his holstered pistol. He was a big guy, about my size, and looked like he'd been around the block a couple of times. The Tech Sergeant and Staff Sergeant backing him up were equally as large and when he stepped forward they took up positions a couple of feet on either side of him.

"Sir, please place your hands on top of your head." He said, the tone in his voice leaving no doubt that he was ready for a confrontation.

Well, so was I. There was no way in hell I was going to cool my heels in the Air Force version of the stockade while Katie was still out there in the hands of a maniac. The anger that was nearly consuming me boiled over when he finished speaking, and I lunged, delivering a massive uppercut to his chin, yelling at Dog to stay. As furious as I was, I didn't want Dog to kill these guys for just following a lawful order.

The lead cop might have been expecting resistance, but he had probably been expecting me to go for a weapon, not charge in. Without the opportunity to defend himself I landed the blow, feeling the impact all the way up my arm and into my shoulder. The Master Sergeant's head snapped back, his feet left the floor and he crashed onto his back. The two cops in the room with him hesitated when I struck, most likely used to subjects of arrest not fighting back. Or if they did fight, it was once the cuffs started going on.

Their delay in reacting was what I expected. Letting the momentum of my attack carry me I spun an elbow into the temple of the guy on my right and he dropped like a marionette without the strings. The third guy grabbed my arm as shouts of alarm came from the group in the hall. I turned into his grasp and crashed my forehead into the bridge of his nose, sending him sprawling to the tile floor.

I turned to meet the charge from the hall just in time to absorb a flying tackle from the first cop through the door. He wasn't as big as the first three I'd already put down, but he hit me squarely in the chest with his shoulder and drove me back onto the large table in the middle of the room, arms locked around my mid-section.

Up to that point Dog had obeyed and stayed out of the fracas, but seeing me tackled was more than he could take. The cop screamed when Dog clamped down on his leg and began dragging him off of me. When his grip loosened I hit him in the face three times, fast and hard, then he was on the floor holding his face and moaning as the rest of the squad flooded the room.

As I scrambled back to my feet I saw the first Taser raised and heard the pop when it fired. The darts couldn't penetrate my vest and I reached for the cop who had fired the device but never got my hands on him. There were now eight more Security Forces pushing in on me and two more Tasers fired, one of them finding exposed skin on my right arm.

The jolt of electricity hurt like hell and made my head spin, but I was able to grab the wires leading from the barbs embedded in my skin back to the battery pack in the butt of the Taser, ripping them loose. The current stopped surging through my body, but the jolt had slowed me. Four of them charged in, trying to bury me under their mass.

I was ready for them, jumping back to clamber across the table and open some space, but the table must have been weakened when I was first tackled onto it. This time it collapsed, dropping me flat on my back with four cops piled on top of me. I could hear Dog's snarls then a yelp of pain and I fought harder, gouging an eye, squeezing a pair of balls hard enough to feel one of them pop, but more cops rushed in and the fight went out of me when a handheld Taser was pressed against my neck and triggered until I couldn't move.

16

Rachel flushed the toilet in the latrine, exited the stall and began to wash her hands. Looking up she saw her reflection in the mirror and paused, staring into her own eyes. She was upset. Happy for John, yet distraught for herself. She had always known there was a possibility he would find Katie, but deep down she'd never believed that the woman could still be alive.

Now, just when she was starting to believe that John was hers… Damn it! She had no ill will for Katie. That wasn't it. She just felt like her heart had been broken. Not intentionally, and she realized it was no one's fault other than her own for allowing herself to fall in love with a married man. John had never led her on. He'd been candid and upfront since the day she'd met him in Atlanta, but that didn't make her ache any less for what could have been.

What did she do now? She loved him, but she knew that once he got Katie back she wouldn't be able to stay around. There was nothing that could be done about her feelings, and the thought of seeing John every day but not being able to touch him was not something she could live with. But what the hell did she do? It wasn't like she could just pack up and move to a new city to start over. That world was gone.

She would help John do whatever he needed to do to save Katie, then she'd be on her way. Somewhere. Somehow. With a sigh, she looked down at the running water and the thought hit her that maybe Roach had already killed Katie. For a moment the idea gave her some comfort, then she got mad at herself for even thinking about the other woman's death being a solution to her heartache.

Turning the water off, Rachel was reaching for a paper towel to dry her hands when the sound of a disturbance from the hall made her pause. The first thought that went through her head was "infected", but after a couple of seconds of listening to the shouts and sounds of a fight, she knew this was something else.

Rachel quickly stepped across the room and was almost hit in the face when the door was suddenly pushed open. Captain Blanchard dashed through the opening and before she could utter a sound, he grabbed her and clamped a hand over her mouth.

"Shhhhh…." He hissed softly in her ear and after a moment she relaxed a notch and nodded her head. Blanchard slowly removed his hand and turned to face the door as it finished closing.

"What's going on?" Rachel whispered in his ear as the sounds of fighting continued to grow.

"The Air Force is trying to arrest the Major by order of the President. He's not going quietly." He whispered back.

Rachel immediately stepped forward, but Blanchard grabbed her arm and held her. "We can't help him if we're in the cell next to his." He said, staring into her eyes. Finally she nodded and he released his grip.

The sounds of the brawl continued on for what seemed like forever, finally stopping as quickly as they had started. After a few moments Blanchard stepped to the door and cracked it open half an inch, peering through with one eye. He watched for a long time, then waved Rachel over to join him. He motioned at the opening and moved aside so Rachel could see into the hall.

No less than a dozen Security Forces cops were clustered around the door into the conference room, all of them trying to see what was happening inside. Movement amongst their legs caught Rachel's eye as Dog slipped through the crowd. She hissed his name as loudly as she dared, his head turning in her direction. She spoke his name very softly and he moved down the hall towards the latrine door.

Rachel was concerned as she watched Dog approach. He was unsteady on his feet and favoring both left legs. When he reached the door she darted her eyes up to make sure none of the cops were looking in her direction. Their attention was still focused inside the conference room and she quickly stepped back and pulled the door open far enough for Dog to slip through.

Door closed, he moved past her and sat down with a slight whimper. Rachel kneeled next to him and ran her hands over his body, but failed to find any injury. She rubbed his head and pressed her face to his, Dog letting out a long sigh.

"What did they do to him?" She asked. "I don't see anything, but something's wrong."

Blanchard knelt next to her and placed a hand on Dog's head, giving him a moment to accept the contact before also checking him over for injuries.

"They must have used a Taser on him." He finally said after a thorough inspection. "He'll be OK in a bit. Just feeling the after effects at the moment."

Rachel wrapped her arms around Dog's neck and held him for a few moments, then stood up and glared at Blanchard.

"What are we going to do? Did they arrest the Colonel, too?"

"I don't know. He had left the room to have a conversation with Admiral Packard. I'm sure they will if they can find him, but if he's got a heads up they won't have an easy time of it." Blanchard said.

"That's good, but what are we going to do? We have to help John." Rachel said, anger threatening to boil over.

"We're going to wait until there's not a small army of Air Force cops standing just down the hall, then we're going to get out of here and round up a few platoons of Rangers. Once we have some combat muscle behind us we'll get the Colonel and Major back." He said.

Rachel was momentarily surprised. She had always seen Blanchard operating in his role as Colonel Crawford's aide. That job required him to maintain a calm and diplomatic demeanor, and she had never looked at him as a leader of rough men, despite the Special Forces tab he wore on his uniform. Apparently there was more to the man than she had given him credit for.

"OK," she said, giving him a smile. "Two months ago I didn't know what a Ranger was, but now I think they're about the best people on the planet!"

Rachel looked down when Dog stood up and shook. He was steady on his feet and looked like he had gotten past the shock of the Taser.

"Will the Marines help? John knows one of them and…"

"All the Marines got sent to Texas to secure an oil refinery. That may or may not be another problem. I'm supposed to be coordinating air support between them and the Air Force. I'm a little worried this turn in events may leave their asses hanging out in the wind." Blanchard said, shaking his head.

"Besides," he continued. "This is going to be a little tricky. The President has the authority to do what she's doing, no matter what any of us in the military think. She is the Commander In Chief."

"So you think this is OK?" Rachel glared at him.

"That's not what I'm saying. I know the facts, and if times were normal... Well, let's just say nothing is normal any longer. We have a President who was a political appointee. There's no Congress, no media, no public opinion, no international partners, nothing to guide or temper her decisions. In effect she has unchecked power as long as the military will follow her orders. That's not the way it's supposed to work."

"Then why is the Air Force arresting John?" Rachel didn't understand what Blanchard was trying to explain to her.

"It's General Triplett who is following the orders of the President. It's not an Air Force thing; it's an officer following the oath he took. I know Colonel Crawford and Admiral Packard were already concerned about President Clark and were prepared to refuse orders they felt weren't in the best interest of the country. But there will be officers that will follow the President blindly. This is quickly becoming one hell of a mess, and I only hope it doesn't end up with the complete fracturing of the military and two armed camps facing off against each other."

17

Master Gunnery Sergeant Matt Zemeck stood atop a hastily erected barricade that surrounded the Texaco oil refinery outside of Midland, Texas. It was late morning, the sun hot on his shoulders as he held a pair of binoculars to his eyes, surveying the scrub desert spreading out to the south. Next to him, standing in an identical pose, Marine Colonel Jim Pointere cursed as for the fourth time his binoculars lost focus for some mysterious reason.

"Here, sir. Use mine." Zemeck held them out, taking the Colonel's in exchange. Pointere looked through them, grunted his thanks and scanned the horizon.

They couldn't see the approaching herd. Yet. But it was coming. It was being watched on satellite and from drones that were tracking the mass of infected humanity. Arrival of the leading edge was expected at about 1900 hours, or just before sundown. And right behind that leading edge were more than two million bodies determined to kill every living thing in their path.

"Bravo platoon will be making contact in about 5 minutes." Zemeck said.

Bravo platoon was comprised of 35 Marines spread across four Humvees and four, eight wheeled LAVs or Light Armored Vehicles. Their unenviable job was to decoy the herd away from the refinery by distracting the front ranks of infected and leading them in a safe direction. No one knew if it would work, but it was an idea courtesy of Army Major John Chase and was the Marines' only hope of saving the vital infrastructure so it could continue to provide fuel.

The sheer numbers of the infected precluded any successful armed resistance. The infected, once zeroed in on prey, don't quit. They can't be scared off or their will to fight broken like a normal army. All that can be done is to kill every single one of them, and while Zemeck knew his Devil Dogs were the best fighters on the planet, they didn't have enough men, rifles or bullets to kill over two million attackers.

Colonel Pointere had hoped that the refinery could be shut down and abandoned until the herd passed, but was disappointed to learn that it takes days to safely shut one down that is operating at full capacity. There simply wasn't time to evacuate ahead of the herd's arrival. But the shutdown process was underway, and it was up to the Marines to hold back the tide of infected long enough for the workers to shutter the plant and escape. Once the herd was no longer a danger they could return and restart the production of fuel.

"How many Ospreys are up?" Pointere asked.

"We've got two flying cover for our guys." Zemeck answered. "Sure is nice to be staging out of a gas station."

Pointere, a man of no more words than absolutely necessary, grunted again in acknowledgement. Lowering his binoculars he turned to face Zemeck.

"You trust this Army Major knows what he's talking about? There's a chance this will work?" He asked.

"He knows his shit, sir. If it weren't for him my head would be decorating some jihadists wall in sand land. But this was an idea, not something anyone's tried before. What he does know is that we can't hold the herd back. Too damn many of them, and not enough Marines or ammo."

Dirk Patton

The Colonel stared at him for a few moments then nodded his head in understanding.

"You've got to tell me the story sometime." He said.

Before Zemeck could answer a voice came over his radio earpiece. Pausing, he lifted his hand to his ear to make sure he heard the communication clearly. He listened for a couple of moments before turning to Pointere.

"Bravo platoon in contact, sir. They're lighting up the leaders to get those fuckers' attention."

Pointere grunted, did a quick pat check of the twin combat knives strapped to the small of his back, then resumed looking to the south through the binoculars even though the action was too far away for him to see.

"Let's go see what's going on," he said after a few moments. "Everything's quiet here. Let Captain Simon know we're going."

"Yes, sir." Zemeck answered, making a call on his radio as he turned to follow the Colonel.

Five minutes later they were on board an Osprey, the rotors spinning up a maelstrom of dust and debris as they reached take off speed. The pilot took exaggerated care in every movement once they were clear of the ground, the hulking refinery close enough to present a hazard if he didn't pay close attention. Moving clear of the facility he fed in full power and transitioned to forward flight, the aircraft streaking across the desert.

Once they were in stable flight, Pointere and Zemeck moved forward into the cockpit, the Colonel crowding in with the pilots and Zemeck eclipsing the hatch with his bulk. Directly in front of them a massive dust cloud was clearly visible on the horizon.

"Jesus Christ," Pointere breathed. "How many does it take to stir up that much dust just from walking?"

The question was rhetorical, and Zemeck didn't bother to answer. He well knew how large the herd was, having seen it on sat imagery as well as video feeds from orbiting drones. But no matter what you see on a video screen, no matter how good the image is or how large the screen, nothing prepares you for the sight of several million infected all moving together.

Pointere spoke an order to the pilot who fiddled with some controls on the radio. Moments later the voices of the men in Bravo platoon came over speakers mounted in the ceiling of the cockpit. No calls for help or any indication of problems, but one of the Marines was being a little too talkative and flippant about the whole situation for the Colonel's taste.

"Who is that?" He asked, turning to Zemeck.

"That would be Lance Corporal Bradley, sir." Zemeck replied. "I'll take care of it."

Stepping out of the hatch, Zemeck activated his radio and placed a call to the offending Marine. The conversation was short, and Bravo's voice traffic died down to nothing more than the exchange of essential information.

"I'll have a conversation with him when we get a moment, sir." Zemeck said.

Pointere grunted his response and leaned forward for a better view as the vehicles of Bravo platoon and the front edge of the herd came into view. The vehicles were no more than a hundred yards in front of a group of charging females, spread out and driving due east in their attempt to change the herd's direction.

As they moved across the desert, gunners fired occasional bursts to knock down the fastest females and keep those behind them interested. But the million dollar question was would the body of the herd turn to follow the head. Could a mass of infected this large be tricked into following the leader?

The pilot started to slow, intending to go into a hover to observe the operation, but Pointere told him to keep flying south over the herd. Adjusting some controls he put them back on a southerly course, nothing visible below other than dust and a sea of raging humanity. It took a long time to reach a point where the infected weren't a solid mass of bodies. The pilot checked an instrument and let the Colonel know the herd was nearly six miles long.

"OK, take us back to the front." Pointere said after a moment's thought.

Once they were turned and heading back, Zemeck checked the Osprey's compass. Their heading was only a few degrees to the east of due north. The infected beneath them were stretched out like a fat snake, and if Bravo platoon's efforts were working he expected to see a bend in the snake as they approached the leaders of the herd.

But that bend wasn't there. Thousands of females were sprinting out ahead of the herd, chasing after the Marines on the ground, but the bulk of the infected were staying on course.

"Why aren't they taking the bait?" Pointere asked, eyes glued on the action below.

"I don't know." Zemeck answered. "Maybe we're not making a big enough distraction. Maybe we can't make a big enough distraction. This is all theory."

"If it's a bigger distraction that's needed, let's give them one." Pointere said, turning to the pilot and telling him what he had in mind.

The pilot nodded and a few minutes later transitioned into a hover a hundred feet over the heads of the infected. The Osprey was positioned about half a mile back over the herd from the leading edge, and as soon as the aircraft was in a stable hover the co-pilot began hosing down the bodies below with the belly mounted minigun. The pilot slipped them sideways as the weapon continued to devastate the bodies below, dropping until he was only fifty feet above the ground. Giving his co-pilot a few seconds to keep wreaking havoc, he then moved them to the east in the direction of Bravo platoon.

But the infected didn't follow. The females looked up and screamed at them, the males tilting their heads in the direction of the noisy aircraft, but none of them changed course.

"Save your ammo." Pointere said, the minigun falling silent immediately.

"We need that air support the Air Force promised, sir." Zemeck said. "And we need it now if we're going to slow or turn them."

Pointere grunted and told the pilot to take them back to the refinery.

18

Rachel, Dog and Blanchard stayed quiet in the latrine as the Air Force Security Forces went about the business of restraining John. Before they had him out the door and on his way to a holding cell, sirens could be heard approaching the building, shutting down as they pulled into the parking lot. Blanchard moved to a small window set high in the wall and used an overturned trash can to gain enough height to see out.

"What's going on?" Rachel asked quietly.

"Two ambulances," he said without taking his attention away from the view. "I hope the Major isn't hurt too bad."

"I'll bet it's cops they're hauling out on stretchers." Rachel said.

They stayed that way for a while, Rachel sitting with her back against the wall, facing the door. Dog sat in front of her, also keeping an eye on the door as she stroked his head.

"You're right," Blanchard, still watching the parking lot finally said. "They just brought the Major out and he's walking. He's in cuffs and leg irons. They just loaded three MPs on gurneys into the ambulances, and there's another three limping along."

"Does he look OK?" Rachel asked. "John, I mean."

"Other than pissed off, looks fine." Blanchard turned and almost lost his balance when the door from the hallway suddenly opened.

Martinez paused halfway through the door when she saw them, automatically reaching a hand out to Dog when he ran over to her. His initial attack charge to protect Rachel had changed to a greeting when he'd recognized Martinez. She glanced over her shoulder, down the hall in the direction of the conference room, then moved quickly into the latrine and pushed the door shut with her back, the pneumatic closer hissing in protest as it was forced to move faster than normal.

"What's happening?" Rachel asked, climbing to her feet and moving across the room to meet Martinez.

"The President ordered Major Chase's arrest." Martinez answered. "Charges are the murder of Brent Cummings and Treason."

"Is he hurt?" Rachel asked, reaching out and touching Martinez' arm.

"They finally got him down with a Taser after a bunch of them piled on top of him. He put three in the hospital and put the hurt on a few more before he went down."

"You know this is bullshit, right?" Rachel asked.

"Don't worry about me," Martinez said in a hard voice. "I was there. Remember? And I've been through some nasty shit with him. But what can I do? I'm just a Captain."

"Have they arrested Colonel Crawford?" Blanchard had jumped down off the trashcan and joined them.

"I don't think they can find him." Martinez said.

"I can," he said. "We need to get out of here and join the Colonel."

"We need to get John back!" Rachel said, turning to glare at Blanchard.

"Agreed, but that will be a whole lot easier with the Colonel and a few hundred Rangers helping." He stared back at her and after a moment Rachel nodded her head and looked away.

"Are you with us, Captain?" Blanchard turned his gaze to Martinez.

"You realize you're talking about subversion, treason and half a dozen other things that could get us shot?" She met his gaze and didn't blink.

"Before the world ended, yes. Now? With a traitor for a President and people dying all around us? I took the same oath you did, Captain, but part of that oath is to defend our country against *domestic* enemies too. If betraying us to the Russians, who were the ones that orchestrated this whole thing, doesn't qualify as a domestic enemy, I don't know what does. Time to pick sides, Captain." He said. "Join us, or forget you saw us here."

"Of course I'm with you. Damn but the Army has sticks up their ass. And I thought Marines were bad." She grinned. "Now, how do we find your Colonel?"

"Wait. What about Irina and Igor?" Rachel asked. "What's going to happen to them?"

"They'll probably be held and turned over to the Russians." Blanchard said. "Who will most likely put them on a very public trial in Russia before executing them."

"Then we have to help them, too." Rachel declared. "As good as it felt to punch that blonde bitch in the eye, we can't let them be handed back."

"They're in a room down the hall. Under guard." Blanchard said. "We won't get them without getting our hands dirty."

"What do you mean?" Rachel asked.

"It's what I was trying to explain earlier. About the military fracturing? General Triplett has apparently decided to follow President Clark's orders. That means, with a few notable exceptions," he nodded at Martinez, "the Air Force personnel under his command will be following his orders. We just became the rebels, and rebellions are never clean and sanitary. People get hurt and killed. Men and women we were fighting alongside yesterday are now the enemy."

"You're saying we're going to have to kill Air Force personnel?" Rachel asked, shocked at the thought.

"I'm saying that we may very well find ourselves in a situation where we don't have a choice. I don't like it one bit, and I'll do everything I can to avoid it, but if we're going to resist then you have to be prepared for that to happen. Can you deal with that, Captain?" Blanchard turned to look at Martinez.

"I won't kill unless it's to defend one of our lives." She answered. "Is that good enough for you?"

"Don't misunderstand me, Captain. I'm not blood thirsty, ready to go hunting anyone wearing an Air Force uniform. I'm just pointing out that the situation will most likely arise where we have to make a difficult decision and I need to know, if the time comes, can you make that decision and live with it?"

Martinez stood still for a long moment, staring at the floor, finally looking up and meeting Blanchard's eyes.

"Yes. To save one of our lives, I'll do what has to be done. But nothing more than that."

Blanchard nodded but didn't feel the need to add anything further to the discussion.

"That's good, but I'll ask again. What about the Russians?" Rachel said.

"She's right," Blanchard said. "As soon as things calm down they're probably going to be moved to a more secure location."

"Leave it to me." Martinez said, pulling the door open and exiting into the hallway.

Less than two minutes later the door opened again and Irina walked in, Martinez on her heels. Irina stopped when she saw Rachel, but Martinez put a hand on her back and guided her the rest of the way into the latrine so she could close the door.

"Told the guard I was checking on them, then that Irina had to use the latrine." Martinez smiled.

"What's going on?" Irina asked, looking at their faces.

Blanchard gave her an abbreviated version of the events that she was unaware of. "We expect Barinov to demand President Clark hand you and Igor over."

"They'll execute us!" Irina had gone pale.

"That's what we think as well, which is why we're going to get you out of here." Blanchard said. "Martinez, how many guards on Igor?"

"Just one. In the hall. And it looks like they're wrapping up in the main conference room. I don't think we're going to have much time before someone thinks to put our guests into confinement."

"OK. If I remember right, the room he's in is around a corner and there are windows in the room that open to the rear of the building." Blanchard said.

"Correct. We're going out the window?"

"Yes. You and I will escort Irina back to the room. Rachel, you and Dog right behind us. The guard shouldn't know everything that's transpired, and we'll be able to walk right up to him. I'll take him out, non-lethal, and we get Igor then haul ass. Everyone ready?"

As they walked around the corner in the hall, Martinez slowed but didn't stop when she saw the guard was missing. She glanced over her shoulder at Blanchard who quickly pushed past Irina and drew his pistol. Martinez frowned at him, but he ignored her.

Waving the small group to a halt, he slowly continued down the hall, suddenly accelerating when the door to the room where Igor was being held began to swing open. Prepared to launch a blow at the guard he expected to see, Blanchard skidded and nearly fell when Colonel Crawford leaned out of the opening.

The Colonel nodded at them and motioned them into the room. Once inside they glanced around, spotting the unconscious and restrained guard lying to the side. Igor stood next to an open window, watching the area behind the building.

"Good to see everyone," Crawford said in a low voice. "Let's get out of here before the Security Forces come looking for our Russian friends."

He turned and led the way to where Igor was keeping watch, sending Blanchard through the opening first. The rest of the group quickly followed, clambering through the awkward sized opening. Crawford lifted Dog up and handed him through to Igor's waiting arms, then levered himself up and through.

The back of the building faced a large, grassy area that covered at least two acres.

Despite the events that had transpired over the past couple of months, it was still neatly mown and edged. Rachel found it a little surreal, but knew the maintenance of the grass was a routine the military would maintain until prevented by circumstance.

Far to their left was another cluster of low buildings and a hundred yards to the right a wide, tree lined road that led to the area where the homes of senior officers were located. Crawford signed for them to follow and he set off at a fast walk directly towards the middle of the lawn. On the far side were more buildings, each with large parking lots and multiple military and civilian vehicles were visible.

When they were half way across the grass, Crawford reached up to touch an earpiece in his left ear and mumbled a few words. A minute later the first of a dozen Humvees pulled into the closest parking lot, the convoy swinging around and stopping, pointing back the way it had come. Half a dozen Rangers in full battle rattle stepped out of each vehicle and quickly formed a defensive perimeter.

The sound of racing engines came from behind them and Crawford glanced over his shoulder to see two Security Forces Hummers jump the curb and start across the neat lawn in pursuit. Without breaking stride he spoke into his radio again. Moments later a Ranger stepped forward, dropped to the ground and sighted in on the Air Force vehicles. He was using a sound suppressed .50 caliber rifle and disabled each vehicle with a single shot to its engine, then maintained his aim without firing any additional rounds.

"Colonel!" General Triplett had stepped out of one of the stalled Hummers and shouted.

Crawford stopped and told the rest of the group to continue on to the waiting vehicles. Blanchard stopped by his side, turning with him to face the General. Triplett was walking across the field with ten armed Security Forces in tow. Blanchard turned and hand signed to the Rangers, a moment later twenty of them running forward and forming up behind their Colonel. Their rifles were up and ready, but not pointed directly at the approaching Air Force personnel.

The field was large and it took a few minutes for General Triplett to reach the area where Crawford waited for him. He came to a stop ten feet away, the Security Forces spreading out behind him. They looked nervous, as well they should have. They were cops, not combat troops, and they were only armed with pistols. They were seriously outnumbered and outgunned if things went bad.

"Colonel Crawford, by order of the President of the United States, you are under arrest for sedition and treason. You need to surrender yourself peacefully." The General said in a loud, commanding voice.

"General, what seditious or treasonous acts have I committed?" Crawford asked. "You've been involved in every discussion and decision that has been made. You can't seriously be following this order. The only sedition and treason here is what our President has done."

"Colonel, it's not our place to question the orders of our superior. We took an oath to obey those appointed above us, and this is a lawful order from the Commander In Chief."

Crawford let out a long sigh and took a couple of steps closer to the General. One of the Security Forces drew his weapon when the Colonel stepped forward, immediately getting half a dozen rifles aimed directly at him. He froze, muzzle of the weapon still pointed at the ground. Triplett looked around at his man, then at the Rangers and the determined looks on their faces. He waved for the man to holster the weapon, and when it was, the aim of the rifles was moved a few degrees off target.

"General, the world we knew has ended. It ended courtesy of the Russians. The very same people to whom our President has betrayed us. There are people out in Oklahoma City that are turning every day, and there's millions more infected on the way here. Exactly where the Russians are drawing them. You were at the briefing. You know what's going on. Do you really think it's prudent to follow these orders and divide our forces? We need to be working together, not fighting each other."

"You're right about needing to work together, but we also need to follow orders." Triplett responded. "Surrender yourself and place your men under my command."

Crawford stared at the man, read the conviction in his eyes. "General, I respectfully decline to obey the order."

"Colonel, don't make me come and get you."

"Sir, to attempt to do so would be a grave mistake. We have bigger concerns. Don't put us in the position of having to start shooting at each other." Crawford took another step forward, wanting Triplett to see his face clearly and understand that he was serious.

After a few moments of silence Crawford turned and walked through the line of Rangers, heading for the waiting Humvees. Blanchard fell in behind him, the Rangers slowly following, making sure the Security Forces didn't try to advance.

19

The holding cell the Air Force put me in wasn't large, or particularly comfortable, but at least it was clean. When they put me on the floor in the small room my hands were still cuffed behind my back and my ankles were shackled together. The lead Sergeant was pissed that I had resisted and hurt some of his men, but he should have been glad all I'd done was hurt them. I was starting to regret my restraint.

Use of my Kukri and pistol would most likely have gotten me out of there and on my way to find Katie. Right now all I cared about was finding her. I was through holding back. The next person that got in my way wasn't going to survive the encounter.

Four of them were crowded into the tiny space, and before they removed my restraints I received several solid kicks to my head and ribs. Fortunately I didn't feel anything break, but I almost passed out from a well placed blow to my temple. Finally they stopped kicking and one of them leaned in and Tasered me on the neck again.

Days Of Perdition

My body went rigid and I lost control of my voluntary muscles. And it hurt like a son of a bitch. While my nervous system was still scrambled, they removed the leg shackles then flipped me over and took the cuffs off. The last one out the door paused and looked down at me.

"Not so fucking tough now, are you asshole?" He punctuated his words with a kick to my balls that caused bile to rise in my throat, then stepped out and slammed the heavy steel door.

I just lay there for a while, slowly curling into a fetal position as the effects of the Taser wore off. The floor was smooth concrete and there was a small, metal drain cover set in the middle. I let the coolness of the floor seep into my battered body as the pain in my lower abdomen began to subside. Not go away, just ratchet down from a ten to a six or seven.

Eventually I was able to sit up and look around. The cell was stark. The walls and ceiling were also concrete that had been finished smooth, the only way in or out a solid steel door with an access slot at the top and another at floor level. A light was recessed in the ceiling, protected by thick glass covered with heavy wire mesh. A combination stainless steel toilet and sink were bolted to the wall in the back corner.

On the opposite wall was an iron bunk that was bolted to the wall and floor, a thin mattress rolled neatly and resting at one end. Otherwise, the room was completely void of any furnishing or decoration. Slowly climbing to my feet I unrolled the mattress and eased myself onto the bunk, suppressing a groan of pain as my weight came down on my pelvis. Opening my pants I inspected myself, relieved to find that while there was some swelling it didn't appear that the kick had ruptured anything important.

Taking a deep breath I took another, closer look around the inside of the cell. Nothing I hadn't seen the first time. The only way out was if someone opened the door. In what seemed like a lifetime ago I had undergone Army SERE – Survival Evasion Resistance and Escape – training. I had failed to evade and resist arrest. Now it was time to think about escape.

But unlike a Hollywood movie, I wasn't going to be tunneling through solid concrete, or disappearing down a sewer drain. My shot would come when they opened the door, which they would. Someone would want to talk to me.

Lawyers would be involved. I could probably make a good case for needing medical attention. Every time that door opened I had an opportunity. Some would be better than others, and I had to be ready to take the right one when it presented itself.

Step one was to not cause any problems for the guards. Right now they were keyed up and on high alert, expecting me to go Neanderthal on them after the way the arrest had gone down. I needed them to relax. Think I was going to be a docile prisoner. Let their guard down a little. Until that happened, I wasn't going to have a chance.

Step two was to be physically ready for any opening. That meant resting and letting my body heal as much as possible. But rest was going to be difficult with the throbbing pain between my legs. Gingerly standing I hobbled to the door and banged on the upper access slot with my fist. After almost a minute it slammed open and I found myself looking at a pair of angry eyes.

"Could I please have an ice pack? I've got some injuries." I said in a calm, respectful voice.

The eyes stared back at me for what seemed a long time, then the panel was slammed shut. Shrugging, I turned and went back to the bunk. A few minutes later the access panel at floor level slammed open and a chemical ice pack came skittering across the floor.

"Thank you," I shouted before the opening closed with slightly less violence.

Good. Let them think I'm hurting and subdued. Well, I was hurting. Subdued? Not hardly, but it's all in the timing. Squeezing the pack I broke the ampules inside that released whatever chemical it was that starts the reaction. I immediately felt the cold start seeping through the rough cover. Stretching out on the bunk I opened my pants again and placed the swiftly cooling pack directly on my aching boys.

Laying my head down I closed my eyes and thought about Katie. I was still in shock that she had made it all the way to Oklahoma. I knew she was smart, tough and resourceful, but I had to admit to myself that I was surprised she'd made it this far on her own.

How had Roach identified her? The Security Forces major had said that Roach was in charge of processing refugees, but how the hell had he put it together? Or had he? Was she just a woman that had caught his eye? No. That was just too much of a coincidence. He knew exactly what he was doing and whom he was taking. But why?

I had thought he was dead, killed by the fall into the Mississippi River. Hell, everyone had thought he was. But he'd survived somehow. Not only survived, but had managed to make it several hundred miles to Tinker and put himself into a position to kidnap my wife. The anger began pulsing again and I forced myself to think about something else. I'd just tamp that anger down until it was time to make use of it.

The clang of the lower panel opening woke me sometime later, followed by a scraping sound as a tray of food was slid into the cell. They had arrested me in the early afternoon and this was the first food I'd been given, so it must be the evening meal. That told me it was roughly 1800 hours. I'd slept for maybe three hours.

The chemical reaction had stopped in the ice pack and it had grown warm from my body heat. Removing it, I closed my pants and carefully swung my legs off the bunk into a sitting position. I still hurt, but it was manageable. Retrieving the tray, I balanced it on my lap and devoured every bite. Placing it back in front of the slot I lay back down and waited.

Half an hour later the tray was collected and I was just settling down to try and get some more sleep when I heard the rattle of keys in the steel door. The lock scraped, then the door was pulled open. I remained still on the bunk, raising my head to see what was happening. A large Security Forces Sr. Airman stood blocking the opening. Over his broad shoulders I could see two more guards standing in the hall. All of them were wearing tactical gear, and I suppressed a grin that they were being that cautious around me.

"Your lawyers are here." He said, never taking his eyes off of me. "I have to let them in, but if you cause any problems they'll have to leave and you can spend the night in the punishment cell. Understand?"

"Understood." I replied, still staying still.

He stepped back into the hall and motioned to someone down the hall that I couldn't see. A moment later, Tech Sergeant Zach Scott stepped into the cell, followed by Martinez. Scott's arm was still in a cast supported by a sling, and he was wearing an Air Force Captain's uniform. Martinez was dressed in an Air Force issue dress uniform, complete with skirt and low heels. She wore Staff Sergeant chevrons.

Once they were fully through the door, Scott turned to the guard. "I'm going to have a privileged conversation with the Major. You and your men wait down the hall."

The guard nodded, then closed and locked the door. Martinez quickly moved to it and pressed her ear against the steel. She listened for a few moments then nodded to Scott. I stood up and smiled at him.

"Congratulations on your promotion, Tech Sergeant." I said in a quiet voice.

"Colonel Crawford's idea." He said. "A better idea than this." He held up his cast and frowned at me.

Scott had broken his arm when we were extracting from Los Alamos. I'd gone to visit him in the hospital at Tinker and he'd been asleep, so I'd personalized the virgin white plaster for him. I was mildly surprised he hadn't covered up my message. In bold, black letters it read, "I've fallen and I can't get it up".

"Get *IT* up? Really?" He said, with a shake of his head.

"Isn't that how it goes?" I asked innocently.

"If you two are done, how about we get the hell out of here." Martinez said.

"I'm ready. What's the plan?" I asked.

Scott reached up and fished around inside his sling, pulling out a Taser. Martinez hiked her skirt up around her hips and retrieved two, small pistols that were strapped to her upper thighs. Handing me one, she smoothed her skirt back down and stepped close to me.

"We only kill in self defense." She said, face close to mine as she looked directly into my eyes. "Agreed?"

"Agreed." I finally said. She kept looking at me until she was satisfied I was being sincere.

"OK, there are the three guards you saw in the hall. Out the door to our left is a gate that leads to a processing area. The gate is locked, but the lead guard has a key for it. We're going to put them in here and lock them in, use his key to get through the gate where there's one more guard. I'll go through the gate first, distract him, then you two get him back here and in a cell. Then we walk right out the front door where our ride's waiting." Martinez said.

"Seriously? That sounds way too easy." I said.

"This is a holding facility, not a prison. It is easy. Ready?" Scott asked.

I nodded my head and he stepped over to the door and banged on it sharply. The Taser was concealed in his good hand. Martinez and I had our pistols held behind our legs, out of sight. A few moments later the lock scraped and the door opened. Martinez quickly stepped past the lead guard as Scott moved close to him and pressed the Taser to his neck and pulled the trigger.

The guard fell like a sack of bricks, the two others freezing in place when Martinez brought her pistol up and aimed it at their faces. Scott stepped over the stunned guard and I quickly dragged him into the cell and removed a ring of keys from his belt. Stepping into the hall I raised my pistol and motioned the two guards into the cell.

"Are you fucking crazy?" One of them asked, a shocked look on his face.

"I just might be," I said. "Now, inside before you find out."

With looks that were a mix of hatred and fear the two men slowly moved into the cell. Scott pushed the door closed and I fumbled with the ring until I found the right key to secure the lock. We moved down the hall past half a dozen empty holding cells with doors standing open, stopping at the gate long enough for me to find the right key.

Gate unlocked, Martinez put the pistol into her purse and slipped through as Scott and I held back. The processing area was a large room lined with benches. Heavy, steel rings were set into the floor in front of each bench for the cops to secure a prisoner while waiting for a holding cell to be assigned. A government issue, gray metal desk sat in the center of the room, a Security Forces Staff Sergeant sitting behind it doing paper work. There was no one else in the room at the moment.

He looked up when Martinez walked in front of his desk, stopping at the far corner so that to look at her his back was completely turned to us.

"I think something bit me," Martinez said, bending at the waist and lifting her skirt to run her hand up the back of her thigh. "Do you see anything?"

I rolled my eyes. I couldn't believe she was doing this. But it worked. The guard nearly fell out of his chair in his haste to lean forward for a closer inspection of Martinez' leg. Scott moved forward and pressed the Taser to the back of his neck and I grabbed him before he hit the floor.

Dragging him through the gate, I put him in the first empty cell I came to, closed and locked the door. I locked the gate behind me, dropped the keys in a waste can sitting behind the desk, tripped the magnetic lock on the exit door and followed Scott and Martinez outside.

The fresh, night air was invigorating. Martinez led the way, heels clicking rapidly on the pavement. We rounded a corner and ahead I heard a Humvee's diesel engine clatter to life, then roar towards us. Captain Blanchard pulled up next to us and we piled in, the vehicle rolling before we even had a chance to close the doors.

"Any problems?" He asked.

"Smooth as silk." Martinez answered. For about the hundredth time I reminded myself I was glad she was on my side.

20

The infected were relentless. The Air Force had arrived and had been bombing the herd for hours, killing tens of thousands, but at best had only slowed their advance. Dead infected were just another obstacle for them to negotiate. Nothing more. Nothing less.

The Marines securing the refinery had spent the afternoon waiting for the coming battle. Hours with nothing to do other than think about the millions of hungry mouths that were bearing down on them. Enough to drive most people crazy, but like fighting men the world over, waiting was just another part of combat. Sometimes the worst part, but these were well trained and well disciplined men.

They had kept it together, and now they were ready for battle as the leading edge of the herd came into small arms range. Zemeck had made more trips up and down the line of Marines than he could count, making sure everyone was alert. Colonel Pointere had made at least as many, not the type of officer to leave the morale of his troops to his NCOs.

They had four snipers with them, two with .50 caliber rifles, two more with 7.62 mm rifles. The snipers had started engaging targets at 800 yards. Bodies dropping from sniper fire would have stalled the advance of any normal army, but the infected could care less. Zemeck and Pointere watched in dismay through their binoculars as the herd continued unabated, trampling the ones that were shot into the dirt.

"Guess your Army buddy was right," Pointere said. "They don't even notice when the one next to them goes down."

"No, sir. They don't." Zemeck answered, then turned his head when he heard a low rumble approaching from the west. "Fast movers coming."

The sun was almost down, but low on the horizon the two Marines could see the silhouettes of a dozen jets streaking towards them at a low altitude. As they approached, they slowed until it seemed they were flying too slow to stay in the air. Then they spread out and commenced their attack runs.

The jets were A-10 Warthogs. Ugly and slow, they were originally designed as a weapon to destroy Soviet armor. With a seven barrel, 30 mm

Gatling gun, they could fire 4,200 high explosive rounds per minute, and that's exactly what they did.

The display of raw power was amazing, the Marines cheering as the Warthogs began chewing up the ranks of the infected. Pass after pass destroyed everything in their path until the final plane in the flight fired its last round. Easily 50,000 infected had been killed in the attack, but those behind them immediately began climbing over the shattered bodies to continue their trek.

"Shit on a stick," Pointere said.

"We need napalm," Zemeck answered. "Roast these motherfuckers."

Pointere turned and looked at him, then turned and looked at the refinery at their backs. Zemeck looked too, then met his eyes and grinned.

"Aye aye, sir. I'm on it!" He said and turned, running off to find the refinery manager.

A Lance Corporal ran up to the Colonel a minute later and held out a secure satellite phone. "Admiral Packard for you, sir."

"Pointere." He said into the phone.

The conversation lasted five minutes, then he clicked off and handed the phone back to the Marine. While he was disturbed by what the Admiral had told him, he wasn't surprised.

"Fucking Secretary of Energy." He muttered to himself.

The devastation from the Warthogs' attack had bought them some time. A sea of bodies stretched out from the barricade, and the closest infected were now a mile away. They had maybe fifteen minutes before the infected were pushing up against them. Half that time was gone when Zemeck returned.

He started to speak, but paused as two Ospreys lifted off and raced away to the north.

"Not napalm, but we've got a plan." Zemeck said.

After almost a minute Pointere turned to him, "Is this one of those jokes about how to keep an asshole in suspense?"

"Sorry, sir. We're going to spray them down with fuel oil and set the fuckers on fire. There's a big agricultural site a few miles to the north and one of our pilots swears he saw a couple of crop dusters sitting there when we flew in."

"We're going to crop dust the infected?" Pointere smiled.

"Pretty much," Zemeck smiled back. "Load up with fuel oil from something called a cracking tower, don't ask me what the hell that is, then soak these bastards down and toss a match."

"Is that a good idea? That much fire this close to a refinery?" Pointere asked, turning back to look at the approaching herd through his binoculars.

"It's better than being the appetizer to keep them excited about getting to Oklahoma City. Sir."

Pointere nodded but didn't say anything else on the subject. "We've got another problem, Master Gunny."

"Sir?"

Pointere filled him in on his conversation with Admiral Packard.

"Your thoughts, Matt?" He asked when he finished speaking.

Zemeck was quiet for a minute, processing what he'd just heard. He'd been with Pointere for a long time, and knew he could speak freely in this situation.

"I think we've got one big fucking mess that's bad enough to deal with without a traitor trying to hand what's left over to the Russians. I haven't spent over twenty years of my life and had my blood spilled on three continents just so some goddamn bitch can roll over and spread her legs for the enemy. Sir."

"Well put, Master Gunny." Pointere said. "Here's what else you need to know. The Admiral has dispatched a couple of SEAL teams to Alaska to arrest President Clark. If we're in, we're in all the way."

"Why don't we just ignore her?" Zemeck asked.

"We could, but there's officers that are following her orders. We've got to take her out of the picture and try to get them back in line." Pointere said, then continued to fill in Zemeck on the situation at Tinker.

"What's funny, Master Gunny?" He asked when Zemeck started grinning.

"The thought of them thinking they're going to arrest and hold John Chase." He answered. "He is the most god awful terrifying son of a bitch in battle I've ever seen. And with a few hundred Rangers right there in the middle of the base? They don't know the can of worms they've opened." Zemeck answered, then they both looked up when first one, then a second bi-plane roared overhead.

"Guess they got the crop dusters flying." Pointere said drily.

"Looks that way. If you'll excuse me sir, I want to be on hand while they're loading up."

Pointere nodded and Zemeck trotted away in the direction the planes had flown. Looking through his binoculars Pointere could clearly see the leading edge of infected. It was all females and they were now less than five minutes away, charging as fast as they could over the broken corpses left behind by the Warthogs.

An Osprey went into a hover between the barricades and infected, minigun sweeping across the ranks of females with devastating results. But it was only a delaying action. They had nowhere near enough ammunition to stop the herd. Tens of thousands had already been killed, but millions still pressed forward from the rear. Pointere took a moment to say a silent prayer that Zemeck's idea with the crop dusters would work. They were out of rabbits.

It was close to ten minutes later when the first bi-plane roared into the sky. Its tanks that normally held fertilizer or pesticides were full to the top with partially refined fuel oil. Marine Captain David Williams was at the controls, not at all bothered by the thought of flying a gigantic fuel bomb. He gained altitude and turned toward the herd.

Lining up with the long axis of the mass of infected he swooped down over the refinery and as he approached the leading edge, pulled a lever in the cockpit that activated a high pressure pump driven by a wind turbine. The pump forced the fuel oil through nozzles designed to break liquids up into billions of tiny droplets.

The crop duster's spray nozzles are mounted along the trailing edge of both wings, and as the plane flew less than fifty feet above the heads of the infected it left behind a dense fog of highly combustible fuel oil that slowly drifted down and soaked everything on the ground. The second plane flew in formation to his left, slightly higher and just behind so there was no chance of it passing through the flammable mist.

The herd was half a mile wide and several miles long, stretched to the south like a huge, undulating snake. At the one mile mark they banked sharply and separated to spread farther to the sides so they could cover the full width of the leading mile. Tanks running dry, they banked sharply again and returned to the north side of the refinery for a fresh load.

As soon as the crop dusters were clear, an Osprey roared in and transitioned to a hover over the front of the infected. The rear ramp dropped and a Marine secured with a safety tether stepped to the edge and looked down at the seething mass beneath his feet. With a deep breath he leaned out, aimed an emergency flare gun straight down and pulled the trigger.

The red flare streaked to the ground, encountering residual vapor from the atomized fuel oil still hanging in the air above the heads of the infected. In a fraction of a second the vapor ignited, the flame spreading instantly across the entire gas cloud. The resulting explosion nearly knocked the Osprey out of the sky and the blast wave flattened every Marine that was standing. Including Pointere.

When he climbed back to his feet and looked at the herd, he couldn't help but smile. Nothing was alive or moving for well over a mile to their south. Close to a quarter-million infected must have been killed in that one blast. The shattered remains of their bodies smoldered, littering the desert floor in every direction. "This is what hell will be like," Pointere thought to himself.

Tamping down the gloomy thoughts, he smiled again. Zemeck had managed to create one of the most destructive weapons of war other than nukes, a Fuel Air Explosive or Thermobaric Bomb. Simply, unlike conventional explosives that contain their own oxidizers, a FAE uses the oxygen in the atmosphere around it. FAEs held the record for the largest non-nuclear explosions in the world.

The best part was that they hadn't killed themselves with the blast. Now to repeat a few more times and wipe out the remaining infected so they could get back to dealing with the Russians and a traitorous President.

21

Air Force Captain Tillman circled the large building with the helipad on the roof, making sure it was safe to land. He was surprised the massive building was a casino and couldn't imagine why the madman in the back wanted to go there badly enough that he had kidnapped Vanessa and strapped a bomb to her chest.

The flight from Tinker had taken a little under an hour and he was anxious to drop his passengers and get back to the base as fast as the Pave Hawk would fly. He felt bad for the woman that Roach had subdued and tied up to bring along with them, but his only real concern was for his wife.

A few minutes into the flight the effects of the Taser had worn off and despite being bound at her wrists and ankles, the woman had tried to fight. She'd even landed a solid kick with both feet to the side of Roach's head, but the Taser's metal darts were still embedded in her neck and he'd pulled the trigger to send another surge of electricity into her body.

Every few minutes for the remainder of the flight Tillman had heard the rapid clicking of the device as Roach kept her immobilized. His heart went out to the woman, and several times he'd thought about making a sudden maneuver to distract or disable Roach, then he thought about Vanessa and lost all desire to antagonize the man.

Satisfied the helipad was clear, he transitioned to a hover and lowered the helicopter until its landing gear settled on the large H painted in the center of the pad. He didn't cut the engines, planning to get the information he needed from Roach and immediately take off when they exited the aircraft.

He jumped when Roach suddenly appeared next to him, having squeezed into the cockpit between the two seats.

"I did what you asked. Where's Vanessa and how do I disarm the bomb?" He said, turning to face his hijacker.

Roach smiled and pointed at the ceiling of the cockpit with his left hand. Tillman automatically looked, raising his head, and Roach struck. A ten-inch dagger was in his right hand and he slammed it all the way into the pilot's head, the point going in through the soft tissue under the jaw, the blade slicing all the way into his brain.

"Now you're with your wife again, just like I promised." Roach said, pulling the blade out and wiping it clean on Tillman's sleeve.

Roach hadn't been in many helicopters, but he had always paid attention and knew what to do to safely shut one down. He followed the procedure he'd memorized the last time he'd been in a Pave Hawk, a moment later the engines going quiet and the large rotor spinning down to a stop. Raising his short barreled rifle he fired several rounds into the avionics, disabling the aircraft.

Working his way back he checked on Katie who was currently immobilized from her most recent shock. Tears induced by the pain rolled down her cheeks, but her eyes burned with a ferocity that excited him. She was a fighter, he already knew that, but seeing the rage and desire to murder reflected in her gaze made him smile. This was going to be fun.

Sliding the side door open, Roach jumped down onto the landing pad, patted Katie's hip and slid the door shut. He didn't particularly like the idea of leaving her alone in the Pave Hawk, but there was no way she was getting out of the thick, plastic ties that secured her.

Looking around he spotted a small block structure, a bulkhead, that protruded up from the roof of the casino and held the door that opened to a stairwell which descended into what had been described in the scouting report as a VIP area. As he approached the metal door, Roach heard several infected female screams and changed direction to the edge of the roof.

Leaning over he saw about twenty females standing in a ground level service area, staring up at him. They had been drawn by the sound of the helicopter landing and were screaming their frustration at not being able to get to the prey on the roof. Roach scanned the area to make sure there wasn't an exterior ladder or stairs that they could climb, relaxing when all he saw was sheer, vertical walls.

He ignored the infected and moved to the side of the bulkhead, opening the smallest of the electrical panels fixed to the exterior. Inside, just as noted by the scout leader, was a large key. Smiling, Roach took the key, closed the panel and walked around to the door. The key fit smoothly into the sturdy deadbolt, turning easily in his hand.

He twisted the knob, pulled the door open and looked down a well-lit stairwell.

Red carpeted stairs descended into the building. Roach pulled his pistol and fired a single shot in the air, then holstered it and raised his rifle, aiming into the stairwell. He stood there for a full five minutes, waiting and listening. The air smelled stale and there were no sounds from below. No females charging up in response to the report of the pistol fire. No males tripping and bumbling as they blindly climbed.

Satisfied he was safe for the moment, Roach propped the door open and returned to the Pave Hawk. When he slid the side door open he was ready, twisting away to avoid Katie's two footed kick. Wrapping his arm around her ankles he reached for the Taser but stopped when he saw the two bloody darts lying on the deck. She had managed to get a grip on the wires and rip them out of the back of her neck.

Pulling his dagger, Roach placed it against Katie's face, the tip hovering half an inch in front of her right eye. She stopped struggling against his grip.

Days Of Perdition

"What the fuck are you doing? What do you want?" She asked in a quiet voice.

"Now isn't the time for conversation," he said. "We'll have plenty of time to get to know each other better. Right now you need to understand that if you don't behave I'm going to cut that pretty face, then I'm going to start working on your other assets. Do you understand me?"

Katie stared back at him, eventually speaking through clenched teeth, "I understand."

"Good!" Roach smiled broadly. "I knew you would. Now I'm going to cut your feet free so you can walk. If you give me any problems, remember what will happen to you."

Roach held the blade against her face for a few more moments, then sheathed it and roughly turned her over onto her stomach. Holding her down with one hand he retrieved a length of paracord from his pocket and threaded it through the plastic tie binding Katie's wrists behind her. Pulling the end, he looped it around her neck and secured it with a slipknot. Cutting the tie at her ankles he hauled her out of the Pave Hawk and onto her feet, spinning her around to face him.

"If you're not a good girl, I'll have to punish you." He leaned in as he spoke, smiling in her face.

Katie smiled back at him, snapped her head forward and delivered a wicked blow with her forehead to the bridge of his nose. Roach was knocked back, momentarily stunned and Katie started to move sideways to snap a kick into his damaged face. Years of aerobic kickboxing to stay in shape made her feet more dangerous than her hands, but her ankles had been bound for an hour, restricting blood flow.

When she tried to move her left ankle buckled and she fell to the roof. The paracord was still gripped tightly in Roach's hand and pulled taut as she fell, the slipknot around her neck tightening and cutting off her air supply. Trying to gasp even a tiny breath, Katie struggled; panic seizing her when she couldn't breathe. Roach slowly moved over her, blood running across his lower face and chest from his broken nose. He smiled, revealing bloody teeth.

"I'm glad you like it rough, bitch. I do too."

22

Blanchard drove us across Tinker, careful to stay within the speed limit and not draw the attention of a Security Forces patrol. I should have been relieved to be out of custody and breathing free air, but all my freedom did was remind me that Katie was still somewhere out there in the hands of a raving psychopath and I wasn't any closer to finding her.

"Captain, did you have any luck finding out where Roach went?" I asked from the dark of the back seat.

"I got separated from my laptop in the confusion of your arrest, but I've got the Navy working on reviewing sat imagery and tracking the helicopter. I'll call them as soon as we get to the Colonel." He said, never taking his eyes off the road. Nodding, I leaned back in the seat and let out a frustrated breath.

"Who's Roach?" Scott asked from beside me. I spent the rest of the drive filling him in on who and what was going on.

"He's got your wife? Dude, that asshole needs to die!" Scott exclaimed when I finished telling him the story.

"He's slipped away too many times," I said. "This time I'm not stopping until I'm holding his fucking heart in my hand and squeezing every last drop of blood out of it."

"Whatever you need, Major." Scott said as we pulled through a double cordon of Rangers and up to a large hangar.

Blanchard parked and we stepped out, Dog running up and nearly taking my legs out from under me in his enthusiasm. Rachel walked up and looked at me, hesitating a moment before wrapping me up in a hug. I hugged her back, but wasn't in the mood to do anything other than start looking for Katie. I turned to Blanchard but he pre-empted me.

"On my way to place that call now, sir."

I nodded as he trotted away, Colonel Crawford walking up and shaking my hand.

"Good to see you." He said.

"Thank you, sir. And thank you for sending in the cavalry."

"Her plan," he said, tilting his head towards Martinez.

"I thought you said it was the Colonel's idea." I said.

"His idea, my plan." She smiled.

Crawford escorted us into the hangar where he had set up an operations center. I could see Blanchard talking on a satellite phone near an open door so he could get a good signal.

"How big is the mess, sir?" I asked Crawford.

"Big enough. As you know, General Triplett has decided to follow President Clark's orders. So have a few other key officers that still have intact commands around the world. At the moment it's a cold war between the General and me. He wants to arrest me, but is smart enough to not try and fight his way in.

"Admiral Packard has dispatched some SEALs to arrest the President. They should be on the ground in Alaska in about six hours. It may get really ugly up there, as the General in command of Fort Wainwright has sided with the President. The soldiers won't know the reality of what's going on, just whatever the President and their General tell them. We expect they'll resist the SEALs."

"There's what... a full Stryker brigade and an entire infantry division at Wainwright?" I asked. "The SEALs won't stand a chance."

"They're not going head to head. Penetrate and extract are their orders. We don't think General Carey knows they're coming. If he does, you're right, they'll be wiped out. But our belief is that the President feels secure in the middle of an Army post and the SEALs can get in, get her, and get out without firing a shot. We hope."

We could have continued debating the issue, but Blanchard wrapped up his phone call and walked over. Grabbing a laptop he opened a mapping application, checked some coordinates he had written on his hand and punched them into the computer. A moment later he leaned back and waved me over.

"We've got them, Major." He said, pointing at the screen where a red dot pulsed to indicate the location he had entered. "The Navy tracked the Pave Hawk they left in and it's still sitting where it landed. They just looked in real time to verify."

"Where the hell is that?" I asked, trying to make sense of the map.

"About a hundred miles north-northeast of us." He said, adjusting the zoom on the map and pointing at our current location in relation to the red dot.

"What is it? Why did he go there?" I asked, staring at the map and already thinking about how I was going to get there.

"It's an Indian casino. Huge. Something like forty or fifty thousand square feet. There's a helipad on the roof, and that's where the Pave Hawk is sitting." He answered.

"OK, point me at some weapons and let's go. Martinez can fly me there in under an hour." I said, straightening up, ready to start moving.

There was an uncomfortable silence for a few moments before Colonel Crawford spoke up. "We can't get to any of our aircraft. The Air Force is guarding them. It'll be a full on fire fight if we try."

"I don't give a fuck," I said. "My wife is out there with that freak. She's already been out there for over twelve hours. I need to go get her now!"

"Stand down, Major." Crawford's voice hardened. "I understand what you're feeling, but we can't start shooting Air Force personnel. We need to give the SEALs time to do their job and take the President into custody. Once that happens we can probably break this stalemate and the first thing we'll do is get you on a chopper."

"That's not good enough..." I started to say.

"It's not open for discussion, Major!" Crawford snapped and stepped up to face me. "Is that clear?"

I seethed. Anger rocketed through me; churning my stomach and making my face feel like it was on fire. But Crawford didn't flinch and didn't back away. He stood there and held my eyes with his.

"I'm sorry," he finally said. "I don't like it either, but we're not going to start killing our fellow service members if there's any way around it."

"Yes, sir." I finally said. "You're clear."

Without waiting to be dismissed I turned and walked out of the hangar, Dog trailing along behind me. I spotted a Ranger that I knew smoked and asked for a cigarette. He gave me the whole pack, saying he had more. Thanking him, I wandered over to sit on a low wall at the edge of the parking area. Dog rested his chin on my leg and watched my every movement as I lit a cigarette and took my first drag.

Less than a minute later Rachel walked up and sat down next to me, taking the cigarette out of my hand and smoking it. With a snort I lit another, blowing smoke at the dark night sky.

"You OK?" She asked.

"Not really," I answered. "I'm about ready to lose it, to tell the truth."

Rachel reached out and took my hand in hers. "What do you want to do?"

"He wants to get his wife." Martinez spoke from the darkness behind us. I looked over my shoulder to see her and Scott standing there. Irina and Igor were with them.

"Let's go get her." Scott said.

"Da!" Igor said after Irina translated for him. "I help too."

"How?" Rachel asked. "You heard the Colonel. We can't get to a helicopter, and there's infected at the fence. We've got no way off the base."

"We can get a helicopter." I said, looking at Scott and Martinez. They both nodded.

"How?" Rachel asked.

"We take one." I said. "I don't like the thought of hurting some Airman that is just doing his job, but I've got to get to Katie before it's too late. If it's not too late already." The thought soured my already piss poor mood and I threw my cigarette down and ground it under my boot.

"Fine. Say we get one. Did anyone get the coordinates Captain Blanchard typed into the computer? I sure didn't. How do we know where to go?" Rachel asked.

Martinez recited a set of GPS coordinates without hesitation. Rachel turned and looked at her, amazed.

"I'm a pilot," she explained, shrugging. "It's an occupational hazard. Get a set of coordinates within range of my eyes and I remember them."

"Crawford's going to be pissed." Rachel said.

"He'll either get over it, or arrest me when I get back. If I get back." I said. "Either way, I don't care." Rachel nodded and squeezed my hand.

"We'll be back," Martinez said, slapping Scott on the shoulder to get him to follow her. They walked away in the dark, taking Irina and Igor with them, heading to the hangar.

"Do we need to talk about us?" I asked Rachel, dreading the answer.

"No. Not now." She said after a long moment. "We get Katie back. That's the priority. We can worry about everything else later. Besides, if we talk about it now I'll probably go into a funk and not be any use to you. And before you say it, I'm coming along. I made you a promise right after we met that I'd help you find your wife. Nothing has changed in that regard. I'm keeping my promise."

Dirk Patton

I looked at Rachel for a long time, finally wrapping my arms around her and holding her close. She circled her arms around me and held tightly. We were still sitting like that when my small team of rebels returned, arms loaded down with gear and weapons.

23

It took us close to twenty minutes to prepare, most of it spent loading ammunition into magazines. Once we were ready I circled the small group and discussed what we were going to do and how we were going to do it. Out of deference to Martinez I agreed that we would only use lethal force if we had to defend one of the team, even though I was ready to shoot, hack or slash my way through just about anyone to get to a helicopter.

The first step was to find a likely aircraft. We knew the general direction where the Black Hawks flown in by the Army were parked, and I remembered seeing numerous Air Force helos in the same area, but I didn't have any idea how much security was guarding them. Leaving everyone huddled in the dark I slipped around the side of the hangar to go conduct some reconnaissance.

There was a cordon of Rangers acting as perimeter defense around the area, and the first problem was to get past them without being detected. This was going to be an even bigger issue, as I had to get back inside the perimeter and retrieve my team once I found us a ride.

The Rangers were spaced at fifty yards, doubled up so there was always a pair of eyes looking in every direction. Shit! I squatted there in the dark, hidden by a thick bush, and watched them. They were alert and paying attention and I reminded myself that these were elite troops, not just some soldiers thrown on sentry duty. I wasn't getting past them without a distraction.

Creeping back to the corner of the hangar I rejoined my team and explained the problem to them. Scott suggested tossing food at them since they were Army. He grinned when I told him to fuck off. Rachel let out a sigh and asked Martinez to borrow one of her knives. Blade in hand she set to work and in a few minutes was ready.

This time we all moved around the hangar, staying close to the wall and concealed by the shrubbery. When we were in place Rachel looked at me, smiled, turned to Dog and whispered in his ear. Pointing out into the dark she smacked him on his ass and he took off like a shot, racing past the closest pair of Rangers.

There was a shout of surprise and one of them started to raise his rifle but relaxed when his partner laughed at him and pointed out it was just a dog. Rachel moved out from behind the bushes and headed directly for them, calling out when she was half way to where they stood.

"Hello," she said. They both turned to look and both did a double take.

Rachel had used Martinez' knife to cut the legs off her pants, and she'd cut them very short. She'd stripped down to a thin tank top, removing her vest and combat shirt. I had her pack and weapons. Walking the rest of the way up to the Rangers she put a roll into her hips and just the right note of distress in her voice.

"My dog ran off. Have you seen him?" She asked, casually moving to their right so they were facing away from half their area of responsibility.

I motioned the group and started moving, slow and quiet. Rachel had the mens' undivided attention as she chattered brightly, reaching out and touching one of them on the shoulder as she laughed. In hindsight, I could probably have driven a parade float behind these guys without them knowing, but I wasn't taking any chances as we moved in single file out into the dark.

It took us over five minutes to go far enough that I felt safe in calling a halt. Dog ran up out of the dark, pleased with himself and happy to see me. I rubbed his neck and told him to speak so Rachel would have an excuse to come out into the field to look for him. He just stared at me. OK, so Dog can't do everything.

I was startled when a dog barked behind me, whirling around to see Scott with his head tilted back. His imitation of a dog wasn't perfect but I was willing to bet it was good enough. I frowned at him and he shrugged his shoulders and grinned. I decided I didn't really want to know why he could imitate a barking dog so well.

A few minutes later Rachel joined us, quickly pulled her shirt and vest on, buckled on her belt with a pistol and shrugged into her pack. Once her rifle was slung I couldn't help but chuckle at her.

"What?" She asked.

"You look like a teenage boy's wet dream." I said.

"Yeah. Nice booty shorts." Martinez chimed in.

Rachel looked at us for a moment before punching my arm. Hard. "Are we ready to go or does anyone else want to make a comment?" She asked, hands on her hips as she glared at the group.

"You lead the way, we'll keep an eye on your rear." Martinez said, trying to suppress laughter.

I told all of them to shut up before I started laughing, then got us moving towards the flight line. We had to cover most of a mile, occasionally flattening ourselves on the grass as a vehicle passed on the road a hundred yards to our left. We moved past a couple of dark buildings and came to a stop behind a parked truck.

We were in a large parking lot that fronted a warehouse adjacent to the flight line. On the far side of the area a low fence separated it from the acres of smooth and level concrete where dozens of helicopters and jets of all sizes were parked. Closest to us was a large group of Black Hawks and Apaches with Army stenciled on their tails, and they were heavily guarded. Too many guards to get to them without starting a fire fight.

Martinez fished a pair of binoculars out of her pack and took her time scanning ahead of us. After a few minutes she handed the glasses to me and pointed at the far end of the tarmac. I looked through the glasses and it took me a moment to realize what I was seeing. Or not seeing.

Half a dozen Air Force Pave Hawks sat by themselves, and there was only one guard within 300 yards of them. Whoever had set up the security had falsely assumed that if we tried for an aircraft it would be one of the ones we'd brought with us.

"Think they'll be fueled and ready to go?" I mumbled to Martinez.

"They should be," she answered. "We're at war. Aircraft sitting on the tarmac don't do you any good if they aren't ready at a moment's notice."

I nodded and took the time to brief the rest of the team on what Martinez and I were talking about. Everyone up to speed, I led us around the corner of the warehouse into the deepest shadows at its rear. There was a narrow strip of grass then a road running parallel to the perimeter fence. As soon as we came around the corner a chorus of screams from infected females started up from the far side of the fence.

We hesitated as a group for a moment, then I broke into a run, the others following close behind. If we didn't get away from the fence, fast, someone was going to come to investigate the commotion and find us. Sprinting along the back of the big building I should have slowed when I reached the corner but was in too much of a hurry and was distracted by the screaming females.

An Air Force guard, coming to see what had the infected riled up, stepped around the corner and directly into my path. I ran into him at full speed, both of us tumbling to the ground. He fell one way and I the other and I was just starting to scramble to subdue him when Igor lunged forward and wrapped a thick arm around his neck, dragging him into the dark behind the warehouse.

Igor had him in a sleeper hold, compressing the carotid arteries on either side of his neck. The guard struggled for a moment then quickly lost consciousness. Igor gently lowered him to the ground and stepped back. Martinez moved in, checked his pulse, then pulled some plastic zip ties out of her pack and secured the Airman's hands and feet. A strip of fabric served as a gag.

Nodding my thanks to Igor I set off at a run for the next building. The females were still screaming and though I couldn't see them in the dark I could tell they were moving down the fence line, following us. I ran harder, making it past two more buildings before we encountered another curious guard. This one stepped around a corner thirty yards in front of us, looking to his left and right for whatever had the infected worked up.

When he spotted us I saw his eyes go wide, even in the dim light, then he was swinging his rifle up in our direction. I was too far away to do anything to stop him, cursing and raising my own rifle. At twenty yards my weapon was up and ready to go, my finger along the trigger guard as I sighted in. At fifteen yards he realized I had the drop on him, his rifle still not up to his shoulder, and he froze. Thank God!

The Airman looked no more than 18 years old, just a baby to me, and relief flooded through me that he had the sense to not keep bringing his weapon up. I came to a stop five yards from him and motioned him behind the building where Igor and Martinez grabbed and disarmed him. A minute later he was bound and gagged and stashed against the base of the wall.

"That was too fucking close," I said to the group in general. "I almost had to kill that kid."

"We need to get away from the infected before a whole squad comes back here to see what's going on." Scott said.

I agreed with him, but we either stayed behind the hangars and in view of the infected, or moved to the front in view of the guards. We didn't have a whole lot of options. There were only three more buildings between us and where Martinez had spotted the lightly guarded Pave Hawks, so I decided our best option was to just keep running and hope for luck.

We covered the remaining distance without any more incidents. I breathed a big sigh of relief when we reached the back corner of the hangar closest to the helicopters. We'd made it without hurting any of the Air Force guards. I knew I would have if I'd been forced to, but not having to carry that load on an already burdened conscience was an almost physical relief.

"Shit," Martinez muttered. She was leaning around the corner looking at the Pave Hawks through her binoculars. "They're red tagged."

"What does that mean?" I asked, afraid I already knew.

"They're grounded, waiting for repair or maintenance." She said. "Sorry. I couldn't see the tags before."

"Not your fault. Do you think they're really down, or could one of them fly?" I was grasping at straws.

"As far as we're concerned, they're down. If I had time to do a thorough a pre-flight inspection, check the logs and do an engine run up, maybe we could find one that could make it, but as soon as we walk up to one they're going to spot us. If it's not ready to go as soon as we climb in…"

I nodded and looked around at the small group of females pressed against the perimeter fence, screaming at us. We needed to get out of sight and come up with a new plan. I turned my head to the right when metal clanged at the fence. A couple of males were pushing on a small access gate that rattled in its frame but was well secured with a heavy chain and padlock.

"Over here," Scott hissed. I turned to see Igor finish picking the lock on a steel access door into the back of the hangar we were hiding behind and pull it open. We all quickly moved into the dark interior, Scott softly closing the door behind us, muting the sound of the screaming females at the fence.

"Have you lost your mind?" Irina blurted a few minutes later when I explained what I planned to do. "There's too many of them. You'll never make it."

"Yes I will," I said. "There's a bunch piled up against the fence, but there's still a lot of people that haven't turned. I've faced a lot worse odds."

I looked around the small group and was met with grim expressions. All except for Dog who was curled up at Rachel's feet taking a power nap. They hadn't thought much of my plan when I explained it to them. I didn't either, but I was out of options and wasn't going to let something like a few thousand infected stand between me and rescuing Katie from Roach.

"It's simple," I repeated. "I go out the gate behind this hangar and once I'm past the infected I can find a vehicle and drive to where Katie is. I'm not asking for anyone's permission, I'm just telling you what I'm going to do."

"How do we find the location? It's a hundred miles away." Rachel said. For the moment I ignored the "we" part of that.

"I…" started to say but was interrupted by Scott.

"He'll use this," he said, pulling a small, handheld GPS unit out of his pack and handing it to Martinez. She powered it up, hit a couple of buttons then punched in the coordinates she had memorized, watched the screen for a couple of moments then handed the device to me. The screen was small but a blue dot pulsed noticeably at the location she had just entered.

"Press the green button," Scott said.

I did and the screen refreshed, displaying my current location and a large blue arrow pointing the direction I needed to go. In the top right a small group of text told me I was 107 miles from my destination. I met Scott's eyes and thanked him with a smile and a nod.

We talked, and argued, for another five minutes. Everyone wanted to go with me. I immediately overruled Scott because of his broken arm. It's hard enough to battle the infected face to face, but doing it with your dominant arm in a cast would be a recipe for a quick and ugly death. I also vetoed Irina because of her lack of combat experience and finally convinced Igor to stay with his Captain. That left Martinez and Rachel.

"Don't even fucking say it, sir." Martinez stared me down. "I'm coming with you and you can't stop me." Smiling at her I shifted my eyes to Rachel.

"We've had this conversation too many times," she said. "Do we really need to have it again?"

I let out a sigh and shook my head.

"Thank you." I said to Rachel and Martinez.

With that out of the way we spent some time redistributing what was in our packs. Scott and Igor gave us all of their spare magazines and ammunition. MREs from those staying behind and an extra set of batteries for the GPS from Scott and we were as ready as we'd ever be.

Moving to the access door, Irina opened it and stepped out of the way. Igor and I each took a knee in the opening, shoulder to shoulder, and raised our rifles. My first target was the padlock securing the chain on the gate. It took four rounds from my rifle to damage the lock enough for it to drop free of its shackle, then Igor and I started targeting the infected.

We were only 60 yards from the fence, easy shooting with a rifle, and an infected fell dead every time one of us pulled the trigger. We took out the females first for obvious reasons, then began clearing the males. There was enough noise from jets landing and taking off and the impact of the infected trying to claw through the chain link fence that none of them noticed our sound suppressed rifle fire.

Soon there was a twenty yard wide gap in the infected, the gate in the center of the open ground.

"Let's go," I hissed and ran for the fence, Rachel, Dog and Martinez on my heels.

Igor and Scott ran with us, Igor continuing to shoot, bringing down any infected that started moving towards the gate. Scott had a length of heavy wire in his good hand that he would use to re-secure the chain on the gate once we through so the infected couldn't come flooding into the base.

Reaching the gate I ripped the chain out of the way and pulled it open, stepping through with my rifle up and immediately engaging a pair of females that were charging in from the right. They dropped and I kept moving forward, careful with my footing so I didn't trip over any of the bodies in the immediate area. Dog was tight to my right side, a moment later Rachel moving up to my left and Martinez patting me on the shoulder to let me know she was behind me and ready.

We moved, each of us firing as we walked, targeting the few females still in the immediate area that were homing in on us. Behind, I heard the gate clang shut and the sound of a chain being pulled through the frame. We were clear of the base and as on our own as Rachel and I had been in Atlanta. There wouldn't be any answers to calls for help. No Black Hawks swooping in to pluck us out of danger. No platoons of Rangers to provide fire support. It was three rifles and a dog against a city descending into chaos.

24

Infected from up and down the fence line started closing on us as soon as we came through the gate. All three of us were firing almost continuously, but we were keeping them at bay. For the moment.

On the outside of the fence there had been a five-yard wide strip of gravel at the edge of a multilane road that carried much of the traffic in this part of the city. The power was still on in the area, in pockets, and after firing three more shots I had a moment to scan across the businesses that lined the far side of the road.

The civilian areas immediately adjacent to military bases seem to never be good areas. I guess it makes sense that if you could live elsewhere why would you want to be next to the noise and traffic of a base? I wasn't surprised to see a couple of cheap apartment complexes, low rent hotels, payday loan stores, liquor stores, fast food of every description and a small used car dealer.

Changing directions I led us across eight empty lanes and into the dealership's parking lot.

We were still having to engage fast moving females but for the moment there weren't as many of them coming at us. Reaching the edge of the lot, Dog leapt and took down a female that had apparently been waiting for us behind a rusting minivan. He finished her off quickly and came back to stay close to my side.

The car dealer was a small, local business. The lot was paved with crumbling asphalt and a couple of dozen cars, trucks, vans and SUVs were scattered haphazardly across it. The sales office was a singlewide mobile home with a sliding glass door for an entrance. I moved us to the base of the metal stairs that led up to the door and turned to face out into the lot. Only a couple of females were approaching and I dropped both of them as Martinez and Rachel engaged the slower males.

"Rachel, take Dog with you and go check inside. There should be keys in there. Get us a truck." I said without letting up my rate of fire.

A couple of moments later I heard glass break as Rachel battered her way through the locked sliding door. Eight shots and eight dead infected later she was back at my side with a key in hand.

"Chevy truck is what it's labeled." She said. "It was the only one that said truck, but I see five Chevy trucks in the lot."

"Did you get the other Chevy keys?" I asked, shooting a male that was completely nude. Not a dignified state of dress to be in when you turn, but I suppose you won't care in the end.

"Yep. Where do you want to start?" Rachel asked.

"That one," I gestured at a rusting four-wheel drive truck sitting on mostly bald tires. It was closest, and at the moment I just wanted to get us out of there.

The volume of infected was increasing. More females were arriving at a sprint, drawn by the noise of the others. Martinez and I were keeping up with them, but we were burning through a lot of ammo in a hurry. Ammo that would most likely be desperately needed as we made our way through the city.

Rachel ran to the truck, Dog at her heels, and started trying keys in the door lock. Dog took up position behind her, protecting her while she was distracted. At the last moment he noticed the male that was crawling under the truck, spinning and attacking just as the infected's fingers brushed Rachel's ankle. She didn't pause in her efforts, trusting Dog to neutralize the threat at her feet.

"Got it!" She shouted a moment later, yanking the door open and letting all the unneeded keys drop to the ground.

Jumping behind the wheel, Rachel started the engine and shouted for Dog to get in. I told Martinez to head for the truck, moving behind her as she lowered her rifle and ran. The infected began collapsing in on me from all directions as I ran backwards, slamming to a stop against the side of the idling Chevy.

Four more shots to take down charging females and I risked a glance to make sure everyone was inside and ready to go. Seeing they were safe, I slid down the side of the vehicle and squeezed behind the wheel, yanking the door shut behind me moments ahead of the arrival of several males.

The truck was a single cab with one bench seat and we were stuffed in like sardines. Rachel had scooted all the way to the passenger door, Dog sitting on the floor with his upper body in her lap. Martinez was crammed into the middle, leaning hard into Rachel to make room for my shoulders. I still had my pack on and it forced my upper body forward until my chest was only inches from the steering wheel.

Hoping the damn rust bucket didn't have an air bag that could deploy and crush me, I shifted into drive and hit the gas. The engine clattered in protest but we started moving forward, a thick cloud of blue exhaust marking our wake. I steered through the lot, avoiding the other aging vehicles that were offered for sale. Males were constantly stepping in front of us and I had no option other than to run them down, but the females had backed off as soon as the truck started moving.

Reaching the exit to the street I let off the gas in surprise when three females stepped into our path. Two of them looked to be older than me, but the one in the middle was young and very pregnant. My reaction was instinctual, no conscious thought going into it. I heard Martinez mutter something in Spanish that I didn't understand and I was just starting to step on the brake when the pregnant girl twitched the way the infected do.

That twitch overrode any thoughts I had of trying to spare her life and I pressed on the accelerator. The truck didn't exactly surge forward but it did begin to pick up speed. At the last moment the females nimbly moved out of the way, the mother to be moving much faster and with more agility than I've ever seen a pregnant woman move.

Clattering into the street I turned right and kept accelerating, avoiding males when I could, smashing them down with the bumper when I couldn't. The truck's steering was about as vague as a politician's answer to a question, the vehicle taking nearly half a second to respond to any directional change I made.

"GPS is in my right cargo pocket. Can you reach it?" I said to Martinez.

She squirmed around to make room for her hand, a moment later digging the unit out of my pants and holding it up to her face.

"We need to be going north. To our right." She said a moment later.

I nodded and started looking for a road that went in that direction as I continued to do my best to avoid the infected males. They were spaced out, but it required an almost constant adjustment to our direction to avoid them. Reaching a relatively clear stretch of pavement I glanced down at the dash and grimaced when I saw the fuel gauge.

We had an eighth of a tank of gas, at the most. Not surprising when I thought about it. Car dealers don't like to spend the money to fill up vehicles that are sitting on the lot. They also don't want one of them stolen with enough fuel in it to make it out of the area without having to stop to fill up.

"We aren't going to get far in this thing," I said. "Not much gas."

"We go as far as it'll take us, then find something else." Rachel said, her voice muffled by Dog's furry body.

I nodded in agreement and kept driving. A short distance ahead I saw a large intersection where we crossed a four-lane road that headed north. Slowing, I steered us around a couple of abandoned vehicles and onto the new street. Within a mile we had moved into an area where the power had gone out. It was pitch black outside and I fumbled on the dash until I found the switch that turned the headlights on.

Just like the rest of the truck, the lights weren't up to modern standards. Hell, they were barely brighter than a couple of candles shining off curved reflectors and I could only see maybe fifty feet of pavement directly to our front. I guess it was fortunate that the clattering engine didn't seem to be able to push our speed any higher than about 45 miles per hour.

"No infected," Martinez said quietly.

She was right. Since we'd passed into the dark area I hadn't had to make any maneuvers to avoid a shambling male. It should have made me feel better, but it didn't. Perhaps it was the darkness outside the windows of the truck, but something was bothering me. I couldn't figure it out or come up with a reason why, so I just kept my attention focused on the poorly lit road to our front.

"101 miles remaining," Martinez said, her face bathed in the pale, blue light of the GPS unit's display.

I nodded, but didn't say anything. Kept driving, attention to our front, but also keeping an eye on the fuel gauge. We hadn't driven ten miles yet but the small, red needle had dropped noticeably towards the large red E. I didn't think we'd go more than maybe another twenty miles, if we were lucky, before the asthmatic motor under the hood sucked the fuel tank dry.

"Either of you have anything we can use to siphon gas? A length of hose, or something like that?" I asked.

Rachel and Martinez both shook their heads, Martinez leaning to her left to look at the instrument panel. She sighed and leaned back as much as her pack would allow.

"We'd better be watching for any likely vehicles," she said. "Can either of you hot wire a car?"

Rachel and I looked at each other and both of us grinned.

"What?" Martinez asked.

Rachel spent a few minutes telling her about us being trapped in a truck in Atlanta when we first met. How we almost died in that truck until I figured out how to bypass the ignition and get it started.

"OK, we've got nothing else to do while we drive." Martinez said. "I want to hear the story from the start."

After a minute Rachel started talking in a far off voice, remembering where we were when this all started.

25

It was quiet in the truck. Rachel had finished our story, editing out certain parts she didn't want to talk about but still being quite frank about others. The fuel gauge was taking more and more of my attention, the needle solidly pegged against the stop at the E. I was expecting to feel the engine start hiccupping at any moment as the last of our fuel was burned. Fortunately, we hadn't seen any infected for at least twenty minutes.

"So I'm going to be a bitch and ask," Martinez said to Rachel after a few quiet minutes. "You two seem like a couple. I thought you were until I heard about the Major's wife. What's going to happen when we find her?"

Rachel didn't respond. Neither did I, and I didn't have time to get distracted by whatever I felt for Rachel. Right now the only thing that mattered was saving Katie. OK, I could acknowledge that maybe it wasn't the only thing. Rachel mattered. But I'd been in love with Katie since the moment we'd met, and that hadn't changed. Hadn't diminished, regardless of how much I cared for Rachel.

The truck saved me from any more awkwardness. It lurched hard, ran for a few more seconds, then the engine died. We weren't going fast and quickly rolled to a stop in the middle of the road. I had killed the lights while we were still rolling, wanting to have as much time as possible for my eyes to adjust to the darkness.

We didn't have night vision. That was the one thing Martinez and Scott hadn't been able to get their hands on. Each of us had a night vision scope on our rifle, but that was a far cry from a head mounted set of goggles.

"We walk from here, ladies. And Martinez... mind your own fucking business." I said, opening the door and stepping out into the night.

I raised my rifle and used the scope to scan a 360 degree circle. Abandoned vehicles and dark buildings was all I saw. No infected. No survivors. This was starting to not make much sense. We were still relatively close to Tinker, and the last numbers I'd heard was that there were close to a quarter of a million people in the immediate area. Where the hell were they?

Martinez climbed out after me, chuckling at my expense and immediately raising her rifle and joining me in a scan of the area. Dog jumped down and came to stand with his flank pressed against my right leg, nose in the air. I was glad when he stayed silent, not alerting on the scent of any infected in the area.

Rachel stepped out of the truck, came up on the opposite side of me from Dog and slipped her arm around my waist. I lowered my rifle as she leaned in and kissed me softly on the lips.

"We get her back," she whispered. "Don't worry about me."

Now, I'm a hardhearted son of a bitch. I don't get emotional at movies that would send Katie into crying jags. Hell, I didn't even cry when Bambi's mother died the first time I saw that movie when I was a kid. In fact, the last time I remember shedding a tear was when I had to have a very old and sick dog put down several years ago. But Rachel's kiss and comment put a lump in my throat and moisture in my eyes. I started to turn away, but she reached up and held my face with her hand.

"I'm OK. Really." She said.

"Contact," Martinez said softly at the same moment Dog let out a low growl. Thank God, infected!

I swallowed the lump and moved to stand next to Martinez, raising my rifle and looking in the direction she was watching. Half a dozen males were stumbling out of the mouth of an alley a hundred yards behind us, slowly turning and heading south towards the Air Force Base. We watched them for a few seconds then I made another full scan of the area, not wanting to be surprised because we were watching some males that weren't a threat at the moment.

Traversing across a roofline I thought I saw movement and quickly reversed direction, but couldn't see anything when I focused back on the spot where I might have seen something. I stayed focused on the spot, telling Martinez and Rachel to keep scanning. Dog stopped growling as the males continued to move away from our position and after a minute I passed off what I thought I'd seen as a ghost in the optics.

"Clear," I said softly.

Rachel and Martinez both confirmed they weren't seeing any threats and I relaxed half a notch and began looking around for an alternate means of transportation. There were several cars parked along the curb closest to us and I walked over to them and began trying doors. All but one were locked up tightly. The door on a small Honda sedan opened, but there were no keys in the ignition.

I'd gotten lucky starting the Ford truck in Atlanta, but it was at least twenty years old and hadn't had any fancy anti-theft features built in. The Honda was fairly new and I was reasonably certain it took the kind of key that had a microchip built in. Without that key the on-board computer wouldn't allow the engine to start and run no matter what wires were connected.

Sure, there's probably a way to steal one of the damn things. In fact it seemed like I'd seen an article a few months ago that said the Honda was one of the most commonly stolen cars in America. But that didn't mean I had a clue how to go about doing it. Maybe I needed to start bringing a teenager along.

Covering all my bases I checked the back seat, then popped the trunk in case there was something we could use to siphon fuel for the truck. Nothing. Other than an empty chewing gum wrapper the car was as clean as the day it rolled off the assembly line.

Making sure the girls were keeping an eye out for any unwelcome guests, I went back to the vehicles that had been locked and used a small flashlight to check their interiors. Lots of trash in some of them, others neat and clean like the Honda. The cargo area of a Hyundai SUV was stacked with boxes of cooking pots and pans, but I was striking out in finding anything that resembled a hose.

Walking to where Rachel and Martinez were standing watch with their backs to each other, I came to a stop and turned back to look at the SUV. Would it work? No reason it wouldn't. Reversing course I came up to the rear of the vehicle and fired a couple of rounds from my suppressed rifle through the rear glass.

Vehicle safety glass doesn't shatter when you shoot it. The bullet punches a hole through and weakens the laminated layers of glass and plastic in the immediate area. Reversing my rifle I used the stock to batter a hole through the glass large enough to reach in and release the catch. The door rose with a hiss of hydraulics and I grabbed three large stockpots and set them down on the pavement.

I shrugged out of my pack, dropped it on the ground and clicked the flashlight back on. Lying down on my back I slithered under the SUV, dragging one of the pots with me. I didn't have to look hard to find the bottom of the gas tank. Moving one of the pots into position I drew my Ka-Bar and placed its tip against the thin metal wall of the tank. Holding the knife in my left hand I used the heel of my right to hammer on the pommel.

When you've been injured and your injuries are finally healing and no longer causing constant pain, you tend to forget about them. The first blow on the pommel of my knife reminded me that it wasn't that long ago I had been nailed to a cross and not nearly enough time had gone by for my hands to completely heal. Fuck, that hurt!

Shaking my head I settled for crawling back out from under the Hyundai, aiming my rifle carefully and putting a round into the tank. A small, neat hole appeared in the bottom and gasoline began to slowly trickle into the pot. Yes, you can fire a weapon into a container of gasoline without causing it to ignite, regardless of what

Hollywood has conditioned everyone to believe over the years.

Gasoline requires a spark, open flame or extreme heat to cause it to combust. A bullet will generally not provide any of those. Notable exceptions are tracer rounds that have a small chemical charge in the base that is ignited when the bullet is fired. There are also steel jacketed rounds that can spark upon striking steel, iron or stone. I was using US Military issue Full Metal Jacket bullets, but just because they're metal doesn't mean they will cause a spark. Anyway, I pulled it off without blowing myself up.

Watching the slow trickle of fuel I stood and moved to the side of the SUV where I pried the locked fueling door open with my knife. Twisting the fuel cap I removed it and went back to the rear and squatted down to see underneath. Removing the cap and creating a large vent hole worked. The fuel was now pouring out in a steady stream, quickly filling the pot.

I stood to check on Rachel and Martinez then had to squat back down and slide a new pot in place as the first one was mostly full. Careful not to spill any of the gasoline I carried it to the side of the truck and set it on the ground to open the fuel door. Snorting when I saw a locking gas cap, I started to raise the knife to break it off before thinking to check the keys in the ignition. Finding a key for the cap, I unlocked it and stood back looking at the filler neck.

There was no way I was going to be able to pour fuel out of a cooking pot into the tank without spilling nearly all of it. While I tried to come up with a better idea, I had to go change pots again before the second one overflowed. As the new pot filled, I dug through the kitchen supplies in the vehicle and smiled when I found a stack of kitchen funnels. Grabbing the largest, I went back to the truck and after shoving the narrow end into the fuel neck lifted the pot and poured its contents into the tank without spilling a drop.

I was walking back to the SUV to change pots when I heard the sound of an approaching engine. Not trusting in the kindness or benevolence of strangers, I shouted for Rachel and Martinez and they came running, Dog trotting between them. The vehicle sounded loud in the silent city streets and it was hard to estimate how far away it was, but I didn't want to waste time standing there guessing. Grabbing my pack off the ground I led the way into a narrow alley, looking through my rifle's night vision scope long enough to make sure we weren't walking into a nest of infected.

26

The alley was full of trash. Empty boxes were piled up near the entrance, crumpled sheets of newspaper spilling out of them. Even abandoned, I could smell the rank stench of body odor. Not the ripe stink from soldiers in the field for days on end, rather the cloying smell of a body, or bodies, that hadn't seen soap and water for months. Glancing around I realized this had been where homeless had taken refuge, but they were gone now.

Rifle up as I crouched behind a box that had once held a washing machine, I watched the street. Dog was stretched out on his belly next to me, Rachel and Martinez farther back in the alley keeping an eye on our rear. The engine grew louder, noise reflecting off the hard faces of the buildings that lined the road. Then the vehicle turned a corner at an intersection a quarter of a mile away and headed our direction.

It was a Chevy Suburban, lifted up with big off-road tires. A heavy grill guard protected the front and a large bank of high-intensity LED lights was mounted to it. They were on, illuminating the whole area in a stark, white light. The vehicle approached slowly, engine burbling in the dark behind the brilliant lights, coming to a stop nose to nose with our truck.

They just sat there for a few minutes, most likely surveying the area for any danger. They certainly weren't using night vision, at least to look to their front. There was just too much light which would have washed out the electronics. Finally the front doors popped open and two men stepped out onto the pavement.

Both were dressed in jeans and khaki shirts, military-ish boots on their feet. Holstered pistols were on their belts and each carried a rifle like they knew how to handle one. While the driver held back, scanning the surroundings, the passenger walked forward to check our truck. He approached cautiously, rifle up and ready, swinging wide around the open driver side door to see inside then squatting to peer underneath.

Satisfied there was no immediate danger he lowered the rifle and walked the rest of the way around the truck, pausing to survey the open fuel door with the funnel sticking out of it. He raised his head and looked around but the Hyundai was slightly behind the Suburban and concealed by the darkness behind its lights.

The guys knew to be careful and how to handle weapons, but they weren't being very smart with their approach. The contrast between the blindingly bright light thrown by the light bar and the darkness to the sides and rear of their vehicle meant they could only see in one direction. The human eye just can't adjust to drastic differences in lighting that quickly.

Moving back to his partner, the passenger spoke briefly before stepping back around to his side. The driver leaned in the open door and pulled out a radio microphone, keyed the transmit button and started speaking. When he let off the button I could hear a voice answering him but not well enough to understand what was being said.

Who the hell were these guys? They certainly appeared to be organized and well supplied. For some reason they dressed the same, as if they were wearing some sort of uniform. But what were they doing? Had the survivors in Oklahoma City formed some sort of militia? That, or these were bad guys who both happened to like khaki shirts and faux jump boots.

I wanted them to be good guys. Wanted to ask for help getting to Katie's location, but since the day of the attacks I had yet to see any civilians working together for any reason other than to prey on their fellow survivors. The thought of just shooting both of them and taking their vehicle passed through my head. As attractive as that beast of a vehicle was, I couldn't just attack what might be a couple of the best guys left in the world.

The driver finished his radio conversation and moved forward to stand next to our abandoned truck. He looked around, hands on his hips. I was able to get a good look at him in the light from his vehicle. He was in his 40s, still in good shape with strong features under a tan Stetson hat. My eyes moved over him and noted the duty belt with holstered pistol. Then they traveled up and caught a glint off something on his chest.

Raising my rifle I peered through the scope, clearly seeing a gold star pinned to his chest. Cops? OK, definitely dressed and acting like them, but the guys in Nashville had been dressed like real cops too. But I wasn't getting the same vibe off these guys as I did in Tennessee. Making my decision I waved Rachel and Martinez forward and filled them in.

"You sure that's a good idea?" Rachel asked, concern creasing her face.

"No, but if they're legit it will make things a whole lot easier." I said. "Besides. You two are going to stay here in the alley, and if it starts to go sideways I'm trusting you'll take them out for me. They're wearing body armor under their shirts. Your rifles should punch through at this range but don't count on a body shot."

Martinez nodded and Rachel reached out and squeezed my arm. Telling Dog to stay I stood up and stepped out of the alley. My rifle was slung, hanging down at my left side and I held my open hands out at waist level.

I had only moved a couple of steps into the light when the driver spotted me. He grabbed his rifle and moved it to the low ready position, shouting for his partner. I had paused when he moved his rifle, but when he didn't point it at me I resumed slowly walking towards him. His partner ran up to stand a few yards away from him, rifle also at low ready. Well, at least they didn't start shooting as soon as they saw me.

"That's close enough." The driver called when I was ten yards away.

I stopped and looked at them, trying to decide if I was blocking the line of fire to either from the alley. I was pretty sure I was directly in line with the passenger so I moved a couple of steps to my left. The driver watched me move laterally, eyes squinting as he looked back in the direction I'd come from.

"How many rifles you have on us?" He asked.

I smiled. "Enough," I answered. "We didn't start shooting when you rolled up, and you didn't start shooting when I showed myself, so maybe we can all just relax a little."

He thought about that for a moment before nodding. "OK. We're Oklahoma State Police. You Air Force from Tinker?"

"Army," I said, introducing myself. "Sorry for the precautions. We haven't had the best of luck with survivors."

"Don't I know it," he said. "Shit heels are taking the opportunity of a lifetime to cause problems. Got a lot of half-wit assholes running around thinking they're all King Shit of the Apocalypse."

I relaxed another half a notch, grinning. He certainly had a way with words. I stepped forward to get out of the direct light and each of us took a moment to survey the other before he held his hand out.

"Jesse Timmons," he said. "Sergeant with the OSP. That there's Bobby Small, my partner." I shook his hand and nodded a greeting at Bobby.

"What the hell are you doing out here and not behind the wire at Tinker?" He asked, watching me but also scanning the street behind to my rear. That was OK, good in fact. I was doing the same thing, not wanting any surprises because we were busy talking.

I almost lied. Wasn't sure I wanted to share what was really going on. But this guy dealt with liars, cheaters and thieves for a living. He most likely had a finely tuned bullshit detector and I'd rather have his help than have him dismiss me because he didn't like my answer. So I told him an abbreviated story of what was going on.

"I know that casino," he said when I told him the location I was trying to reach. "The missus and I used to go up there once a month to lose one of her paychecks. It's a huge fuckin' place."

I was encouraged that he not only knew the area but also knew the specific building.

"Don't suppose you want to take a road trip and make this official?" I asked, not really expecting an affirmative answer. He stood there, hands on hips, chewing on his lip and thinking.

"Well," he said, drawing the word out into two syllables. "I'd say this is a military problem since she was taken on an Air Force Base. Then he flees to a casino, which is Indian land and that makes it an FBI problem. But seeing as I don't much care for people who mistreat women, I think I can make a case for the State Police to get involved."

I was surprised, and it must have showed on my face.

"You don't have to look so goddamn shocked," he said with a smile. "Why don't you call your friends up and let's get rolling. Don't like to stay in one spot too long. If the infected don't find you there's always some fucker with a rifle just waiting to take a shot at you."

I've seen it happen time and time again, both in combat and in just normal, everyday civilian life. I can't explain it, not sure it's anything more than a coincidence, but as I've gotten older and lived through more shit I've learned not to tempt fate. Don't think or talk about something bad that might happen. Kind of like driving down the road and thinking it's been a long time since you've had car problems, then out of nowhere you get a flat tire.

A flat tire would have been preferable to the rifle shot that punched through Bobby's chest a moment after Timmons finished speaking. Yes, they were wearing body armor, but the vests police wear are designed to stop handgun rounds, not high velocity rifle slugs.

As I dove for the darkness underneath the Suburban I heard a follow on shot and recognized the sound as coming from a large caliber rifle. Probably a .300 or .308. Either was capable of taking down targets at a thousand yards. Punching through police issue body armor probably hardly slowed the bullet.

27

Sergeant Timmons hit the ground with a grunt and rolled, coming to a stop next to me under the big SUV.

"You hit?" I asked, twisting to scan the street level to make sure there weren't any infected approaching.

"I'm OK," he said, which most likely meant he had taken a bullet, but for the moment was still able to move and fight.

The shots had come from just down the street and above ground level. Damn it! That was the location where I'd thought there was movement earlier. Pissed off and cursing, I wormed my way out from underneath the Suburban on the far side from the shooter. Getting my knees under me I crawled to the rear corner and poked my head around.

A muzzle flash from the roofline spotted our attacker, but I had to duck when a bullet punched through the metal bodywork a few inches from my head. Don't know if I've mentioned this, but I hate snipers! Well, to be accurate, I hate *enemy* snipers.

A good man with a rifle can pin down a vastly superior force, and nothing will demoralize combat troops more than the fear of a bullet screaming in from seemingly out of nowhere.

I rolled back under the vehicle and slowly crawled to the rear, keeping the heavy steel wheel between the sniper's position and me. Slowly, I eased my rifle around the big, all-terrain tire and peered through the night vision scope. I was counting on the shooter not having night vision and the area I was in being dark enough that he wouldn't spot me.

It took me a couple of minutes to spot him, and I was mildly surprised to see it was a her. I've heard of a few countries, most notably Israel, fielding female snipers, but it was a rarity. Don't ask me why. In my experience a woman can be just as good with a gun as a man. It's about raw ability to start, then practice, practice, practice. Maybe it's one of those things that more men have that basic physical attribute than women. Maybe not. At the moment, I didn't give a shit. So far the bitch on the roof was proving herself to be quite adept.

She held a large bolt-action rifle with a high-powered scope, but as I watched her through the night vision it quickly became apparent that she wasn't military trained. There was plenty of concealment available for her to use, even a couple of spots that would have allowed her a covered firing position, but she was propped up on the third story parapet without any apparent concern over return fire.

"See him?" Timmons asked with a frightening wheeze in his voice.

"Her," I said, thumbing my fire selector to semi-auto.

I was zeroed on her face. She was young, probably no more than seventeen, but that didn't matter once she started shooting at me. As I began to take up the slack in the trigger I heard shouting from the alley where Rachel, Martinez and Dog were hiding. Several shots were fired, and though I should have taken the sniper out when I had the opportunity, I turned to look in that direction. I couldn't see anything, but the sounds of a fight reached my ears, Dog's snarls letting me know he was in the thick of it.

The mouth of the alley was on the same side of the street as the girl sniper, and when the commotion started she leaned out over the edge in an attempt to see what was going on. I turned back to my scope, sighted on her head and squeezed the trigger. I watched in the night vision when the round punched through her skull and all animation left her body, which slumped across the parapet.

The heavy rifle slipped through her lifeless fingers and fell to the sidewalk below, the wood stock shattering on impact. She had been leaning way out when I shot her and in slow motion her body began to succumb to the pull of gravity and slide over the edge. Picking up speed it slithered free of the roof and tumbled as it fell, striking the sidewalk next to the rifle with a sickening thud.

I scanned the roofline but didn't see any other threats, so I rolled out from under the Suburban and sprinted to the alley where the sounds of the fight were growing louder. Rounding the corner with my rifle up I paused when I didn't see what I expected to see.

Two dogs lay dead on the ground, apparently having been shot, and Dog was fighting with a third. Rachel and Martinez both were aiming their rifles at the fight but the dogs were moving too fast for either of them to risk a shot that might hit him. Rachel was screaming at him to stop but he ignored her and pressed his advantage, finally taking the strange dog to the ground by the throat. A moment later it was over and Dog moved away from his kill and walked to Rachel, limping slightly as he moved.

Feral dogs. I was surprised we hadn't run into any before now. Dogs aren't any different from humans. Strip away the comfortable home and the ease of grocery store bought food and it doesn't take long for the wild side to come out. Not every human or every dog, but it's still there, just under the surface, waiting for the right moment.

I turned back to the street and made a quick scan. A hundred yards to the south the males I'd seen earlier were approaching, having been attracted by all the shooting. I didn't see anything else at the moment. Pointing out the infected to Martinez I told Rachel to come with me and ran to where Timmons was sitting with his back against the front wheel of the Suburban, Dog limping along between us.

Timmons didn't look good when we got to him. He was pale and his shirt was soaked in blood from a high chest wound. Looking up as we approached he tried to smile but it was more of a grimace, blood trickling from the corner of his mouth. Rachel dashed past me and dropped to her knees next to him, ripping his shirt open and barking at me to help her remove his body armor.

We were as gentle as we could be, propping him back up once the vest was worked over his head. I clicked on my flashlight so Rachel could see the wound, turning my head when I heard Martinez open fire. She was putting the infected males down and didn't need my help so I turned my attention back to Timmons. He had reached out and taken Rachel's hand in his.

"Going to die," he wheezed out, looking into Rachel's eyes.

I could see the tear form and trickle down her face as she nodded. "I'm sorry. There's nothing I can do without a hospital."

"That's alright then, pretty lady. Wasn't liking life too much without my missus anyways." He tried to laugh but it turned into a strangled cough. Bright red blood poured out of his mouth and he died, hand slipping out of Rachel's to flop onto the pavement.

"There was just too much damage," Rachel said, no longer trying to hold back the tears. "Big bullet and it most likely started tumbling from going through his vest. There's no exit wound so it probably bounced around inside him."

I wanted to hold Rachel and comfort her, but I didn't think we had time. It was hard to imagine the girl with the rifle had been by herself. Anything's possible, but that doesn't mean it's very damn likely. But if there were others with her, why hadn't they attacked by now? Was she a lookout? Put there to keep an eye out for whatever her group was interested in?

That made sense. And lookouts usually have radios. Had she called for reinforcements? But then why they hell had she started shooting? Just young and inexperienced and eager to do something? That was all that was making sense, and that meant it was time to get the hell out of there. Fast.

Whistling to get Martinez' attention I waved her over to the idling Suburban. She ran and jumped into the back seat with Dog, Rachel and I getting in front.

"What the hell?" Martinez said, reaching forward and banging on the heavy wire mesh that separated the back seat from the driver.

"Cop car," I said, finding the switch to shut off the bank of lights on the front. Shifting into gear I spun us around and headed north, the powerful V8 roaring as I fed in gas.

"If either one of you so much as thinks about making a crack about a Mexican in the back seat of a police car, I'll…" Martinez didn't get to finish her thought as bullets began slamming into the vehicle.

28

Navy Lieutenant Randy Parker looked down over the lowered rear ramp of the C2-A Greyhound that had launched from the aircraft carrier USS Harry S. Truman over eight hours ago. The twin turbo-prop aircraft was flying at slightly over 32,000 feet and they were less than five minutes from the jump point of their HAHO – High Altitude High Opening – insertion into Alaska. Parker looked behind him at the rest of his SEALS, twelve of them stacked up in line. Everyone had switched over to their portable oxygen supply and were ready to go.

"Arrest and extract the President of the United States," was what Admiral Packard had ordered Parker and his men to do.

After a lot of soul searching, and the most detailed background briefing for an operation that he'd ever received in his Naval career, Parker had accepted the order. Not without reservations and certainly not without doubt. But the "normal" world that would have made this act unthinkable a few months ago had been ripped away. There was no normal left. Only the fight to hold on to what you had, and the thought of the President handing the remains of the country to the Russians on a silver platter was what had swayed his decision.

"Fifteen seconds." The jumpmaster's voice over his radio. "Godspeed, Lieutenant."

Parker looked up at the small "Christmas Tree" over the open rear door. A stack of lights resembling a traffic signal with red and green.

As he watched, the red light on top of the stack faded out and the green began glowing. Then the world turned on its side as the aircraft suddenly banked hard and began rapidly losing altitude.

Parker was thrown against the men behind him and wound up pinned to a bulkhead by the violent maneuvers of the aircraft. He started to shout out on his radio but a blinding white light consumed the Greyhound and all souls aboard.

"We have a confirmed shoot down, Madam President." An Army Sergeant said a few moments later, looking up at Kathleen Clark in the darkened operations center at Fort Wainwright, Alaska.

"Thank you," she said, turning to face General Carey, the base commander.

The General looked decidedly unhappy about having shot down a Navy plane full of American sailors. But a sympathizer within Admiral Packard's command had contacted him and warned of the SEAL mission to arrest the President. Carey wasn't happy with the decisions she had made, felt they weren't in the best interest of the United States, but she was the President and he was obligated to carry out her orders and protect her.

When he'd told her about the impending SEAL raid she'd flown into a rage. Wanted him to attack the aircraft carrier the Admiral was based on and sink it. He'd finally calmed her after a long explanation that he didn't have any way to carry out that order. His compromise to her insistence that the Admiral be punished was to agree to use one of his Patriot missile batteries to shoot down the SEAL's plane. He'd argued for letting them parachute in and having troops waiting to capture them alive, but she'd overruled him and insisted that a statement needed to be made so the Admiral didn't make any more attempts.

"You're welcome, Madam President." He finally responded, not meeting her eyes.

The President smiled and swept out of the operations center, three MPs assigned as her personal security detail going with her. General Carey met the haunted eyes of the Sergeant who'd released the missile that had killed their fellow servicemen, then walked out and headed to his office for a stiff drink.

"That's definitely a shoot down, sir." The Navy Chief Petty Officer said to Admiral Packard.

They were deep within the bowels of the USS George Washington in the CIC - Combat Information Center – watching a real time satellite image as the debris from the Greyhound fell towards the ground. The sailor clicked his mouse a couple of times and the image jumped, displaying the aircraft in flight.

He adjusted a setting and the playback slowed just as a streak of white appeared and intercepted the plane. Milliseconds later there was a bright flash that obscured the entire screen, then as it faded pieces of the shattered airframe could be seen spiraling down, trailing smoke.

"I never saw any canopies," Packard said, hoping the Chief would rewind some more and show him that at least the SEALs made it out alive.

"No sir. They hadn't jumped yet." The man said in a low voice.

Packard shook his head and balled his hands into fists in his frustration. His first inclination was to order a squadron of bombers off the Truman to reduce Fort Wainwright to rubble, but he wasn't about to start killing soldiers because of the bitch occupying the virtual White House.

"Get me General Carey at Wainwright," he said to a communications specialist. "I'll take it in my cabin."

The Admiral turned and stormed out of the CIC, sailors in the passageway leaping out of his path as he strode through the giant ship with murder in his eyes. Three minutes later he slammed through the door of his personal quarters and snatched up the phone that was ringing.

"General Carey on the line, Admiral." The specialist said before connecting the call.

"What the fuck do you think you're doing, General?" Packard barked into the phone. There was silence on the other end for a long time then Carey spoke in a subdued voice.

"How many?" He asked.

"How many what?" Packard snapped.

"How many men were on that plane?"

Packard paused, his anger tempered by the obviously contrite manner of the General.

"Thirteen SEALs and four in the flight crew." He answered in a less brusque tone.

"Jesus Christ," Carey breathed into the phone. "Jesus Christ." The Admiral heard ice tinkle in a glass and thinking it was a good idea pulled open a desk drawer that contained a prohibited bottle of whiskey.

"This is going to spiral out of control," the General finally said.

"Going to? I think it already has." Packard retorted, pouring two fingers of amber whiskey into a water glass and tossing both of them down his throat. "You killed seventeen Americans. And don't even fucking tell me you were just following orders."

"What the hell am I supposed to do when the President's security is threatened and she issues an order? Ignore it and let your SEALs walk in and take her away?" Despite his words, Carey's tone didn't change. Didn't become belligerent. Packard took a deep breath and collected his thoughts.

"Sam, do you really support what she's doing? Crawling into bed with the Russians after what they've done to us? To the whole world?"

"I don't like it, but goddamn it Admiral we took an oath. Doesn't that mean anything to you?"

"It means everything to me, including the part about defending what's left of this country against all enemies. And right now, with a President conspiring with Russia instead of standing up and defending us, I'm choosing to follow my oath. And so should you. That bitch is going to hand everything that's left over without firing a shot, and what does she get in return?

"You saw the same radio intercept I did of her conversation with Barinov. She has a fucking mansion waiting for her in Russia. All she has to do is get us to stand down so the infected and Russian troops can finish off the last of us."

"What the hell are you talking about?" General Carey's voice rose for the first time. "I've not seen any intercept."

"Son of a bitch!" Packard exploded. "Something's rotten somewhere. I ordered you copied on that a couple of days ago! I'll call you back."

The Admiral slammed the handset back onto the phone, picking it up a moment later and ordering the CO of the Washington, Captain James to report to his cabin. It was time to find out whom he could trust, and who else was responsible for the deaths of his sailors.

29

Katie looked over her situation for the third time, frustrated that she couldn't come up with any way to escape. Roach had forced her down the stairs from the roof and left her in the VIP lounge while he explored the massive casino. Her hands were bound behind her back and her ankles were once again restrained with plastic ties that securely held her to the furniture. The paracord noose around her neck was stretched up to the ceiling and tied off to a light fixture. There was just enough slack in the line for her to sit on a red velvet couch as long as she remained sitting up very straight.

She had thought about trying to pull the light out of the ceiling, but if she exerted any pressure on the rope it would tighten around her already bruised throat. Without her hands she would die quickly as once tightened, the cord wouldn't loosen by itself.

Katie had tested her bonds until her wrists were raw and bleeding, but she didn't think even John would be able to break out of the restraints. There was a bar with rows of gleaming glasses on the far side of the room. If she could reach it and break one of them she could cut herself free, but Roach had effectively ensured that she wasn't moving off the damn sofa.

With nothing but time to think, Katie wondered if John was really alive or had Roach lied to get her to willingly come with him? She still didn't know what he wanted, for sure, but every time she thought about it there was only one logical answer. He wanted her. She would let her thoughts get that far before shutting them down, refusing to think what her immediate future held.

Katie had no illusions about her looks and the behavior of men. She wasn't narcissistic like many beautiful women are, just realistic. Unwanted advances from men was something she had dealt with since she was a teenager. She'd dealt with college professors who made thinly veiled proposals of how she could receive easy As.

Then co-workers at the predominantly male CIA. On one occasion she'd drawn the attention of a department head whose behavior qualified as stalking, his training helping him go so far as planting cameras in her home and listening in on her personal phone calls. She had confronted him, but he had effectively covered his tracks and she had no evidence. After their very public confrontation in the halls of Langley his spying on her had only gotten worse. Until she broke down one night and told John.

This was years ago, her still with the Agency and John still in the Army. He'd been somewhere in the Middle East, or at least that's what she thought. They had been talking on encrypted satellite phones and she was sure that half way through the conversation she'd heard a faint *adhan* in the background. The adhan is the Muslim call to prayer, and in many Middle Eastern countries it is played over loud speakers five times a day to remind the faithful to prostrate themselves before Allah.

The next morning when she arrived at work everyone was talking about the department head that had been the victim of a vicious street mugging the previous evening while walking his dog. He was in the hospital with multiple broken bones, bruised kidneys and a severe concussion. The odd thing was his dog's leash had been carefully tied to the tree next to where he was found, the animal unharmed and with enough slack to be comfortable while it waited for its master to get up.

Katie had thought about asking John what he knew about the incident when they talked a few days later, but knew his response would be something innocuous. He had been in the Special Forces community a long time at that point and had friends all over the world, in every branch of the service as well as in service to several other nations. One phone call and he could reach out from half a world away and solve her problem. At first she'd been upset he'd taken it on himself to get involved, but then if she hadn't really wanted his help she wouldn't have told him about it in the first place.

Years later the topic came up late one night when neither of them could fall asleep. She had poked him a little, saying if she'd wanted to kick her stalker's ass that she was more than capable of doing that herself. He'd just grinned, crushed her to him in his big arms and whispered, "and what would have stopped him from having you arrested and prosecuted? Do I really need to explain plausible deniability to you, of all people?" She'd thought about what he said for a moment then smiled and snuggled against him, feeling as safe as a CIA case officer can ever feel.

Then, three weeks later the bottom had dropped out of her world. She'd been at her desk at Langley when she'd received a phone call asking her to come to the Assistant Director's office on the seventh floor. Arriving, she'd been met by her immediate supervisor who was waiting in the reception area for her. He'd escorted her into an office where an Army Colonel in dress uniform stood stiffly next to the AD.

They'd invited her to have a seat and offered coffee or tea, but the presence of an Army officer told her something had happened to her husband. Rather rudely she'd told them to get to the point. The men exchanged glances then the Colonel told her that John had been missing for four days after leading his team to rescue a squad of MARSOC Marines. She nodded her head and asked a few questions which were answered evasively. Thanking the officer she'd turned and walked out of the office and directly to a sub-basement room that housed the operations center for the Middle East.

Her best friend, Anne Hoffman, was an analyst that spent most of her time with her nose buried in satellite photos of that part of the world. Katie told her what was going on and as she suspected, Anne knew all about the mission, just not that John was involved. Together they spent two days and nights looking through images until Anne got lucky and found one taken at a very oblique angle as a satellite was being moved over the horizon.

The photo showed a firefight raging between a small force of men who were noticeably paler than the larger group they were battling. While the resolution was nowhere near good enough to recognize anyone, the fighting was happening at the right location and time. It had to be John and his unit. With the photo as a starting point they eventually constructed two timelines. One was the exfiltration of John's unit and the Marines, without John. The other was two men, both still unrecognizable, who were cut off by hundreds of freshly arrived jihadists and had set off into the desert.

By the time Katie and Anne had found them and were able to set up a real time satellite feed, the two were within a mile of a Mediterranean beach with nearly eighty men in pursuit. Katie had snatched up a phone, and only because the call was coming from the CIA had spoken directly to the Army Colonel who was the current duty officer for CENTCOM. Anne had shared the feed with the Army's operations center at Fort Bragg and flash traffic started flying around the globe.

Twenty minutes later the two men made it to the beach and dug in, holding off the much larger force. They were running low on ammo and about to be overrun when three F-18s from an American carrier operating in the Med appeared on the image the two women were watching. Forming up in a line the jets streaked in, strafing the jihadists over and over until they started running. Katie had stood up and cheered, drawing disapproving looks from other analysts working on the far side of the quiet room.

The fighter jets had stayed on station, occasionally swooping down and loosing a rocket into the enemy that had taken shelter in the shallow caves of the area. Twenty minutes later a Navy rescue helicopter, escorted by two attack helos, had arrived and quickly winched the two Americans aboard. John had called her a few hours later, safely aboard the carrier. When she'd asked what he was up to, he replied that he'd been sitting on a beach sipping a drink with a new friend who just happened to be a Marine. She'd smiled and never told him her role in his rescue.

The CIA had taken a dim view of Katie and Anne's unauthorized involvement in a military matter. Both had received letters of reprimand, which were placed in their permanent records. Anne lost out on a promotion that she had already been told was hers, and in utter disgust with the politics and bureaucracy Katie resigned from the Agency.

Thinking about John brought tears to her eyes, but she fought them back. Forced herself to remember the training she'd received. Remembered the necessity to remain calm and not let emotions cloud her judgment or interfere with her thinking. Sniffing softly she had just returned her attention to her bindings and the cord around her neck when Roach walked into the room.

"Good, you're still here." He said with a broad smile on his face.

"Where else would I be?" Katie answered, her voice rough from the cord having been tightened around her throat earlier.

"Well, infected could have come along and helped themselves to you. Or maybe some survivors. Pretty little thing like you would tempt even the most respectable of men." Roach leered at her for a moment, then reached for her.

It took every ounce of self-control that Katie had to not flinch away from his touch, but she sat still as he placed his hands on her hips before slowly sliding them down her legs to the tie around her ankles. He let out an exaggerated breath of pleasure, then drew his knife and cut her legs free. It took a few seconds, then the pain hit as blood rushed back into her feet.

Roach grabbed her upper arm and roughly pulled her to her feet and spun her around. He took her left forearm in his hand, raising her bound wrists into the air so he could cut the last of her bonds, but took the opportunity to caress and squeeze her ass before he did.

Stepping away he watched her roll her shoulders forward to start working out the stiffness, then wring her hands as the blood flow was restored. She finally turned around, looking warily at him.

"What's going on?" She asked.

"The building is clear," he said. "And there's nowhere for you to go. All the exits are chained and locked from the inside, and I'm tired of having to keep you tied up. If you give me any trouble I'm going to hurt you. Understand?" He waved the knife in the air.

"I understand," Katie said, carefully reaching up to remove the cord from around her neck. "But I don't understand why you're doing this."

A cloud passed over Roach's face as it turned purple with rage, then he stepped forward and screamed in Katie's face, spittle flying, holding the tip of the knife a fraction of an inch from her stomach. "Because he left me no choice! You're my leverage out of this! Now don't ask me any more stupid questions!"

Katie kept her face neutral but her concern ratcheted up a few notches. Until now she'd thought this guy was just some nut job that wanted her to live out some sick end of the world fantasy with him. Now she realized he was stark raving mad. Throw him in restraints and shoot him full of Thorazine mad. That changed her whole plan about how to deal with him.

30

Backup for the dead sniper had arrived, and they had come in force. Three pickups had pulled up at the closest intersection, staying just far enough back to be out of sight. Several men, I didn't get a good headcount, had started moving down the street in our direction, hugging the dark storefronts.

Martinez, cursing in Spanish, shoved Dog onto the floor and reached for a button that wasn't there to lower her window. She had forgotten it was a police Suburban with the seat she was in intended for the transportation of prisoners. She screamed at us and Rachel fumbled around and hit a switch that lowered all the windows in the vehicle at the same time.

Shoving the muzzle of her rifle between the bars protecting the side window glass, Martinez started returning fire, a moment later Rachel joining in. All I could do was drive and try to get us out of range as fast as I could. Gas pedal flat to the floor, the engine roared as we picked up speed, the two women keeping up a steady rate of fire.

Bullets were finding the big, black vehicle, but Rachel and Martinez' return fire was forcing them to keep their heads down and their accuracy was suffering. I thought we were almost home free when another pickup screamed out of an alley on my side of the road. I swerved and the other driver turned at the last second so instead of a T-bone collision the two vehicles struck on their front corners.

The impact was loud, metal rending and glass shattering, but both vehicles were big, heavy American steel and kept going. The truck was pushed away by the force of the collision then slammed back into the driver's side of the Suburban, metal grinding on metal as it accelerated and stayed pressed against me. Four men in the back of the pickup were struggling to regain their balance and bring their weapons to bear. If that happened, they were at point blank range and we were dead.

I yanked the wheel to the right to get a few feet of separation then steered back into them. The heavy vehicles slammed against each other, knocking the men in the bed of the pickup off balance. Martinez had swiveled around in the back seat and opened up with her rifle. One of the men took three rounds in his chest and rose up, his body going above the cab of the truck. The slipstream caught him as he died and flipped him over the tailgate where his body came to rest on the pavement.

The pickup slowed a half a second before one of the men in back was able to start firing his rifle. His rounds struck the rear side of the Suburban instead of punching through Martinez' door as he intended. Without conscious thought I realized what the other driver was trying to do. He had slowed enough to align his front bumper with my rear bumper and was going to slam into it sideways and send me into an uncontrollable spin.

This is called a PIT – Precision Immobilization Technique – maneuver and was originally developed by a police department in Virginia, but made famous by the LAPD with all of their high-speed chases. The best way to counter it is to not keep driving in a nice, straight line and let the pursuit vehicle get in position to deliver the blow. Lifting my foot off the gas I stomped on the brakes as hard as I could, the SUVs big off-road tires screaming as we suddenly decelerated.

The pickup had already started swerving towards us, but my sudden braking prevented him from executing a successful PIT. Instead, the truck shot past us, its lateral momentum causing it to keep drifting until its right rear side impacted the Suburban's left front. I jammed the accelerator back to the floor and steered hard left into the truck as it slammed into us.

I had a scary moment when I thought I was going to lose control but finally got us back in a straight line. The pickup was ahead of us now, fishtailing as the driver sawed the wheel back and forth to overcome the violent sideways shove I'd just given him. The pickup was whipping violently across the road, one of the men in back finally losing his grip and tumbling out.

We were less than thirty feet behind and I had the throttle wide open when his body struck the grill of the Suburban. I more felt than heard the thud as he was thrown over the hood. For an instant his face was against the windshield, terror filled eyes staring at me, then the glass shattered, bowing in towards us but holding in its frame at the last moment. He was thrown over the roof of the SUV and I heard a couple of bumps as he tumbled along the top before falling to the pavement behind us.

I stayed on the gas, closing the gap with the pickup. The driver was starting to get it back under control when I rammed into the rear bumper. It was a hard impact and I had hoped it would be enough to cause the truck to lose control, but it did the opposite and helped him straighten out the heavy vehicle. Moments later bullets started punching through the damaged glass as the guys in the back found their balance and were able to bring their weapons up.

"Knock the glass out!" I shouted to Rachel, swerving to not make it any easier for our attackers.

"How?" She screamed back over the roar of the engine and wind noise whistling through the bullet holes.

"Use your feet! Kick it out!" Martinez shouted from the back seat.

Rachel lifted her feet onto the dash, scooted her ass forward and braced her shoulders against the seat back as she started battering the compromised windshield with the soles of her boots. She did an admirable job of focusing on the task as I kept us swerving and the occasional bullet punched through, showering us with powdered glass. Finally it popped lose and I reached forward and helped push it out of the way.

Now I could see, but the wind whipping directly into my face was intense, immediately causing tears to form in my eyes and blurring my vision. The truck in front of us was swerving, the driver intent on not allowing me to get next to him and attempt my own PIT maneuver. Rachel laid her rifle on the dash and started pumping bullets at them. I drew my pistol and joined the fight, driving with my left hand while I shot with my right.

Neither of us was finding a target, but we did manage to keep their heads down and stop the incoming fire. Ahead I could see an intersection as a major east-west road crossed our path. At the last moment I jammed on the brakes and cut the wheel to the right. We were still going fast, probably close to 60 miles an hour, and the Suburban started to drift to its left as I held the wheel to guide us through the turn.

The pickup shot through the intersection, unprepared for my turn. From the corner of my eye I saw the one unbroken taillight come on as the driver stood on the brakes but I didn't have time to check on what they were doing. The SUV was still drifting, the rear trying to come around and send us into a spin. Steering slightly to the left I fed some throttle, hoping to straighten us out, and slowly we started to come back into line.

"Look out!" Rachel screamed.

I took my eyes off the pavement directly to our front and looked up to see a road full of infected coming our direction. There wasn't time to tell male from female before we blasted into the front ranks of the pack at speed. Some bodies were knocked aside, some battered under the tires, others flying off to the side. That would have been fine, but a female was flipped over the hood and slammed through the opening where a windshield would normally be, bouncing off the dash and landing on Rachel and me.

The infected are tough. Impervious to pain and injuries. A normal human would have already been in shock and immobile by the time she landed face down in my lap, but the female began thrashing and trying to bite the instant she landed. I couldn't risk using my pistol and having a bullet travel through and go into me, so I settled for grabbing her hair and yanking her teeth away from my legs.

Dirk Patton

She screamed and fought harder, but
fortunately she had sustained a lot of injuries when
first hit by the Suburban's grill guard. She might
not have felt or reacted to them, but she must
have broken both arms as she was unable to use
them to any degree of success.

"Kill this bitch!" I shouted at Rachel,
keeping my foot down on the gas and pushing us
through the herd.

"Here!" Martinez shoved an eight-inch
stiletto through the wire cage separating the back
seat from the front. Rachel snatched it from her
hand and rammed it into the back of the female's
head. The infected went limp and Rachel started
to lift and drag her lower body towards her open
side window.

"No. Put her up on the dash. Her body will
give us some protection." I shouted over the
constant thuds of infected against the vehicle as
we smashed our way through.

It took some doing and a lot of help from
Rachel, but we finally got the female's body over
the steering wheel and resting on the dash. She
blocked the entire lower half of the opening, and
no sooner did we have her in place than another

infected was thrown over the front of the hood. This was a male and he slammed into the dead female, almost pushing her back into our laps, but Rachel and I braced the body until I was able to lean forward and shoot him with my pistol.

Finally the small herd began to thin, then we were through, roaring down a dark, empty street. I looked in the mirror and could see the herd pursuing, but there was no sign of our attackers in the pickup. But just because they weren't chasing us through a herd of infected didn't mean they weren't racing down a parallel street to intercept us.

Keeping the speed on, I wrenched into a tire screeching left at the next intersection to get us heading back north. The male slid off the hood, body tumbling across the pavement where it slammed to a stop against an abandoned car. The female stayed in place, more inside the vehicle than out.

"Everyone OK?" I shouted to be heard above the engine, road and wind noise, looking around to try and see my three companions.

"I'm good," Rachel responded in a shaky voice, turning to look through the cage into the back seat. Dog stared back at her and stuck his tongue through the wire to lick her hand when she held it up.

"Fine," Martinez said from the back seat, but I didn't like the way she said it.

Scanning the area I didn't see any immediate threats and braked to a hard stop in the middle of the road. Jumping out I yanked the rear door open, pushed Dog aside when he greeted me and climbed into the back seat.

"Rachel!" I shouted and a moment later she opened the far door, supporting Martinez who had been using the door for a backrest. With the doors open the dome light was on and I could see blood soaking the front of Martinez' shirt.

31

Rachel worked on Martinez while Dog and I stood in the street keeping watch. I shot a couple of females that came running out of an alley, but so far they were the only threats we'd seen. Stepping to the driver's door of the idling Suburban I reached in and shut off the engine so I could listen for any approaching vehicles. The fuckers that had attacked us were still out there somewhere, and I had no doubt the only reason they weren't climbing up our asses at the moment was they just hadn't found us.

I didn't understand their mentality. Never had. I'd witnessed the same behavior in half a dozen third world countries over the years. There always seems to be a group of guys who think that because there's no civil authority they have the right to impose their will on anyone and everyone. Most of the time they're the only ones with guns and the people can't stand up to them. More than once I'd been pleased to show the bad guys the error of their ways.

Reagan had been President when I earned my beret, and he had never hesitated to send in some boots to kick ass when some two-bit warlord decided to act out. Granted, it usually happened to coincide with US security interests in the region, but there were still plenty of times it was just because he didn't like bullies. After Reagan, the backbone in the White House steadily softened until we wound up being openly challenged by every piss ant dictator on the planet.

They knew they could thumb their nose at us and we wouldn't do anything except whine and cry to the UN and go through a series of self-flagellating exercises in front of the world's media. Personally, I wished for Teddy Roosevelt to return from the grave. Walk softly and carry a big stick.

The US military was the biggest stick the planet had ever seen, but somehow our politicians decided it was better to talk and threaten and gnash their teeth for months or years while people were dying, or while some regime led by a mad man developed nuclear weapons and openly stated they wanted to use them on us or one of our allies.

International politics are really no different than high school. If someone knows they can do something to you and get away without any real repercussions, guess what? You're going to find yourself stuffed into your locker with your underwear around your head. But if they know they'll get a bloody nose for crossing your path, life is generally a much more pleasant experience.

I shook my head, dismissing my musings before I got any more distracted. There wasn't time to be worrying about things I could do nothing about, or that no longer mattered. I needed to be focusing on watching for infected and listening for shit heels, as Sergeant Timmons had called them. I couldn't help but grin, thinking I'd probably have become friends with the man if circumstances had been different.

Circling the Suburban, I glanced at Dog who was on high alert but not showing that he was detecting any threats. Stopping at the driver's side rear door I looked in on Martinez. She sat in the middle of the seat, vest and shirt off as Rachel worked with a suture kit.

"How is she?" I asked, turning my head to check the area.

"Nothing life threatening," Rachel answered without looking up. " She took two rounds. One through her left bicep. Tore the muscle up, but missed anything vital. The second one was a through and through in her right breast."

"Ouch," I said, taking a closer look at Martinez' chest.

"No shit, sir." Martinez gasped in pain as Rachel kept sewing. "But at least now I've got an excuse to get the boob job I've always wanted."

I snorted, tried to hold in the laughter but failed. "There's probably some tire inflator in the back. Want me to grab a can? We can pump up your tits through one of the bullet holes. Save you a fortune in plastic surgeon fees."

"There's something seriously wrong with you two," Rachel said, shaking her head as she worked. "You, go away so I can concentrate. And you, quit laughing unless you want your stitches to look like something from a Frankenstein movie."

I took the hint and moved on after giving Martinez a wink. Damn the woman was tough. She was sitting there joking but had to be hurting like hell.

Dismissing those thoughts I turned my head when I heard the faint sounds of an engine. The vehicle was still a good distance and the noise echoed in the empty streets, but it sounded like it was approaching from the south. We needed to start moving before we were found again. If they showed up in force we were in trouble.

"How long, Rachel?" I asked.

"Five minutes." She said.

"You're going to have to sew while I drive," I said, Dog and I climbing into the front after I shut the rear doors. "We're going to have company before then."

She didn't say anything, just reached up and turned on the overhead light that had gone out when the last door closed. I started the engine and gently accelerated, not wanting to make the suturing job any more difficult than it already was.

I got us up to 45 and held that speed. Any faster and the wind in my face was too strong and I was constantly having to wipe tears out of my eyes. What I wouldn't give for a set of goggles or even a pair of glasses. Anything to protect my eyes. Dog, on the other hand, seemed to love the idea of a missing windshield. He sat up straight on the passenger seat, head thrust forward and looking straight ahead into the wind; nose twitching and I swear a smile on his furry face.

A few minutes later Rachel trimmed the final stitch, smeared some antibiotic ointment on the wounds and set the med kit aside. She dug through Martinez' pack and found a clean shirt which she helped her slip over her head, then got her vest back in place.

"How do you manage it?" Rachel asked me as she dug through the med kit.

"Manage what?" I asked.

"Driving around with topless women," she said. "First me in Atlanta, now Martinez. You must think you lead a charmed life."

While speaking, Rachel had found a vial of antibiotic and a large syringe which she filled and held up to the light. Tapping it to work bubbles to the top she gently pressed the plunger to purge the air. I chose not to respond to her comment, instead pulled out the GPS while Martinez leaned over on the seat and pulled her pants down so Rachel could administer the injection.

96 miles to go. Not far, but too damn far in today's world. I concentrated on my driving and what I was going to do to Roach when I got my hands on him.

32

The casino was massive. There was no other word for it. After cutting her free, Roach had followed Katie through a door that opened onto the main casino floor. Row upon row of slot machines sat silent, seemingly stretching into infinity. Glass fronted rooms with giant poker tables and plush chairs looked out onto the gaming area and every couple of hundred feet was a restaurant or snack bar.

Roach kept Katie to his front, his short barreled H&K rifle not quite pointed at her, but if he wanted to shoot her it would only require an adjustment of a couple of inches. She surveyed the area, careful to appear docile. She needed to get an idea of the layout, and at the same time lull him into believing that she was cowed and wouldn't put up any form of resistance or make an attempt to escape.

"How are the lights on?" Katie asked, realizing they'd also been on in the VIP suite.

"Solar," Roach answered. "We've got power, food, water and a secure location until time to move."

Happy she'd gotten that much information from him, Katie decided not to push her luck and ask any more questions. Instead she kept walking forward at a slow pace, casually looking around. Roach seemed content to let her lead the way, following half a dozen feet behind. Close enough to maintain control with his rifle but far enough away that she didn't have an opportunity to attack.

Working their way the length of the building they passed several more poker rooms. There was no sign anywhere in the building of a struggle. No overturned tables or chairs, no spilled drinks, no chips scattered on the red and blue carpeting. It looked like the casino had been neatly shut down and abandoned.

"In there," Roach finally said, gesturing at a set of wood paneled swinging doors that blended well with the décor.

"What's in there?" Katie asked, hesitating.

"Food. Aren't you hungry?"

Realizing she was, Katie pushed through the doors and entered a large, commercial kitchen. Roach followed her and pointed at a giant walk-in pantry.

"Plenty of food in there," he said. "Don't open the cold storage. The refrigerators must not be connected to the solar so they're out and full of rotting meat and vegetables. The stoves still work. They're propane and there's a whole row of tanks outside. Water's on. It's from a well and the solar is powering the pump. Make us something to eat. I'll be right here."

Roach settled down on a hard chair where he could keep an eye on the pantry and most of the kitchen. Walking into the room, Katie was momentarily taken aback at the amount of canned and boxed food stacked on the shelves. She was getting a good idea of why Roach had selected this building.

As long as there was sunshine they had power and water. If there really was a whole farm of propane tanks they'd be able to cook for a long time, and just this one room had enough food to last the two of them for months, if not a year. As she thought about what his plan might be, Katie slowly selected cans, taking the opportunity to check the room for anything she could use as a weapon. Finding nothing, she returned to the kitchen and set about preparing their meal.

Sometime later they sat across from each other, eating the food she had prepared. Roach hadn't said anything to her since he'd shown her the kitchen, but she felt the weight of his eyes constantly watching her. Watching to make sure she didn't do anything, but also watching *her*. He even watched her as he ate, rifle resting on the table with the muzzle pointed directly at her.

She'd hoped to be sitting close to him. Wanted an opportunity to get her hands on the weapon. She knew if she could get a grip on the rifle she could most likely take it away from him, but he was alert and cautious. An opportunity never presented itself. She wanted to talk to him. Ask questions. Find out if John was really alive and in the area, or if somehow the mad man had found out who her husband was and just made up the story.

But as much as she wanted answers to her questions Katie had been a very good case officer. She knew when to press, and when to let things take their natural course. There was no doubt that Roach was bat shit crazy, but that didn't mean he wasn't smart. She had to be smarter and pick her opportunities.

She also knew he wanted her. Badly. Wanted to see her, touch her. What she didn't understand was what was holding him back. If he decided to do anything to her, there was very little she could do to stop it as long as he was armed. Slowly chewing her food she considered playing to his desires. Flirting just a little. Maybe undoing a button on her shirt at the right moment. But she also knew that could backfire on her before she realized she had gone too far. There was no predicting the actions of a deranged man.

On the other hand, playing a little seduction might get her close enough to him to get her hands on his rifle. Twist it in his grip; strike his throat with her elbow and balls with her knee to slow him. Turn the rifle and put a few rounds in him. She'd have to move fast and decisively when the time came. Hesitation would give him an advantage.

It had been a long time since Katie had been through the training provided by the CIA, but she'd always been scrappy. She knew how to fight, and she knew that when the time to attack came she had to make the most of it. There wouldn't be a second opportunity if she failed. "Attack with certainty that you intend to kill," John had told her a couple of times when they'd worked out together. "Make sure you walk away from the encounter alive and everything else will work itself out."

She understood, and even though she'd never taken a life, Katie had no doubt she was capable. Somehow she'd made it from Arizona to Oklahoma without having to kill anyone. Well, at least that she knew of. She'd shot at a couple of people along the way but hadn't stuck around to see what the results were. Maybe she was already a killer.

"You don't want to try that," Roach said, startling her out of her thoughts.

Realizing she had been staring at his rifle while thinking, Katie mentally berated herself for making such a rookie mistake. She knew better. Had been taught better. She looked up at Roach's eyes and almost smiled, but shut that down. Not the right way to respond to him.

"Try what?" She asked.

"Whatever you were thinking about that involved my rifle." He said, pushing his empty plate to the side.

Katie glanced down at her half eaten meal, taking a bite to give herself time to think. She needed to distract Roach from the idea that she was thinking about his weapon.

"Actually, I was thinking about my husband." She said, looking him in the eye. "Were you lying to me, or is he really alive?"

"Oh, he's very much alive." Roach smiled. "Running around sticking his nose into business he's got no reason to get involved in. And you'll be glad to know he's replaced you."

"What do you mean, replaced me?" She asked.

"You should see her," Roach's smile spread across his entire face. "Her name's Rachel. Tall thing, like an Amazon. Younger than you with big, perfect tits and legs that go on to Sunday. They actually make a really good looking couple."

"A couple?" She asked, wondering where he was going with this.

"Oh yes. I first met them in Tennessee. He brought her with him from Atlanta. You're from Arizona, right? Did he spend a lot of time in Atlanta before the attacks? I'm just asking because they sure seemed familiar and comfortable with each other." Roach succeeded in putting just the right tone of concern into his voice.

Katie stared back at him, eyes damp. "Yes. Several times a month," she finally said.

"Well, I don't know what to tell you. Maybe I'm wrong, but they sure seem like they're together. Perhaps he thinks he made an upgrade, but I think he's foolish. You're much prettier than she is."

"He wouldn't," Katie said, tears now rolling down her face. "He couldn't."

"I'm not saying he did," Roach said, leaning across the table like he was concerned. "I'm just telling you what I've seen. Maybe there's a perfectly good reason they're still together after all this time, living in the same house on Tinker."

Katie looked back at him for a long time, the tears continuing to stream down her face. With a cry, she leapt to her feet and ran to the far side of the room and stood facing the wall, her whole body racked with sobs. Getting slowly to his feet, Roach walked across the room and stood behind her, watching her cry. Finally he stepped in and placed his hands on her shoulders to pull her into an embrace. To hold her perfect form next to his was the only thought on his mind.

The instant Katie felt Roach's hands on her shoulders she struck. Stepping back she threw a lightning fast elbow into his solar plexus, momentarily paralyzing his diaphragm. Spinning, she batted his arms aside and punched his larynx with bunched fingers, then twisted her hips as she raised her knee into his balls, grabbing the rifle as Roach started to fall to the floor.

The rifle was attached to a sling that was around his shoulders and she had to follow him down to the floor to maintain her grip on the weapon. He tried to struggle with her, but she'd perfectly attacked the three most vulnerable areas on a man and between being unable to breathe and a pair of balls that felt like they had been ruptured, Roach had no strength.

Katie dropped onto him with all her weight, one knee on his throat, the other landing squarely on his bruised solar plexus. What air remained in his lungs whistled out of his mouth.

"Fuck you, asshole!" she hissed in Roach's face as she quickly disengaged the sling from the rifle, leapt to her feet and took a step back. "You think I don't know my husband better than that?"

As her thumb found the rifle's safety she froze at the sound of a shotgun being racked. Looking around she saw half a dozen men watching her, a large, older woman standing only a dozen feet away with a 12 gauge shotgun pointed at her body.

"Why don't you go ahead and put that gun down, sweetie. There's no killing round here lessen I say so." The woman said.

33

Lillian Nosler smiled when her youngest boy told her about the massive casino that was only a couple of miles ahead. She had been on the road with her family for several days, driven out of their home in Arkansas' Ozark Mountains by herds of infected and suddenly aggressive animals. Razorbacks had killed two of her extended family, one niece and one nephew, late one afternoon. Then during the night female infected had begun arriving, first in small groups, but the volume quickly grew until they had to flee.

Mama, as Lillian was known, led close to sixty people out of the hills that night. In her late sixties she was the Matriarch of her immediate family of seven boys, and being the oldest of a dozen blood and in-law siblings she had taken on the roll as head of the family. Her husband had drunk himself to death twenty years ago leaving Mama to fend for herself and her family.

The Noslers had settled in Arkansas in the mid-1800s, claiming land deep in the Ozarks that wasn't good for much of anything. It was too remote, rugged and heavily forested for city folks.

In the late 1800s Noslers had started working in the mines in the area, extracting lead, and for several generations they lived and died in the mines. Then in the 1980s the economy changed and the mines closed down.

Needing a way to make money, Mama's late husband had expanded his still and began producing illegal moonshine, which they sold in several small towns in the area. Her oldest boy, who liked to spend his weekends in Little Rock, came home one Sunday with a new idea to make money.

They were too far back in the woods to worry about the cops stumbling across them, and soon they had a couple of small patches of marijuana under cultivation in the rich soil on the sunny side of a mountain. Once harvested, dried and taken to town, her boy returned with the biggest stack of cash any of them had ever seen. He'd sold every ounce he'd taken with him in less than twelve hours.

The family pitched in and began clearing and cultivating more patches while her husband chose to spend his time with his still, often drunk well before noon. The more successful the pot business became, the more he drank. Late one evening he passed out. This was nothing unusual and Mama and her boys left him in the shed with the still to sleep it off. The next morning they found his body. He had died from alcohol poisoning.

Pot business booming, the Noslers became suppliers for local gangs by the early 90s. They were making more money than they had ever imagined possible, and not knowing any better had started spending it. Cars, trucks, jewelry and every shiny bauble that caught their eye. For years they had stayed under the radar, driving decades old vehicles that were more rust than metal. Suddenly, every member of the family had a shiny new pick-up and someone in the Arkansas State Police that patrolled the area took notice.

Questions were asked and it didn't take long for the cops to discover that the Noslers were the source of the cheap marijuana that had flooded the streets of all the towns and cities in the region. A warrant was obtained and over fifty heavily armed police officers descended on the family's land. Legal or not, they didn't take kindly to an invading army of cops, many of them fighting back.

With a veritable armory of brand new weapons purchased with their drug money they managed to hold out for over a week. By this time the FBI, DEA and ATF were all involved, swelling the law enforcement response to well over 300 men.

When the dust cleared after their assault, 7 Noslers were dead and 15 injured. Everyone over the age of 18 was charged with a multitude of state and federal crimes, and with their drug profits seized by the government they were unable to afford lawyers. The public defenders that were assigned to them weren't interested in fighting a losing battle and soon nearly every adult in the family was in prison. The children were placed into the foster care system and the giant fields of marijuana were torched.

The family's land and homes were seized by the government and sat empty for ten years until some of the Noslers with lesser charges began to be released from prison and returned. They paid no attention to the signs warning that the property had been confiscated, moving right back into their homes.

Prison had been an education for the family. Survival was only possible through strength, and even though there were several family members incarcerated together at multiple facilities, there weren't enough of them. That left them with few options, and most chose to join one of the prison gangs for protection.

By the time the first of them started trickling back to the hills, many were committed to various gangs that were just as powerful on the outside as they were inside. The pot business was restarted, though on a much smaller scale that wouldn't draw attention, and with their new contacts they quickly branched out into running guns and prostitutes throughout their part of the state.

When Mama walked back onto her ancestral land, the family was again flush with illegal cash. Guns and drugs were profitable, but nothing compared with the money they could make off of girls, and the younger the better. They would use female family members to lure young homeless girls and runaways to one of several locations where they kept them as prisoners and forced them to work as prostitutes.

Then one of Mama's brothers, half drunk, suggested they start hosting fights amongst their customers. The winner would get his pick of the girls for free, and the family would control all the wagering on the fights, acting as the house.

Soon there were several fights every Friday and Saturday night. They sold gallons of watered down moonshine and pounds of their pot to the men who stood in line to watch the fights and fuck the girls. Cash from the wagers on the fights rolled in and their biggest problem was how to launder that much money without the cops noticing.

When they'd had to run from the infected, all but a handful of the girls had been left behind, locked in their rooms. Mama wasn't concerned. She knew they could find more as they traveled. Her only concern was finding a safe place for her and her family where they could restart their business. From what she'd seen of the world, cash was no longer something she cared about. But food, weapons and ammunition would be worth more than their weight in gold.

"Tell me 'bout it," she said to the boy who had given her the news about finding the casino.

"Big fucking place, Mama. Doors is locked and I couldn't get inside, but it looks abandoned. And it's a goddamn fortress. All brick and shit. No way's the infected gettin inside." He was excited and tripping over his words as he talked.

She had told him to lead the way, the heavily armed convoy of pickups falling in behind. They covered the two miles quickly, cresting a small rise in the terrain as they approached. In a shallow bowl in front of them sat the massive building, acres of striped blacktop parking lot surrounding it. Mama frowned when she saw the silhouette of a helicopter sitting on the roof, but didn't call a halt.

They pulled into the parking lot, driving around the building until they located a service entrance. The trucks were pulled into a circular defensive perimeter just like a wagon train in the old west. Fifty well armed men sat in the backs of the trucks, facing out; ready to fend off any infected that attacked.

One of her younger nephews had received an education from a professional burglar while he was in prison. He could pick any lock in under a minute and Mama told him to get to work while she walked over to the boy that had found the building, slapping him hard across the face.

"You forget to tell me 'bout that helicopter, boy?" She snarled in his face.

"I'm sorry, Mama. I didn't mean to," he flinched as she raised her hand, but decided not to slap him a second time. There were more than enough of them to deal with the handful of men that could fit on the aircraft.

The lock on the service door clicked and her nephew pulled on the handle. The door opened a few inches before a heavy, chrome chain stopped it. He peered inside a moment, then reached through the narrow opening and began working on the padlock holding the chain in place. It took less time than the deadbolt to open then he was carefully feeding the chain through the inside handle, trying not to make any more noise than necessary. Finally he pulled the door fully open.

"You six with me," Mama said, waving at a group that was four of her own children and two nephews. "Rest of you stay here and keep watch."

As soon as they stepped into the building they all smelled the aroma of food cooking. They slowly moved through the service area, cautiously pushing out onto the casino floor. Less than fifty feet to their left a wood paneled door stood open a few inches and Mama could faintly hear the sound of voices. Walking to the door she paused and looked through the gap.

A man and woman were sitting across from each other at a table, eating. The man was talking and the woman wasn't taking whatever he was telling her very well. After a couple of minutes she leapt up and ran to hide her face against a wall. The man got up and followed, and with their backs to the door Mama and her group pushed into the room, unnoticed.

The man walked up behind the sobbing woman and placed his hands on her shoulders. Mama was surprised when the woman instantly attacked, quickly putting him on the floor and taking his rifle. She was curious, and decided it was time to intervene before the woman finished him off. Stepping forward, she racked the slide of her shotgun.

34

We pressed on in the darkness, driving through an area of the city where the power was out. Infected were a constant presence, but not in significant numbers. Yet. I remembered from a briefing Colonel Crawford had given to Admiral Packard that there were going to be over 200,000 people in Oklahoma City that weren't expected to receive the vaccine in time to prevent them from turning.

That briefing had been a little over 24 hours ago, and at that point the window of time to the appearance of a quarter of a million new threats was seven days at the most. As I thought about this I wondered if Katie had been immunized. She'd apparently been on the base, and I'd heard that everyone on base had been, so that gave me a little comfort.

That also meant that Roach had been as well, but he presented enough danger to her without being infected that I didn't derive any peace from that thought. But what was at the casino? Why had he taken her there? For that matter, why had he taken her at all?

"Because he's fucking crazy. That's why." Startled, I looked in the rear view and met Rachel's eyes. I hadn't realized I had spoken out loud.

"How's Martinez?" I asked, wanting to change the subject.

The last thing I needed right now was for Rachel to decide we needed to discuss what finding Katie meant for us. I already knew the answer to that. I cared for Rachel very much, and if not for Katie could imagine being happy with her. But Katie wasn't just my wife, she was my best friend.

The only reason I'd even let myself go down the thought path of having a relationship with Rachel was I had convinced myself that I'd never see Katie again. I remembered the first time I'd laid eyes on her. She'd been a case officer for the CIA and while working in Central America had run afoul of a local rebel commander. Fortuitously, I'd been there with my team to take the commander out of the equation and we'd wound up rescuing and extracting Katie.

It had pretty much been love at first sight for me. From the moment I looked into her eyes... well, you get the idea. Anyway, I'd had some down time coming after that mission and so had she.

After a couple of days of intense CIA and Army Intelligence debriefing we were released for leave, and I'd convinced her that we should spend our time off together. Thinking back on it I hadn't had to work very hard to talk her into it.

Both of us had had our fill of hot, humid jungles, and since it was summer we headed for a beach, ending up on the central Oregon coast. We spent 10 days exploring the beaches, small towns, eating seafood, drinking, making love and generally decompressing. We'd tried a From Here To Eternity moment in the surf but damn the North Pacific is cold, even in July. Leaving Oregon we drove south through California then headed east, stopping in Vegas where we got married in a small, private chapel by a guy wearing a powder blue leisure suit.

That was more years ago than I wanted to think about, and I didn't regret a single moment. Sure, we had our ups and downs. Katie could be a moody bitch. I could be a rigid asshole. But we were good together. Mostly because she didn't put up with any of my shit.

"She's OK," Rachel said from the dark backseat. "Nothing life threatening, but she'll be hurting for a while."

I had forgotten I'd asked about Martinez, completely lost in my reminiscing about Katie. My hands were aching and I realized I was squeezing the steering wheel as hard as I could. Taking a deep breath I relaxed my grip and forced those thoughts out of my head. The emotions were distracting me from the task at hand and if that happened I could wind up getting all of us killed, then there wouldn't be anyone to rescue Katie.

Clearing my head, I checked the GPS. 91 miles to go. Maybe another 20 miles of Oklahoma City, then sparsely populated suburbs and open country as we drove north to the Indian Reservation where the casino was located. I'd feel a whole lot better once we got out of the city and away from the possibility of running into large numbers of infected, or desperate survivors.

Ahead I could see light as we approached an area of the city that still had power. There were a couple of vehicles moving, and I came to a stop. We might or might not draw unwanted attention from survivors if we drove through an area that still had a degree of normality to it, but there was still a dead infected female lying on the dash of the Suburban.

There was little doubt we'd draw a lot of attention with a corpse decorating our vehicle. The world felt like it was heading that way, but we still hadn't reached the level of the apocalypse depicted in the Road Warrior. Bodies draped over the hood just might be a little over the top.

"Why are you stopping?" Rachel asked. I took a moment to explain before stepping out and dragging the dead woman off the SUV and letting her tumble to the pavement.

Back behind the wheel I got us moving north again, passing a sign welcoming us to Midwest City just a few yards before we entered the area where the lights were on. The street was a large boulevard, lined with businesses and mid-level motels. A big, glass fronted restaurant on our right was full of people, the parking lot jammed with mostly pickups, but also a large contingent of police cars. It looked like they were having a meeting as we slowly passed.

A tall, fat man dressed in jeans, sports jacket and a cowboy hat was standing on what looked like the salad bar and everyone was gathered around listening to what he had to say. A dozen heavily armed men stood watch in the parking lot, all of them turning to look at us. For some reason I wasn't comfortable under their scrutiny and accelerated to open up some distance.

"Not liking the look of that," I commented as we lost sight of the building.

"Why?" Rachel asked.

"It's the middle of the night, and that didn't look like a PTA meeting. That's someone trying to whip the locals up into doing something." I said, keeping an eye on the rearview mirror.

"Maybe they're talking about setting up some defenses against the infected." Martinez offered.

"Maybe. Or maybe they're not too happy that there's not enough vaccine to go around." I said, tensing when I saw two sets of headlights bounce out of the parking lot and start following.

As soon as I saw the headlights, I reacted. Stepping on the gas I cranked the wheel to the right and turned onto a side street. Foot to the floor I raced for the next intersection, braking at the last moment and screaming through a turn back to the south. Not the way I wanted to go, but if we did have pursuers and they didn't know the way we went they'd start searching north, the direction we had been going.

The mirror was still empty and after a quarter mile I made a fast left and kept our speed up to open as much range between the meeting and us as I could. The power was still on in the area, the street well lit, and soon we began passing bodies lying on the pavement and the sidewalk.

"Infected?" Rachel asked.

"I sure as hell hope so," I said, concentrating on my driving. I hadn't seen or heard anything to make me think the Oklahoma City area had disintegrated far enough that people were killing each other in large numbers, but you never know what spark will ignite a wholesale slaughter.

Ahead the road curved to the north, and I was happy to see we'd be traveling in our intended direction once again. Slowing for the turn I jammed on the brakes when I spotted red and blue lights reflecting in a storefront window. Lots of lights, lots of police cars. Something was going on around the curve and not only wasn't it any of my business, I had no desire to make it my business.

Reversing, I got us turned around and headed back the direction we had come from, looking for another road that headed north. Finding one, I made the turn. This road was much smaller, only two narrow lanes in each direction. Large commercial buildings lined each side, built right up to the sidewalks. We were driving through a concrete canyon and my tension ratcheted up several notches.

This was a perfect place for an ambush. The road was barely wider than the length of the Suburban. Turning around wouldn't be a quick or easy process. We hadn't come to an intersection yet, but I had already decided I was going to turn as soon as I could.

I'd been driving with only the headlights on low, not needing the brilliant light from the LED bar because of the light provided by the street lights, but thought it might be a good idea to see what was waiting for us beyond the reach of the Chevy's lights. Turning on the high beams, then the light bar, I let off the gas when a couple of hundred yards ahead I saw three police cars blocking our path.

Their roof lights came on a moment after I lit them up. Shit!

"Hold on!" I shouted, cranking the wheel and attempting to send the ungainly SUV into a skid to get us turned around quickly.

It was a good idea, and in a car would have worked perfectly. But the physics of the lifted vehicle and its oversized off-road tires worked against me. The Suburban leaned precariously to the right as it started into a turn, our speed not great enough to fully overcome the traction afforded by the large footprint of the tires. I instantly recognized my error and stamped on the throttle, trying to break the rear tires free and let them slide around.

I only made things worse. The rear didn't slide, just powered us into the turn. The sidewalk was directly ahead, a four-story cement wall right behind it, and we were about to crash into it head on. There wasn't anything I could do other than ride out the maneuver I'd started and keep the wheel hard to the left.

It seemed to take forever but the front tires finally struck the curb, the nose of the SUV dipping momentarily like it was gathering itself to launch into the air. That change in the attitude of the suspension shifted weight to the front of the vehicle and finally the rear tires came free. As the front bounced up and over the curb onto the sidewalk, the back end whipped around, but farther and faster than I intended.

The passenger side of the Suburban slammed into the building, shattering all the windows on the right side of the vehicle. My foot had come off the gas when we hit the curb and now facing the right direction I floored it. We started moving, bounced back into the street, and I found myself facing three police cars speeding towards us with lights flashing.

35

I accelerated directly at the oncoming cops. We were boxed in, but I wasn't about to give up. The Suburban was big and heavy and could dish out a lot of punishment against the lighter sedans the police were driving. The engine roared as we picked up speed and I steered for the narrow gap between two of the cruisers.

At first it didn't seem as if they were going to blink in our impromptu game of chicken, but at the last moment they did, both vehicles swerving away from the looming grill of the big SUV. Both drivers had waited until the last moment to turn, and didn't create an opening large enough for me to drive through cleanly. With a rending crunch of sheet metal and a hard jolt I blasted between them, seeing one of them go into an uncontrolled spin in my mirror.

Four more police cars were parked at the intersection ahead, creating a roadblock. The cops were crouched behind their vehicles with weapons resting on hoods and trunks, aimed in our direction. Behind them were a couple of unmarked

SUVs that I was sure were official vehicles of some sort.

Staying on the throttle I worked my rifle up with my left hand, struggling to get the muzzle through the window and aimed at the roadblock. I had absolutely no intention of stopping and dealing with the locals. My patience had expired and all I gave a shit about was getting to Katie. I was through with people getting in my way.

A moment before I got the rifle stabilized and ready to fire I saw a muzzle flash from the cordon of police. Almost instantly the wheel wrenched hard to the side. They had shot out the right front tire. OK, if they wanted to play that way.

Flooring the throttle I fought the wheel with my right hand and began firing the rifle with my left. I didn't have a hope in hell of sending accurate fire downrange, but that wasn't my intent. I just wanted to keep their heads down, which was exactly what I accomplished as my rounds punched into the sides of the police vehicles.

Fighting the vibrating wheel I steered for an opening between two of the parked cars, a few heartbeats later slamming into the sides of each and blasting them out of my way. Unfortunately the already damaged Suburban, riding on a flat tire that was shredding itself to pieces, didn't survive the impact. The wheel was spun out of my grip a moment before the airbags deployed, then we ground to a halt with the back half of the vehicle wedged tightly between the two cruisers.

I popped the door open and leapt down, Dog on my heels, changed magazines and started sending covering fire in the direction of the cluster of cops. Still firing, I held the rifle with one hand and reached out for the rear door handle, jerking it open so Rachel and Martinez could get out. They were quickly at my side; all of us ducking as the police finally got organized and began returning fire.

"What the fuck do they want?" Martinez shouted when she paused to change magazines.

"Don't care," I shouted back. "They're in my way."

I fired another burst at our attackers then spared a glance at the closest SUV. It was a Ford Explorer; painted black with tinted windows and plain, steel wheels. Definitely police issue and I wanted it to replace the now defunct Suburban.

"I'm going for the Explorer," I shouted to Rachel and Martinez, pointing the vehicle out to them. "I'll swing around behind and pick you up. Keep giving me covering fire!"

I didn't wait for them to acknowledge my instructions, just fired off several more bursts as I dashed across fifty feet of open asphalt. At the Explorer I came to a stop by slamming my back against the rear door on the driver's side, startled when I realized Dog had come with me. Fortunately neither of us had any new holes in our bodies so I yanked the front door open and told him to get in.

It was running with the keys hanging in the ignition, facing away from the firefight. Throwing the transmission into gear I stomped on the gas and spun the wheel to pick up Rachel and Martinez. When I completed the turn I cursed and jammed on the brakes. Three men stood behind them, two of them pointing shotguns. The third held a large revolver that he pointed in my direction when I screeched to a stop a few feet away.

Anger washed over me like a breaking wave. Enough is enough. From a pocket on my vest I pulled out a fragmentation grenade, gripped it in my left hand and pulled the pin. If I let go of the spoon, which would trigger the fuse, someone would have a bad night. Kicking the door open I stepped out and drew my pistol, targeting the head of the man with the revolver as I walked around the nose of the Explorer. Dog stayed right with me, welded to my leg.

"Back the fuck off!" I said to him. "Look at my left hand. The pin is out. We can all die here tonight, or you can back the fuck off and we're on our way."

By the time I finished speaking I was standing within fifteen feet of the three men. The man with the revolver, presumably the man in charge, looked at me with wide eyes. The two with the shotguns exchanged nervous glances.

"I'm not fucking around," I said. "We didn't do a damn thing to you or anyone else. You jumped us. We've got more important things to do than play hide the salami with you idiots. For the last time, lower your goddamn weapons and back away."

"You're from the base," revolver man said. "We need the vaccine or we're going to turn into one of the infected. Give us the vaccine. That's all we want."

"Do I look like someone who's carrying vaccine around with him?" I snorted. "Now I'm getting seriously pissed off. Back off. Now!"

My pistol was steady on his head, my focus on him, but I made sure I had my body shielded from the other cops by the Explorer. I was starting to get worried about a sharp shooter. No one could sneak up on me with Dog standing there, but a scoped rifle from a hundred yards away could cause a problem. The man didn't look like he was going to give, and I was out of time.

Without any wind up or warning I flicked the grenade overhanded through the air. As soon as it left my hand a spring pushed the spoon off to go clattering across the pavement and the clock started. My throw was good, the grenade arcing high and sailing over the men's heads.

Everyone's attention was on the green, baseball sized object, every pair of eyes except mine tracking its path. At the apex of the throw I pulled the trigger and shot revolver man in the head, his body instantly crumpling to the ground at the same time the grenade landed on the pavement a couple of feet farther on.

"Down!" I shouted to Martinez and Rachel as I started firing at the two men wielding the shotguns.

My first shot blew out the throat of one of them, taking him out of the fight. The second was more interested in escaping, scrambling across the asphalt to get as far away from the grenade as he could before it detonated. Four bullets hit him in rapid succession, the first three to his body, the fourth taking off the back of his head.

I had just finished saying "four Mississippi" in my head when he went down and I dropped to the ground and pulled Dog with me as flat as I could. A fraction of a second before we hit the pavement the grenade detonated, deafening me. I didn't feel any fragments of the casing strike me and Dog was back on his feet almost before the concussion from the blast had passed over us, so I knew he was probably OK.

Sparing a glance at Rachel and Martinez I wasn't overly concerned when neither were moving. Both were flat on their stomachs, hugging the pavement. Whipping my body up into a one knee shooting stance I raised my rifle and started looking for targets.

The cops were just poking their heads up, a couple of them lifting weapons to re-start the fire fight. I sent a few rounds into the cars they were sheltering behind, causing them to duck for safety, then pulled another grenade out of my vest. Pin out, I let the spoon fly, counted to two and side armed it along the ground in their direction.

It skittered across the asphalt, slowing as it disappeared under one of the cruisers. A second later it went off, shaking the vehicle on its suspension before rupturing and touching off the fuel tank. The explosion and resulting fireball was intense, the heat from the flames threatening to blister my exposed skin.

"Let's move!" I shouted at the girls and leapt to my feet.

Sending more covering fire in the direction of the cops, I dashed to the Explorer and jumped behind the wheel after dog scrambled into the front passenger seat. A moment later the back door was flung open and Rachel threw herself into the vehicle, Martinez right behind her. I floored the throttle before she was all the way inside, screeching away from the roadblock. No bullets chased us, or if they did they didn't find their target before we were out of range.

"Everyone OK?" I asked as I drove.

"Good," Martinez said, Rachel answering the same a moment later.

I lowered our speed a little and reached over to pet Dog. More than affection, I wanted to check him for wounds. After running my hand across his head, body and legs I checked it in the dim lights of the dashboard for blood. Other than grimy from combat, my hand was clean.

Letting out a slow breath, I controlled the shakes that were hitting me as adrenaline bled out of my system. We were incredibly lucky to have survived the battle without any injuries. We most likely wouldn't have survived contact with well trained military troops, but street cops in mid-sized cities aren't prepared to deal with what I'd unleashed on them.

"If I haven't said it, sir, remind me not to piss you off." Martinez said from the dark back seat.

I could hear the smirk in her voice. Several smart comments sprang to mind, but I wasn't in the mood for witty banter and stayed quiet as I drove, eyes constantly scanning ahead of us for threats. After a few minutes Rachel broke the heavy silence in the vehicle.

"You OK?" She asked.

"Fine," I answered. "I just don't feel as bad about killing those cops as I should. They were simply scared of the infection."

"Think there will be more?" Rachel asked after a couple of minutes of thought.

"Maybe. Probably. Maybe not cops, but more scared people. There's nothing I can do about it. I don't have any vaccine and I can't help them. They just need to stay the fuck out of my way so I can get to Katie." I said.

Either the tone in my voice or Rachel realizing we were only miles from finding my wife killed any further conversation. That was fine with me. I wasn't in the mood to talk. I had one thing on my mind. Rescuing Katie, and that was all I was able to concentrate on at the moment.

I get like that. So focused on the task at hand that all else is ignored. That's one thing that made me so good at being a soldier. It also drove Katie to distraction. She was the queen of multi-tasking and had a hard time dealing with my single-mindedness when I had to accomplish something.

We drove in silence for some time as I kept pushing us north. Frequently I had to sidetrack to avoid abandoned vehicles blocking the road. Occasionally we saw other survivors moving around, some driving and some on foot. All too often we came across groups of infected. All of the infected were headed south towards Tinker.

Now that I knew the infected were being controlled, or more accurately they were being "directed", the previously mysterious herding behavior wasn't quite as frightening. Well, as long as I knew the location they were being called to and could be somewhere else when they arrived. I wondered what was being done to identify the Russian satellite or satellites that were broadcasting the signal that attracted the infected. Hopefully something, because the defenses at Tinker weren't great and there were a lot of people that would die if a large herd showed up.

"Fifty four miles to go," Martinez suddenly spoke from the back seat.

I had been so absorbed in my driving and musings that I'd almost forgotten they were back there. I looked into the rearview mirror, getting a good view of both of them as we were driving through an area that still had power and was well lit by modern streetlights. I nodded my thanks to Martinez and cut my eyes to Rachel.

She was looking back at me and I could tell she had been crying. Her eyes were red rimmed and watery, the end of her nose shiny from being rubbed. At that moment my heart went out to her. I wanted to pull over, open the back door and fold her into my arms. But I didn't. That wouldn't help anyone. It would send her the wrong message and would waste time that I didn't have to get to Katie before something truly bad happened to her.

36

Master Gunnery Sergeant Matt Zemeck stood at the back of the Osprey as it descended for a landing at Tinker Air Force Base. Colonel Pointere stood at his side, both men with rifles in their hands, ready to charge down the ramp the moment the aircraft was on the ground. They had successfully defended the precious oil refinery, wiping out the majority of the herd of infected with repeated fuel-air bomb attacks. The few thousand surviving infected had been handled by the Osprey's as well as ground troops.

While Zemeck had overseen the battle, Pointere had been closeted in conversations with Admiral Packard and Colonel Crawford. Always a hard case, his resolve to stand against President Clark had been cemented when he learned about the shoot down of the planeload of SEALs in Alaska. He quickly assured the other two officers that he and his Marines would stand with them.

During their conversation the Admiral excused himself, finally coming back on the line after several minutes. When he rejoined them it was with news that General Carrey at Fort

Wainwright had called him to say that he too was in support of the Admiral's opposition to the President. The President was currently being detained by the same MPs who had been assigned to protect her and was in a secure area without any outside communication.

Both the General and Admiral Packard had called General Triplett at Tinker but he refused to come around to their side, remaining steadfast in his support of the President. As a result the three officers had discussed how best to deal with him. All were in agreement that Tinker Air Force Base was a vitally strategic asset for the severely diminished American military, but they were also hesitant to initiate open hostilities.

It was finally agreed that once the Marines finished mopping up the herd that had threatened the refinery, Colonel Pointere would leave a skeleton crew behind to provide security and return to Tinker to augment Colonel Crawford's Rangers. At that point they would detain General Triplett and take control of the base.

There was concern that the Air Force personnel on the base would view their actions as unlawful, which in the strictest technical sense they were, and resist. The Air Force outnumbered the

Marines and Rangers nearly three to one, and it was a very real concern.

All three men agreed that there was a high degree of risk that it would be necessary to fire on their fellow American servicemen and women. None of them were happy about it, but they also recognized the danger presented by allowing the base to remain under the control of General Triplett. If the military was fragmented it would severely hamper their ability to mount a defense against the infected or the Russians, and there were thousands of civilian refugees on the base that needed protection.

Pointere had briefed Zemeck on the conversation and hadn't been surprised when he immediately agreed with the Colonel's decision and pledged his support. Now they were moments away from touching down, 30 Marines stacked up behind them and ready to go. All of them had their war faces on, not happy about what they were about to do but determined to do it regardless.

There was a slight bump as the Osprey's landing gear touched the tarmac, the rear ramp already on its way down. Pointere and Zemeck stepped forward, climbing the ramp before it reached the horizontal plane, then moving quickly forward into the open air as it descended to fully open. As they moved out the Marines behind them charged forward and spread out in a protective bubble.

Pointere relaxed when he saw the Army Humvees waiting to greet him. Colonel Crawford stood surrounded by a dozen Rangers. Glancing around he saw that Rangers had taken control of the flight line, restraining the Air Force personnel with flexi-cuffs. Slinging their rifles, Pointere and Zemeck walked forward to meet Crawford.

"Any problems?" Pointere asked, sticking his hand out to shake Crawford's.

"None," Crawford replied. "No shots fired. No resistance of any kind."

Both men paused and looked up as four more Osprey's roared in for a landing and quickly disgorged their Marines who melded into the perimeter the Rangers had formed around the area. They turned as Captain Blanchard stepped out of the closest Humvee and walked over.

"Sirs," he said. "We've got eyes on the General's quarters. He and his wife are inside, presumably asleep. Twenty Security Forces are guarding him. They have one Hummer with a machine gun, the rest armed with rifles and side arms."

"Is that normal, or does he know we're coming?" Pointere asked.

"Don't know, sir. We didn't start watching until yesterday." Blanchard answered.

They talked for a few more minutes, reviewing their plans before loading into waiting Hummers and trucks. The drive across the base was short, the heavily armed convoy being eyed by a few people that were out and moving, but no one approached them or tried to interfere. Half a mile from the General's quarters they came to a halt in a large field, the Rangers and Marines dismounting quickly but quietly in the dark.

A handpicked platoon of Rangers formed up and waited at attention for Colonel Crawford. He approached them and starting at the back walked up and down the ranks, looking each man in the eye and shaking his hand. When he reached the front he stood facing the formation.

"Do everything you can to avoid casualties," Crawford said to the determined looking young men. "But we do what we have to do to take the General into custody."

"Yes, sir!" They chorused quietly in unison.

"Master Gunny, I believe we have a mutual acquaintance," Crawford turned to Zemeck as he adjusted his vest.

"That would be Major Chase, sir?" Zemeck replied.

"That's the pain in my ass I'm referring to," Crawford said with a grin. "He's gone rogue. Violated a direct order. He knows where his wife is and he's gone to get her back."

Zemeck's eyebrows shot up in surprise at the news that Katie was alive. "He does tend to be a little impulsive, sir."

"Impulsive." Crawford spoke the word like he was tasting it. Finding it to his liking he smiled and nodded.

"I suppose you'd like me to go find him and bring him back," Zemeck said, a small grin on his face.

"With Colonel Pointere's approval, I would appreciate that very much Gunny. Of course, you'd have to bring back anyone else that was with him, and perhaps even ensure that any civilians being held against their will were retrieved and returned to safety." Crawford said.

"Aye aye, sir. That goes without saying." Zemeck said, then turned to look at Pointere who simply grunted his approval. Crawford waved Captain Blanchard over then sent him off with Zemeck to provide details on where the Pave Hawk carrying Roach and Katie had landed.

The Rangers were ready to go. Colonel Crawford nodded to their platoon leader and after a few quiet commands from their sergeant they were on the move. They were all veterans of multiple tours in Iraq and Afghanistan. Experienced and hardened. Within moments Crawford had silently led them into the dark, heading towards the large house the Air Force provided for the base's commanding officer.

37

We were out of the metropolitan Oklahoma City area, pushing through dark and empty countryside. There was the occasional house set far back from the narrow highway that showed signs of life in the form of dimly lit windows, but we didn't see any people, infected or not. It was quiet in the Explorer as I drove.

Dog was curled up on the front passenger seat, snoring loudly, his paws twitching every now and then as he dreamed about whatever a dog dreams about. Rachel and Martinez were uncharacteristically quiet in the back seat. Every time I checked on them in the mirror Rachel was staring out her window at the bleak landscape and Martinez had her head leaned back and eyes closed. She had to be hurting from her wounds and I was glad to see she was resting and gathering her strength.

A glow on the horizon ahead warned me that something large was burning and as we began to climb a low hill I shut off the headlights and lowered our speed. Charging into an unknown situation is rarely a good idea. At the crest of the hill I brought us to a stop.

Half a mile ahead, what looked like a large farmhouse was completely engulfed in flames. Well over a dozen figures were visible moving around the perimeter of the fire, but I was too far away to tell if they were infected or not. The house was no more than thirty yards from the edge of the pavement and we didn't have a choice other than to drive right past it.

"Everyone awake and ready?" I asked without taking my eyes off the conflagration.

Dog raised his head then stood up on the seat and sneezed explosively, covering half of the inside of the windshield with snot. From the back I heard Martinez start giggling, and when I glanced in the mirror I could see a smile on Rachel's face. Glad they were alert, I slowly accelerated over the crest and towards the burning house.

As we drew closer I could see more figures running around the fire, but still couldn't tell if they were infected or just the homeowners in a panic. That is until I saw one of them stumble out of the flames and charge across open ground towards a large piece of farm equipment. The running figure was on fire, trailing flames as it ran. It had to be an infected female.

Drawing abreast of what I thought was a harvester; the fire provided enough light for me to clearly see inside the glass-enclosed cab. A woman and two young children were huddled inside, looks of terror plain on their faces as they watched the group of infected swarm around their refuge.

Neither the survivors nor the infected had noticed me as I was driving with the lights off and the noise of the flames consuming the wooden house masked the sound of the Explorer's tires on the asphalt. I wanted to keep going, to get to Katie as quickly as I could, but without conscious thought my right foot stepped on the brake pedal and brought us to a stop.

With a sigh of frustration I jammed the transmission into park and after a quick check of my rifle stepped out into the night. Dog climbed onto the driver's seat then jumped down to stand next to me as Rachel and Martinez got out of the back. The heat from the fire was nearly intolerable even though we were well away from the pyre, and I was once again amazed at the ability of the infected to ignore the pain of mortal wounds.

There were nearly twenty infected in the area, mostly females, and many of them were so close to the heat that their hair and much of their clothing had been burned away. Even over the smell of the house and its contents being burned I could detect the stench of cooked human flesh. At first it reminds you of bacon frying, but there's a sickly sweet undertone to the odor that is impossible to describe. Certainly one of the smells, just like a rotting corpse, that once you experience you will never forget.

We all lined up on the backside of the SUV, using its body for shooting rests and began targeting the infected. Our rifles were suppressed, and unlike an uninfected human they didn't notice or care that one of their number had fallen. This was to our advantage as we kept firing until the last infected fell dead.

Out of targets I re-scanned the area but didn't find any more. The infected had never detected us, but the woman in the harvester had. When the last female went down she popped the cab door open and nimbly scrambled to the ground, turning back to lift her children down.

I whistled Dog into the vehicle, safed my rifle and started to climb in after him.

"Aren't we going to help her?" Rachel asked.

"How?" I asked in return. "What more can we do that we haven't already done? She's probably safer out here than where we're going. We don't have any vaccine to give her or the kids. There's nothing more we can do."

I didn't like just driving off and leaving them there, but I also had to be practical. We couldn't save everyone. Rachel stepped around Martinez and put her hand on my arm as she looked at me.

"I understand you just want to get Katie, but what if someone had the chance to help her, but just left her on the side of the road? They've lost everything. It doesn't look like they even have a gun to defend themselves. Think about what you're doing." She held my eyes with hers until I finally sighed.

"Go see if they want to come with us. And if they do, keep a close eye on them. All we need is for them to turn while they're in the vehicle with us." Rachel smiled, leaned forward and kissed me then turned to go talk to the woman.

Five minutes later we were back on the road. Our passengers were crammed into the small cargo area behind the back seat, the children quickly consuming nearly half of our water. The woman wasn't their mother, but a survivor that had sought refuge in the family's home. The parents had been killed defending the house against the small band of infected. The power was out and in the panic one of the children had knocked a candle into a large set of curtains that had burst into flames that quickly spread throughout the house.

The woman's name was Stephanie and turned out to be younger than I'd originally thought at only 20. Technically an adult, but still a child to me. When she found out where we were going her mood brightened as she explained that her sister had worked as a cocktail waitress at the casino for the past five years. She knew exactly where it was and claimed to know the interior layout very well.

I know, I know. Karma. If I'd left her behind I'd never have gotten the valuable intelligence she was providing. I glanced at Rachel in the mirror and she had a smirk on her face that I couldn't get irritated about.

Stephanie talked for the next several minutes, describing in good detail the different areas of the casino. She also had a thorough knowledge of the service areas as she'd frequently filled in for her sister when the older girl had to stay home with a sick child. I didn't bother to ask how a 20 year old was able to serve alcohol.

Rachel had found an aluminum clipboard with some papers on it in the back and at my prompting Stephanie drew a rough sketch of the layout of the building. She kept describing everything as "huge" or "giant" and since I'd seen a satellite image of the building I didn't doubt her. By the time she finished drawing, I had run out of questions and we were within a mile of our destination.

Another hundred yards and the road crested slightly. Below us in a shallow depression sat the massive casino with acres of parking surrounding it. I had cut the lights before we reached the top of the rise and now came to a full stop and killed the engine after putting the transmission in park. Stepping out I moved to the edge of the pavement and raised my rifle to scan the surrounding terrain with the night vision scope as Dog sniffed up a bush before relieving himself.

Moments later Rachel, Martinez and Stephanie joined me, Rachel also raising her rifle to scan our surroundings. As we did this Martinez focused on the building ahead.

"It's beyond the range of the night vision," she said. "But, I'm pretty sure I can see a Pave Hawk sitting on the roof."

"Where?" I asked, focusing on the casino.

"Far right." She answered without lowering her rifle.

I looked where she indicated and was able to just make out the outline of the building. After looking at the area for a couple of moments I agreed with her that the change in silhouette of the roof looked very much like a helicopter. My heart started pounding when I realized I was only a mile away from Katie.

I wanted to jump behind the wheel of the Explorer and race down there, blast my way inside and find her. I hoped that Roach would be in my way so I could rip his heart out without having to go looking for him. Involuntarily I smiled at the thought then started when someone touched me.

Rachel stood close to me, resting her hand on my right shoulder. I lowered the rifle and she slid her hand down my arm to take my hand in hers. With a gentle tug she lead me to the far side of the vehicle where we could have a degree of privacy.

"You shouldn't tell her anything about us," she said in a soft voice. I could hear a note of sadness in her tone.

"I'll tell her everything," I said, holding her hand in mine. "Always have. Not going to start keeping things from her now. Besides, I wouldn't be standing here if it wasn't for you."

We looked at each other for a long moment before she stepped forward and I folded her into my arms. It wasn't a lovers' embrace, just a hug between two people who've been through hell together and care very deeply about each other. As I stood there holding Rachel I finally realized that I had fallen in love with her. Not to the degree that I loved Katie, but far closer to it than I'd ever thought possible. We stood there for a few moments, enjoying holding each other, and might have stood there longer if I hadn't heard the thrum of approaching rotors.

Stepping away from Rachel I turned and looked to the south, the direction the noise was coming from. I noted Martinez had raised her rifle and was looking in the same direction.

"Osprey," she said after almost a minute of watching through the night vision scope. Osprey meant Marines or Air Force, and since the only ones I'd seen at Tinker were the ones the MEU had brought with them I had a good idea who was coming to the party.

It didn't take long for the aircraft to touchdown on the highway, a couple of hundred yards from where we all stood watching it land. I was glad there was a natural visual and sound break in the terrain to shield it from the casino. I didn't want Roach to know I was here until I wrapped my hands around his throat.

Telling Rachel and Martinez to stay put and keep watch I walked forward with Dog at my side and met Zemeck halfway to the Osprey. Two Marines followed him as he walked up and gave me another one of his spine cracking hugs.

"Jesus Christ, Marine. If you're lonely I'm sure there's some sheep around somewhere." I said with a smile.

"That's alright. Not interested in your sloppy seconds." He fired back.

"Crawford send you?" I asked.

"Yep. Supposed to get you and effect the rescue of any civilians that may be in distress or being held against their will." He said with a twinkle in his eye.

God bless Colonel Crawford. Even after all the headaches I'd caused him, including disobeying orders and taking off on my own to rescue Katie, he was sending me some help. The fact that he'd sent my friend instead of a squad of Rangers wasn't lost on me. Some day I'd have to do something nice for the man.

38

US Navy Commander James McFadden stared at the high definition monitor displaying Admiral Packard's image. McFadden was the Commanding Officer of the USS Alaska, an Ohio class nuclear powered submarine. At the moment he was unhappy to be sitting at periscope depth, just below the surface of the Pacific Ocean to facilitate the video link with the Admiral. In the depths of the ocean the Alaska was virtually silent, nearly impossible to detect. She was one of the most devastating war machines ever conceived and built by man. Sitting near the surface, gently rolling in the low Pacific swells, Alaska was a sitting duck.

"The helo that's inbound to your current location has the personnel and equipment onboard that's needed to make this happen." The Admiral said.

"I'm not clear on why we're not going after targets in Russia, sir." McFadden replied.

"I'm not entirely clear myself," Packard said. "But the experts say they can bypass most of the fail safes and allow an orbital detonation, but can't make the device function as a strike weapon.

I don't understand what they're doing, or how they're doing it, but I trust they know what they're talking about.

"You will provide them with any and all assistance they may require. You are to launch as soon as capable. Any further questions?" The Admiral raised his eyebrows but his tone made it clear he didn't expect another.

"No, sir. Good to go." McFadden replied.

"Thank you, Jim." Packard said a moment before breaking the connection.

Closing down his end of the communication, McFadden shook his head, stood up and exited into the cramped passage outside his cabin. He pulled up short in surprise when he nearly ran into an overweight man wearing civilian clothing. Looking around he saw another man in civvies, two Master Chiefs he didn't recognize and the boat's Executive Officer (XO), Lieutenant Commander Danny White.

"Admiral Packard's personnel have arrived, skipper." The XO called out over the heads of the men.

"I can see that, XO," he answered with more sarcasm than he intended. "Get us back below the layer. I'll take them from here."

McFadden was referring to the point in the ocean where there is a significant difference in temperature between the surface that is warmed by the sun and the deep, cold water that remains almost a constant temperature year round. Sound waves have a very difficult time penetrating the layer where the two different water temperatures meet. A submarine is safe when it is deep and quiet, and getting the Alaska back into the dark, cold water would protect it from detection by any surface vessels or aircraft.

"Aye aye, skipper." White said, making a quick about face and disappearing down the passage.

"Gentlemen, follow me." McFadden said to the new arrivals, not taking the time for introductions.

Ten minutes later he had left the specialists in the capable hands of the boat's Weapons Officer, or Weps, Lieutenant Michael Sherman. As he walked into the control room a Senior Petty

Officer announced his presence and he quickly asked for reports on their status.

"We're just passing through the layer, skipper. Heading is 040 and we'll level out at 600 feet with a thousand fathoms under our keel. Sonar is clear." The XO informed him then came over to stand next to McFadden.

"What's up, sir?" White asked.

"You know those sat images we were watching of the huge herds moving across the country?" He waited until the XO nodded. "Turns out the Russians are causing it. They're using high-energy pulses from satellites to create a harmonic tone on the surface that draw the infected in."

"What's that got to do with us?" White asked, his forehead wrinkling in confusion.

"We're going to take out the satellites. The experts that the Admiral sent us claim they can remove enough of the safeties on our Tridents to enable the warheads for detonation in low orbit. When they're ready, we're going to launch eight birds.

"The experts on board the Washington believe that the Russians must be using geostationary satellites that are over CONUS (Continental United States) and that if we spread the missiles across the country and detonate them as the Tridents reach apogee, the EM pulse will take out all the Russian satellites." McFadden answered.

"Uh, sir, that's also going to take out all of our orbiting birds as well as most likely fry the electronics in anything on the ground." White sounded shocked that this was the best plan available.

"And in the air, but apparently that's the trade off we're willing to make. Oklahoma City has the largest concentration of survivors and right now there are three separate herds that have been spotted that the Russians are drawing in to the area. Total numbers of infected bearing down on Tinker are estimated at greater than forty million, and growing. This is the only idea anyone has come up with to stop them."

The XO's mouth fell open in shock at the news. "Why can't we just use a ballistic missile and take out the satellites that are transmitting the signal?"

"We don't know which one, or ones, to target." McFadden answered. "But we're not done with the first eight Tridents. Ten more are going to Russia. We can't strike them, but we're going to fry every piece of electronics they have. After that, we're all back to the stone age and when the bullets run out we can start throwing rocks and sticks at each other again."

White stood there with his mouth open, staring at his Captain. He hadn't lost anyone in the attacks as he was an only child whose parents had already passed away. Single, his life had been the Navy for the past 15 years. For him, the reality of the world coming to an end was finally hitting home.

He'd counseled numerous crewmembers that had lost, or suspected they had lost, their entire families. But the enormity of the deathblow the Russians had dealt to the world hadn't really sunk in until he contemplated life without any piece of technology more advanced than what was around 100 years ago.

McFadden and White turned when Lieutenant Sherman walked into the control room.

"How are our guests doing, Weps?" McFadden asked.

"They seem to know what they're doing, skipper." He answered. "Missiles one and two are done. I watched what they're doing and it's really clever. Never would have thought of it, but one of those civilians is a damn genius."

"Which one?" The XO asked.

"The fat one, sir. Sorry, can't remember his name. He's a lead engineer from Lawrence Livermore Labs. He was on vacation in Hawaii when the attacks happened. He knows this gear better than he knows his wife's ass."

McFadden couldn't help but snort a quick laugh at the image Sherman's comment put in his head.

"He can't enable them for use against terrestrial targets?" White asked.

"No sir. He's exploiting a hole in the security to enable the warhead, but as you know all of our birds are MIRVs. There's no way to get into the systems that control the separation, targeting and detonation of the individual warheads. They'd just thud down and dig a hole without going boom."

MIRV stands for Multiple Independent Reentry Vehicle. Each Trident missile actually carried three nuclear warheads that would separate after the missile reached apogee above the Earth and began reentering the atmosphere. Each of the warheads can be programmed for a different specific target, or all to the same target, but the deeper level of security that controlled the MIRV function couldn't be compromised.

"Thanks, Weps. Let me know as soon as we've got all 18 ready to fly. We'll come up to launch depth, shoot and scoot. I don't doubt for a second the Russians are watching for something just like this and have a present ready to send our way as soon as they see a launch." McFadden said.

39

"There's how many?" I asked, surprised at what Zemeck was showing me.

We were in the back of the Osprey, bent over a small tablet computer that was displaying a two hour old satellite thermal scan of the casino, courtesy of Captain Blanchard. The resolution was quite good and there were multiple white dots within the faint outline of the large building. Each blob represented the heat signature of a human body.

"Sixty seven," Zemeck repeated.

"Infected?" I asked, moving the tablet closer to my face for a better look.

"Don't think so," he replied. "Put the loop in motion. You can see them moving calmly around."

Zemeck stabbed a small, right facing arrow at the bottom of the image with an index finger the size of a sausage. As the time bar next to the arrow began progressing I could see many of the figures moving about, but they moved in a coordinated and apparently intentional manner, unlike the randomness of the infected. Several could also be seen walking what was clearly a security patrol pattern.

"Shit," I said as the loop ended and the motion on the screen reset to the beginning and froze.

"Yep. Does this psycho have a bunch of friends? That why he came here?" Zemeck asked.

"Don't know. Maybe, or maybe it's just another group of survivors that he's hooked up with. Did you notice this?" I asked, pointing to a large concentration of blobs at the edge of the superimposed outline of the building. Rachel and Martinez squeezed forward to see over my shoulders.

"Prisoners is my guess," Zemeck said. "Too many bodies too close together to be much of anything else."

I grunted my agreement and kept looking at the tablet. Putting the loop in motion again I watched the blobs that were working security. Watched how they moved and where they went and how fast they were moving. Pulling out the rough floor plan that Stephanie had drawn for me I compared it to the image on the tablet screen.

"Best way in is from the roof," I said pointing to a spot on the paper. "It's the far end from the main concentration of people and there's only one guard that's going through that area of the casino. Well, there was only one when this was recorded, but if they haven't had any problems they most likely won't have changed anything."

"Agreed. How do you want to do this?" Zemeck asked.

I rocked back on my heels and thought about the question. Between Stephanie's sketch and the thermal scan Zemeck had brought with him I had some really valuable intel, but nothing that told me who these people were. Were they innocent survivors? In normal times the presence of what appeared to be a group of prisoners would have concerned me, but now? They could be holding Roach and other bad guys. There were a ton of possibilities and there was only one way to find out.

"I'm going in alone to recon," I said. "If this is just a group of innocents trying to survive, then I'll introduce myself, collect my wife and be on my way."

Days Of Perdition

"You realize the odds of that are pretty damn slim?" Martinez spoke up.

"I do," I replied, eyes still glued to the tablet. "And if these are bad guys I'll be inside to clear the way. I'll call you on the radio and we'll do what needs to be done."

"You shouldn't go in alone," Rachel said, and I recognized the stubborn tone she could take when I was proposing something she didn't agree with. I started to turn around to talk to her but Zemeck beat me to the punch.

"That's exactly what he *should* do," he said. "He can move faster and quieter by himself and if he's half as good as he was the last time I worked with him they'll never even know he's in the building."

I looked at Rachel and while she didn't look happy I could tell she respected what the big Marine was telling her. Reaching out I took her hand and gave her a smile that she finally returned.

"And I brought you a couple of goodies," Zemeck said.

He released the bungee cords that were holding down a couple of hard sided cases and dragged them in front of where he kneeled. Before he could open them the pilot, a Marine Captain, walked back from the cockpit.

"Gunny, we just picked up a distress call from an Army unit that is in contact with a large group of infected. They're a hundred fifty miles north of us and sound like they're in a world of shit." He said.

"Go get them," I said before Zemeck had an opportunity to respond. "There's a perfectly good Pave Hawk on the roof down there if you don't make it back in time, and I've got the Air Force's hottest pilot right there." I hooked a thumb in Martinez' direction.

"Thank you, sir. I think you're pretty hot too." She quipped.

"Don't flatter yourself," I said grinning, standing up and grabbing the tablet and sketched floor plan. "I was referring to your flying skills."

Zemeck hoisted the cases he had brought along and we all walked down the rear ramp. The two Marines that Zemeck had brought with him were keeping watch at opposite ends of the Osprey, Dog sitting next to one of them with a dejected look on his face. A stick was on the ground next to the Marine's feet and Dog was hoping he'd pick it up and throw it.

We decided to send the two Marines with the Osprey. The pilot didn't know what kind of situation he'd be flying into and trying to effect an extraction during a battle without anyone in the aircraft that wasn't involved in flying could be a hairy experience. Besides, the mood I was in I was ready to take on everyone inside the casino single-handed.

A few minutes later the Osprey's engines started and the ungainly looking aircraft took off to the south, keeping the terrain between it and the large building I was preparing to assault. As soon as they were off the ground we loaded everything into the Explorer and turned ninety degrees to the pavement and drove out into an empty field. We'd been sitting in the open too long for my taste and I was happy to move us into the concealment of a small stand of trees on a ridgeline that overlooked the natural depression where the casino sat.

Sheltered amongst the trees, Zemeck walked me to the back of the vehicle and opened the cases. First he handed me a set of NVGs that I gladly accepted, along with a new, lighter tactical radio set. From the second case he pulled out a short-barreled Sig Sauer rifle and handed it to me with a grin. The rifle was half the length and weight of my M4, even with the long sound suppressor screwed onto the end.

"MPX-K in nine mil," Zemeck said, handing me a fully loaded magazine. "Nice and quiet with the suppressor. Best CQB weapon I've ever used." He meant Close Quarters Battle, which is what fighting in the casino would be.

I nodded my appreciation as I removed my rifle and worked the Sig's sling over my head. I spent ten seconds familiarizing myself with the weapon, then emptied my vest of spare mags for the M4 and loaded up with new ones for the Sig.

"Do you know how to get on the roof?" I asked Stephanie as I was getting the new weapon settled on my body. She shook her head and I turned back to Zemeck. "What else did you bring?"

"I looked the building over on satellite before leaving Tinker and tried to think of everything we might need. Got you covered," he said, pulling a pneumatic grappling hook launcher out of the apparently bottomless case. Smiling, I clapped him on the shoulder in thanks.

I gathered Zemeck, Rachel and Martinez around as Stephanie kept an eye on the kids who were enjoying playing with Dog.

"OK, here's what's happening." I began. "We leave the Explorer here with Stephanie and move to the right end of the building below where the Pave Hawk is sitting. I'm going up while you three stay at ground level. There should be an exterior door that I can open for you once I'm in and recon is complete.

"If you have to back off for any reason, infected or guards, do it. Don't engage if you can slip away. The last thing we need is a commotion to draw their attention. I don't know how long it's going to take me, and I'll keep you updated when I can, but you're going to have to settle in and be patient."

This last part was for Rachel, and to a degree Martinez. Zemeck knew the routine and wouldn't jump the gun, but this was new for Rachel and I knew from experience that she wasn't exactly the most patient person in the world. Not that I am, either, but she needed to understand that she didn't need to start getting antsy if I wasn't back in fifteen minutes.

We talked for a couple more minutes, most of the questions coming from Rachel. When I was as satisfied as I was going to be that the group was ready I whistled Dog over and gave Stephanie a brief explanation of what was happening. Having grown up in Oklahoma she knew how to handle a weapon and how to shoot, so I felt better leaving my M4 with her in case she needed to protect herself and the children. With a last check of the gear on my body I stepped off, leading the way down the gentle slope to the casino.

40

The walk to the casino was uneventful. We moved with me on point, happy to have night vision again, Rachel and Martinez side by side in the middle and Zemeck bringing up the rear. Dog stayed tight to my right leg, ears up and nose constantly twitching as he padded along silently. There was no breeze to carry scents to him, but that also worked in our favor as our smell wasn't being carried to any infected in the area.

My head was on a swivel, watching for both infected and survivors. The thermal scan had shown a few small groups of what had to be infected at different spots around the exterior walls of the casino, and I didn't want them to have any advance notice of our arrival. I was also worried about potential attacks from infected wildlife.

I had no idea if razorbacks ranged into this part of the country or not, but after dealing with the ones in Arkansas, then seeing the obviously infected bats in Texas, I wasn't in the frame of mind to trust any animal we encountered. But, we didn't encounter any, moving to the edge of the paved parking lot without incident.

The lot was so large the building was still over two hundred yards away and I paused when Dog let out with a quiet growl. Holding up a clenched fist I stopped our advance and looked down at him. His eyes were locked on the structure to our front and I was reasonably sure he had caught a sound or scent of the infected group that was clustered beneath the helipad.

After another scan of the area I got us moving forward again, treading lightly across the smooth asphalt. Dog would growl occasionally to let me know there was still danger ahead, but I wasn't able to see them yet. Slowly the details of the building resolved in my NVGs as I drew closer.

We were approaching at an oblique angle to the edge of what had resolved into a truly impressive structure. Even though the interior of the building was only one level, the walls soared nearly fifty feet into the air, which I suspected created an almost cavernous feel to the inside. Made of smooth stucco there was the occasional symbol embedded into the stone that represented something from the heritage of whatever tribe had built the casino.

Despite knowing that I had Indian blood in my veins courtesy of ancestors on my mother's side, I'd never had an interest in the culture and ignored the designs other than to take note of their presence. What I wanted to see was a maintenance ladder that ran from the ground up to the roof. At the moment that was much more interesting to me. But, I wasn't seeing one on this side.

Reaching the wall, I flattened my back against it and gave the rest of the team a moment to join me before sliding along to a corner. I could hear them before I saw them, the snarling of several males. Pausing at the edge I signed for the rest of the group to hold and peeked my head around to get a view of what we were dealing with.

Eleven infected were in the immediate area, five males and six females. All were just standing there, the females' heads tilted back to stare at the parapet far above them, the males swaying slowly back and forth as they waited for something to happen. I was preparing to raise my new rifle and start dropping the females when movement farther out caught my attention. It was two infected lying on the ground.

At least I thought they were just lying on the ground, until I looked closer and was stunned into immobility. A male infected was on his back, a female straddling him as they mated. What the hell? I knew the females were getting smarter, or probably to be more accurate they weren't having as much of their cognitive functions damaged by the virus as it mutated, but to be having sex?

I didn't even want to think about the implications of the infected mating. For that matter, I had no idea how the infected's minds were being impacted by the virus. Was this mating for procreation, or was some part of their disease riddled brains seeking out sexual pleasure?

A touch on my shoulder startled me back to reality and I turned. Rachel was looking at me with a curious expression that was mirrored on Martinez' and Zemeck's faces. Peeling the NVGs off I handed them to Rachel and motioned for her to take a look. We traded places and she peered around the corner. The way her body went stiff I could tell she had spotted the amorous couple.

Finally I tapped her shoulder and she turned around with a look of stunned horror on her face. Next I waved Martinez and Zemeck forward for a look. This wasn't a peep show; I just wanted everyone to be able to confirm what I had seen. There had been hope that the infected would eventually start dying off and the survivors would be able to reclaim the world. But if they were procreating, well, hell, it wasn't good.

I could tell Rachel wanted to talk about this new development, but I waved her off. We had the information. Discussing it could wait until I had Katie safely in my arms. Zemeck had gotten a look and also had a count and mental picture of the location of the infected. Using hand signs I told him his area of responsibility was the left and I would take the right. He nodded and I raised three fingers, counting down.

When my last finger folded into my fist we stepped around the corner together, rifles up, and began engaging the infected. Two females dropped simultaneously then two more before the others realized something was wrong. One of them turned and emitted the beginning of a scream before Zemeck shot her between the eyes.

We kept targeting and firing, quickly putting down all of the females. I paused a heartbeat when I realized the female in the act of mating was still so occupied that she hadn't noticed us. Walking forward I started shooting the males and she finally stopped grinding her pelvis on the male and looked around. I shot the last male standing and stood with a steady aim at her head.

She turned back to the male and lunged down, tearing his throat out with her teeth, dark blood jetting into the air from his severed carotid artery. Slowly she got to her feet and turned to face me, pants around her ankles. My aim wavered as she bent down, grasped the waistband of her jeans and pulled them up to cover herself.

"What the hell is going on?" Rachel said quietly from behind me.

I didn't know how to answer that question. This was a whole new level of behavior from the females and quite frankly it creeped me the hell out. Remembering why I was here in the first place I said the hell with it and pulled the trigger. The female's head snapped back and her body fell across the male she'd just killed after mating.

My heart was pounding and I took several deep breaths to calm down and refocus on the task at hand. A quick scan for any more infected came up empty and I turned to face the group. All of them looked as shocked as I felt.

"We'll talk about it later," I said, reaching out and taking my NVGs back from Rachel.

I scanned the wall and was disappointed to not see any way to access the roof. Turning to Zemeck I nodded and he walked a few yards away from the building before turning and looking up at the roofline. He must not have liked what he saw as he backed up another couple of yards, lowered his rifle and raised the grappling hook launcher.

Aiming high, he pulled the trigger and there was a low thump followed by the hiss of high-pressure air being released. A high strength polymer hook shot into the sky trailing a length of lightweight rope. The hook sailed out of sight over the edge of the roof, then the rope softly slapped against the wall.

Grabbing the line I began pulling to drag the grappling hook across the roof. There were knots tied into the line every eighteen inches that gave me a good grip. They were there to help climbers grip the rope and I'd forgotten just how long it had been since I'd gone up the outside of a building. Putting it out of my mind I tugged hard when the hook grabbed something solid on the roof.

The rope felt secure but before I started up the wall I held onto a knot and pulled myself a few inches off the ground. Everything seemed secure even with my full body weight hanging from the line. Swinging my legs up I clamped my feet together on the rope, boot soles resting on a knot and reached for the next one above my head. Hand over hand I climbed, keeping my feet securely on the line each time I reached for a new grip.

There was a time when I would have let my legs swing and trusted in just my upper body strength. There was a time when I could scamper up a rope like a monkey. Have I mentioned I'm not twenty any more? Now, if I went too fast I could miss a grip and fall. Too slow and my muscles would fatigue and my grip would slip. I tried not to think about either of those scenarios and just went up at a nice, steady pace. I might have been a little slower than I used to be, but I still made it up the rope and over the parapet in a reasonable amount of time.

When my head cleared the edge, I paused long enough to scan the roof for any threats. Not seeing any, I came all the way up and as soon as I was on the roof, stood and raised the rifle for a more thorough scan. Still all clear. Looking down over the edge I waved to let them know all was good then headed to check the Pave Hawk.

I paused when I saw the man sitting in the cockpit. He was either dead or asleep, head hanging down as he slumped forward in the flight harness. Still, I approached the helicopter carefully, pulling the door open quickly with my rifle up and ready when I got there.

There was no need to check. The smell hit me the instant the door came open. It was bad, but nowhere near as bad as it would get. Not knowing how quickly we might need to be able to depart I took a moment to release the harness and work the body out of the aircraft. The man hadn't been dead long as his body was still stiff with rigor mortis. It was difficult to force the rigid limbs into the angles needed, but I kept pushing and pulling until he came free and tumbled to the roof. Dragging the corpse a few feet away from the Pave Hawk I decided to leave the door open to allow the stench of decomposition to air out.

41

The plasti-cuffs binding Roach's hands behind the chair back finally parted. Suppressing a groan as his arms came in front of his body for the first time in hours he leaned forward and breathed deeply until the worst of the pain passed. He was locked in a small utility closet, having been hauled away by the new arrivals. At first he'd been relieved to see them as the Major's wife was about a second away from putting a bullet in his head when they showed up, but they weren't interested in talking to him.

He had been roughly dragged to his feet and marched to a small closet that smelled of cleaning supplies. A steel framed chair had been brought in and he'd been forced to sit on it, his hands pulled behind the back and secured. Each ankle had also been strapped to a chair leg, the large men ignoring his attempts to speak with them as they worked.

Once he was secured they had slammed the door and left him in the dark. Sitting there, throat and balls aching from where Katie had attacked him, he forgot all about that pain as he listened to a conversation from outside the door.

"Jimmy's going to like that one." One of the men said with a chuckle.

"No shit. He'll be happy. Hasn't had a bitch to use since we had to hit the road."

Both men had laughed then moved away from the door. Roach's blood had run cold. He had always looked at women as nothing more than objects for him to use for his own sick pleasures, but had never imagined finding himself on the receiving end. Terror spurred him to start testing his bonds.

The plastic ties were very tough, but he eventually found a rough spot on the chair's metal frame. It was at the very limit of the reach of his bound hands, but there was a tiny, sharp edge where the legs had been welded to the seat that hadn't been ground completely smooth. It wasn't much, but it was his only option.

Torqueing his upper body into an uncomfortable position he began moving his hands up and down, rubbing the tie on the spot. Finally, after several hours of work, his hands were free. Grasping the tie holding his right leg to the chair he pulled, but there was no way he could break loose. Looking around he hoped to spot something he could use to cut free.

A small of amount of light leaked in through a ventilation grate in the lower half of the door. While it was dark in the closet there was still enough illumination for him to see. To his right was a rack of shelves loaded with one gallon jugs of cleaning chemicals. He briefly considered finding one that was corrosive enough to weaken the plastic and allow him to break free, but dismissed the idea out of fear of what the compound might do to his flesh if it was harsh enough to eat plastic.

On the other side of the room were neatly stored brooms, mops and buckets. Nothing there. Twisting his head around he spotted a small workbench with three drawers. Half standing up into a crouch he lifted the chair and hobbled to the back of the closet, pulling the top drawer open. It was stacked full of clean, glass ashtrays. The second one held neatly folded cleaning rags, the third stacked with boxes of paper match books and a row of cork screws for opening wine bottles, both with the casino's name and logo printed on them.

Slipping a corkscrew into his pocket, Roach grabbed one of the matchbooks and sat down on the seat, leaned forward and struck a match. The odor was sharp and acrid and he worried someone outside the closet might detect it and investigate, but pressed ahead and held the flame to the plastic around his left ankle. Soon the smell of burning petroleum was added to the mix as the white plastic tie began to bubble.

Roach pushed with his leg and the bond stretched half an inch before the match burned down to his fingers and he dropped it on the concrete floor. Lighting another he held it at the same point and as the flame burned out his leg broke through the weakened material. Quickly he lit another and began working on his right. Two matches later he was free, suppressing a shout of triumph.

As he stood up the door was suddenly yanked open and the light that shone in after being in the dark for so long momentarily blinded him.

"Anxious little fellar, ain't you?" A deep voice said a moment before he was grabbed and pulled out of the closet.

Roach's eyes hadn't fully adjusted to the light, but he could tell he was facing a very large man. Another man stood behind him, but he couldn't make out his features as he squinted.

"Billy, my new friend and I are going to get acquainted," the giant man said, the undertone in his voice sending a thrill of fear and revulsion through Roach. "Make sure we're not disturbed."

"You got it, Jimmy." The man answered.

Roach was panicking. Barely able to take a breath, eyes darting around as he looked for any escape route. When Jimmy turned his head to nod to Billy, he lunged away and to the side. He didn't know where he would go, just knew he had to get away from the man. He didn't even make it a step before Jimmy's massive fist lashed out and struck him on the side of the head.

He stumbled and fell, nearly losing consciousness. Jimmy stepped over him, reached down and wrapped a huge hand around his upper arm. Lifting him to his feet he leaned in until his face was almost touching Roach's.

"Go ahead and fight, sugar. That just makes it better!" He said with a grin then planted a wet kiss directly on Roach's mouth.

Roach wanted to tear away from the man and run, but the grip on his arm was like iron and he was afraid to antagonize him. Jimmy broke the kiss and stood back to his full height, a head taller than Roach, turned and headed directly to a door with a small brass sign on it marking it as "PRIVATE". Roach had no choice but to walk with him as the man's hand tightened on his arm to bring him along. A scream of "NO" began to build in his head and he didn't know if he was actually shouting it or not.

42

The steel door set into the roof's bulkhead was locked with a deadbolt and I didn't have a key. But the hinges were on the outside and I did have several thermite grenades courtesy of Zemeck. Seems he'd thought of everything.

Thermite grenades have been used by the US Military since World War II to disable equipment, most commonly artillery that has to be left behind and is at risk of being captured by an enemy. Though they are called grenades, there is no explosion, rather the ignition of the combination of magnesium, aluminum and iron. The chemical reaction quickly reaches temperatures of 2,500 degrees Celsius and will destroy the barrel of a canon, or the hinges on a door.

OK, so maybe he hadn't thought of everything. How the hell was I going to keep the grenades in place on the hinges long enough to melt them? Realizing there was no way to use the thermite I raised the NVGs and clicked on a small flashlight to examine the door. It was set flush into a steel frame, the exterior smooth and unbroken except for the deadbolt and a small knob.

In frustration I grabbed the knob and tugged, surprised when I felt the door shift slightly. I pulled a couple more times, watching the whole frame move when I did. Glad that shoddy workmanship was alive and well, I drew my Ka-Bar and inserted the blade into a narrow gap between the doorframe and the bulkhead's wood framing and started working it around the perimeter.

It didn't take long for me to figure out that when the door had been set it had been held in place with small, temporary screws. Someone should have come along and installed the big, heavy lag bolts that were almost certainly required for a security door, but they hadn't. And I wasn't complaining.

Pausing after I started to apply leverage with my Ka-Bar, I looked over my shoulder at the dead pilot. He most likely had a smaller survival knife on him that I could use and not risk breaking a knife I might need. Sheathing mine I strode to the body and found a six inch, fixed blade knife strapped to his flight vest.

Twenty minutes later I had one screw to go when Zemeck's baritone sounded in my ear.

"Got a few more infected arriving in the area." It was just an update and he didn't expect an answer.

I kept working in silence, finally breaking through and the door coming free. The top began to tilt out towards me and I let it move enough to grasp each side and lift it free. Shuffling sideways I set it down then carefully lowered the top until it was flat on the roof. I had managed to work very quietly and was confident that unless someone had been right on the other side of the door they wouldn't have heard me.

The lights were on inside the casino revealing a red-carpeted flight of stairs that led down. Rifle up I began descending, treading lightly and listening hard for any indication that I'd been detected. The area was quiet and when I reached the bottom of the stairs I found myself in what looked like a VIP area. That made sense, as anyone who had a helicopter on the roof would have almost certainly been a VIP.

Looking around I spotted a row of switches and started pressing them until the lights in the room went out. I had to open a door to move into the main area of the casino and I didn't know if it was lit or not. Either way I didn't want the room I was coming out of to be brightly lit and visible to anyone who happened to be looking in my direction.

Cracking the door open half an inch I pressed an eye to the gap and peered through. The main area was lit, but only with dim lights set far apart in the ceiling far overhead. There were lots of shadows along the walls and large pools of darkness spaced out into the distance. Row upon row of slot machines stretched away, none of them powered up.

I stood still for several minutes, watching and listening, but didn't detect any movement. Rifle gripped with my right hand I slowly pulled the door farther open with my left. Poking my head out I took a quick look in each direction and still seeing nothing of concern I swiftly stepped through the opening, softly closed the door behind me and moved into the closest spot that was dark.

Still clear of danger I ran to the nearest bank of slots, rifle up and scanning in sync with my eyes. Pausing behind the eight foot tall row of machines I checked behind me before continuing on deeper into the room. I passed through two areas lit from above before pulling up in the shelter of a giant Wheel Of Fortune slot machine.

Crouching in the dark I caught my breath when I heard a quiet cough from the adjacent row. Remaining stock still I listened for a moment then checked behind me again before continuing deeper into the building. I kept moving like that, dash and pause, dash and pause, until I was approaching the area where the majority of the blobs had shown on the thermal image.

No more dashing from this point. Slow, cautious, steady movement. I could hear the faint sounds of conversations and smell cigarettes being smoked. The aroma of food cooking threatened to start my stomach rumbling. I was surprised as it was the middle of the night and I'd expected most of the people that weren't on sentry duty to be asleep, but that didn't seem to be the case.

Working my way forward I stopped in a shadowy area at the end of a bank of large slots and listened for a moment. A couple of low conversations and faint sounds of pots and pans being banged around. Flattening my body to the floor I slowly poked my head around the base of the machine, the legs of a stool providing some camouflage.

I was near the far end of the casino from where I'd entered and the area along the wall was better lit than the main gambling floor I'd just crossed. A guard carrying an AK47 rifle was walking away from my position, presumably continuing on a set patrol. He didn't look particularly alert and was focused more on the carpeted floor in front of his feet than he was on the surroundings. That was not unexpected and was also good for me. They felt secure, and even though they had posted men to patrol the building the sentries were bored and not really doing their job.

Three men lounged around a low, felt topped table, and this was one of the conversations I was hearing. Two of them were smoking and there was a half empty whiskey bottle on the table, a shot glass resting in front of each man. I could just make out what they were saying and listened intently for a couple of minutes.

They were discussing organizing a fight and trying to decide what form of payment they would accept for an entry fee; food or ammunition. They settled on ammunition, then moved on to women.

This part of the conversation didn't make as much sense at first as they seemed to be debating which woman was the best. Then, as I continued to eavesdrop, I got a sick feeling in my gut when I realized they were talking about women they were holding captive.

Raising my head slightly I made note of their weapons then pulled back around the corner into the dark. I started moving again, further along the row of slot machines, sticking to the darkness and spotting and cataloging different members of the group. Quietly moving past a couple of large poker rooms with glass walls I could see a lot of people sacked out in sleeping bags in each room.

Wood paneled doors with small, oval windows set head height led to the kitchen where the cooking smells were coming from, next to them a man seated in front of another door that had a discreet sign on it marked "PRIVATE". He looked like he was guarding whatever was in the room, a shotgun resting in his lap. He was dozing, his head repeatedly tipping forward until he jerked himself back awake for a few moments.

My count was at fifty-five. I hadn't been able to approach and look into the kitchen, but I made the assumption there was only one person cooking, so I upped the number to fifty-six. Eleven more bodies to find, and presumably two of those would be Katie and Roach, though I hadn't seen either of them yet. Continuing my cautious recon I upped my count to fifty-seven when I spotted the next guard that was sitting in front of another glass walled poker room.

This one was well lit and it took me a moment to realize what I was looking at. Here were the women the men had been discussing. Six of them. All dressed in lingerie typically only seen in a strip club or Victoria's Secret catalog. Where the hell had they found the clothing? Chastising myself for letting my mind wander to a topic that was unimportant, I adjusted my position to get a better view into the room.

The women were stretched out on the carpeted floor, sleeping. They hadn't been provided sleeping bags or even blankets and just lay with their arms folded under their heads for pillows. My breath caught when I spotted one with long, wavy red hair. She was lying with her back to me, legs pulled up towards her body, as she was most likely chilled from wearing next to nothing. Between the distinctive hair and the small tattoo I could see on her right hip, revealed by the white thong she was wearing, I had no doubt. It was Katie.

43

"We're in the building." I heard Zemeck's voice over my earpiece.

I was working my way back to the far end of the casino after spotting Katie and spending some time locating as many more members of the group that was occupying the building as I could find. Roach and two others were still unaccounted for, my final count four short of the sixty-seven that had been spotted on thermal.

There was any number of reasons for the discrepancy. The satellite image was several hours old and people could have left. There were also a lot of private rooms and offices that I hadn't been able to approach and check without risking being spotted by a sentry. I was thinking about all of these as I heard the radio call and looked up to find a location to tell Zemeck to meet me.

Each of the large banks of slot machines I was moving through was numbered. Large signs stuck up from the top of each group so that they were easily visible and identifiable to the casino staff from anywhere on the floor. Spotting one a few rows deeper into the casino I activated my radio.

"Meet at 42. Four two." I said in a very quiet voice.

"Four two. Copy." He replied then the radio went silent again.

Changing directions I began working my way to the rendezvous point. I was far enough away from the concentration of people that I was once again moving quickly from shadow to shadow, pausing every so often to listen. Nearing my destination I dashed to a dark area, shadowed by a row of video poker machines labeled 38, and froze when I heard the sound of a match being struck from the far side of area 37.

Reaching up to my vest I pressed the manual transmit button on my radio two times in quick succession. This would send two clicks to Zemeck, telling him there was a problem and he needed to go still and silent until I gave the all clear. A moment later there were two answering clicks in my earpiece as he acknowledged my message.

I could smell cigarette smoke now as well as see it drifting up into the faint light above the 37 sign. Scanning the area I didn't see anything other than quiet machines so I moved to the end of the bank with my short rifle up and ready. When I came to a stop I was close enough to hear the burning of the tobacco as what I presumed was a sentry took a drag, a moment later the soft sigh of his exhale clear to my ears in the quiet.

Risking a quick look I leaned out; rifle aimed and finger moving onto the trigger. The man was seated at the far end of the row, four machines away from where I stood. His back was to me as he stared towards the far end of the casino. Not wanting to make any noise I lowered the rifle to the end of its sling and silently drew my Ka-Bar.

When I'd first entered the building I'd not been in a hurry to start engaging the occupants. They could have been survivors who sought refuge from the infected in the security of the big casino. They could have been employees who had just hunkered down. But when I'd found my wife, obviously being held against her will and forced to dress like she was, any hesitation to kill on my part had been removed.

Ka-Bar gripped tightly in my right hand, I took two long, quiet strides and clapped my hand over the man's mouth as I thrust the blade into his kidney. A deep strike to the kidneys will send the human body into immediate shock, rendering it unable to fight or flee. Pulling the knife free I stabbed in from the side, the eight inch blade slipping between his ribs and piercing his heart.

Maintaining my hand over his mouth I twisted the Ka-Bar to ensure an instant kill then pulled it out and lowered the corpse to the floor. After wiping the blade clean on his clothing and re-sheathing the knife I took a moment to pull the stools away from the slot machines, roll the body against their base, then put the stools back in a neat row. Anyone walking by would easily see the dead man, but from a few yards away, in the shadows, he wouldn't be readily apparent.

Raising the rifle I scanned the area but came up clear. Two slow clicks on the radio let Zemeck know he was OK to move again and I turned and headed for the 42 sign. I arrived a few minutes ahead of them and took the time to check two rows on either side of the location. Both were clear of any guards and when I moved back to the bank of machines I spotted Zemeck leading Rachel, Martinez and Dog.

"Why'd you come inside?" I asked quietly after Dog calmed down and quit insisting that I pet him.

"Infected showed up," Zemeck answered in an equally soft voice. We were talking in mumbles, not whispers. The sibilant sounds of a whisper carry much farther and are more easily detected by the human ear than a very quiet mumble. "Too many to fight without retreating, so we came up the rope."

I turned and looked at Dog who thought my glance was an invitation for more petting.

"He's a heavy bastard, but at least he knows to stay still." Zemeck said with a grin. "So what's the landscape?"

I filled him in on what I'd found, Rachel and Martinez pushing in close to hear what I had to say.

"No Roach?" Rachel asked.

"Not that I've seen." I said. "He could be gone, could be in an area I couldn't get to, or could be dead."

She nodded and Zemeck spoke up. "So, what's your plan?"

I pulled out the sketch Stephanie had drawn for me and spread it out on the floor. With Dog pushed out of the way everyone was able to lean in and see as I pointed out what I wanted to do. Zemeck asked a few questions, but kept nodding his head as I spoke.

"Rachel, will you get to Katie?" I asked, looking up at her. She looked back at me and smiled.

"Yes. I'll make sure she gets out." She said, meeting my eyes and still smiling.

"Thank you," I said, reaching down, drawing my back up pistol and handing it to Rachel. "Hand her this when you get to her. She knows how to use it."

Rachel nodded again and tucked the weapon into her waistband. We reviewed the plan one more time and when there were no more questions I looked at each of them and thanked them for their help. Zemeck and Martinez nodded, slightly embarrassed. Rachel looked back at me and I could tell she was holding back tears. Martinez noticed too and motioned Zemeck to come with her and give us a moment of privacy.

"I wouldn't be here without you," I said to Rachel. "I don't know how to thank you or tell you how much you mean to me."

She reached out and took my hand in hers, leaning in and kissing me. It was a slow, soft, deep kiss, but there was sadness behind it.

"Let's go get your wife," she said.

44

We moved single file, me on point with Dog at my side, Zemeck behind me with Rachel and Martinez watching our rear. First step was to take out the roving sentries. I'd already gotten one of them on the way to meet up with my group, but there were two more that I'd spotted. Both were armed with AKs and needed to be taken out before we began our rescue effort. Leaving guards running around behind you with automatic weapons is never a good idea.

I heard the first guard before I saw him. We had angled over to be close to the wall farthest from where Katie was being held and as the man walked he dragged the heel of each foot on the carpet. In the tomblike silence of the cavernous building it was easy to hear him coming. I signed for the group to stop, held a hand in front of Dog's face to tell him to stay and moved forward to meet the man.

As I spotted him around the corner of a row of ATMs he was just pushing through a door into a men's restroom. Padding silently, I ran up and pressed my ear to the door. I couldn't hear well, but managed to pick out the sound of his zipper coming down, followed a moment later by the glassy tinkle of a urinal being used.

Raising my rifle I pushed the door open with my shoulder and stepped into the brightly lit room. The man stood with his back to me, legs spread apart and hands in front as he relieved himself. His rifle was leaned up in a corner, well out of his reach. He hadn't heard me enter the room and died with a bullet in his head. The body collapsed to the floor with more noise than I liked, but overall it was a very quiet kill. The new Sig rifle was every bit as silent as Zemeck had made it out to be.

Exiting the restroom I formed back up with the group and we began hunting the other guard. I had observed them making full circles of the perimeter of the casino floor, so I knew he'd be coming along in the wake of the one I had just killed. We stayed one row in from the outside wall and moved forward to meet him.

Covering almost half the distance to the holding area I called a halt when I heard voices approaching from the front. Crawling laterally I took a peek down the perimeter row and was dismayed to see four men strolling towards us, all armed with AKs. This was not how they'd been patrolling when I'd been snooping around, and while I had no doubt that Zemeck and I could quickly take the whole group, I was afraid to risk one of them getting a shot off and alerting everyone in the building.

I pulled my group another row away from the wall and quickly told them what was coming our way.

"You need them distracted so you can get close," Rachel said. "I'll take care of that."

Rachel was still wearing the extremely short shorts she had used to distract the Rangers at Tinker so we could escape, and now she reached up and peeled her vest and shirt off, leaving only a thin, nearly transparent tank top covering her bare breasts. Handing her clothes to Martinez she went down our row until she was past the approaching men. Zemeck and I moved to a corner at the perimeter row, rifles up and ready.

"What are you doing here?" We heard one of the men ask in surprise a moment later.

"I was lost and this looked like a good place to hide. Are you the Army?" Rachel was getting quite good at putting the right amount of 'ingenuous' in her voice.

"How did you get in?" The same man asked.

"That door right back there."

That was our cue. I knew they were already facing away from us, looking at Rachel, but now she would be pointing at an area behind her and all of them would be looking for a door that they had somehow missed.

I was closest to the row, Zemeck tight against my back with his left hand on my shoulder. When I moved he came with me, both of us stepping into the open, rifles already up and ready. As one we fired, the two outside men dropping from headshots that killed them instantly. We adjusted aim and both fired again as the first set of bodies hit the floor, the remaining two dying instantly as well.

Rachel stepped around them and ran to us, retrieving her clothing and gear from Martinez. She dressed as we started moving again. I had originally planned to head directly across the casino floor once the second sentry was dead, but something had changed to send four of them together. Maybe they were all friends and had decided to keep each other company, but I wasn't going to bet ours and Katie's lives on that assumption.

We circled the building but didn't encounter any other guards, roving or static. Soon we were opposite the guard that was sitting outside the door marked as private. His post was around a corner from the guard watching the captive women, as were the doors into the kitchen area where I'd heard movement earlier.

Ignoring him for the moment we kept moving, turning into a new row to stay hidden. It didn't take long to reach the well-lit poker room where the women were being held and I wasn't at all surprised to find the guard sound asleep, head tilted back and snoring. I intended to rescue all of the women that were being held, but I took the time to single out Katie and make sure everyone knew which one she was.

Moving on we came to a stop in front of the two glass walled rooms that were full of people sacked out in sleeping bags. We had already discussed the plan and Martinez took up position. If things went well we'd take out a couple more guards and make a quiet exit with Katie and the other women. If they didn't, Martinez was there to make sure these people weren't able to join the fight.

Back at the sleeping guard, Rachel, Dog and I stopped as Zemeck continued on. When he was in position to take out the guard at the private door he'd let me know over the radio and we'd both attack at the same time. He and I would then clear the kitchen first, followed by the private room while Rachel and Dog woke the women and got them ready to move.

It took him a couple of minutes then I received a single click over the radio. I clicked once in response then began counting in my head as I sighted on the sleeping guard. When I reached five I pulled the trigger, punching a bullet through the man's forehead. The body was already relaxed and supported as he slept and other than a twitch from the impact of the bullet it didn't move, remaining seated in the chair. Rachel and I both went into motion, her heading for the closed glass door that opened into the room, Dog at her side, as I headed to meet Zemeck at the swinging doors into the kitchen.

We arrived at the same time, each of us putting our backs against the wall on either side of the opening. First Zemeck, then I, we leaned forward slightly and peered through the oval windows into the large room beyond. Zemeck shook his head to indicate he didn't see anyone but I held up two fingers.

There was an older woman and a large young man seated at a long stainless steel counter. They looked to be halfway through a meal. The meal I'd heard them preparing earlier that had smelled so good. At the sight of the food my stomach growled loudly in complaint of being so empty.

Zemeck looked at me and pulled a face. I was sure he had something incredibly witty to say at my expense and was glad we were in a situation that required stealth. Taking another look, each of us confirmed that nothing had changed. With a nod I held up my left hand, three fingers extended. I began folding a finger into my fist at regular intervals, Zemeck bobbing his head as I reached each count.

When I folded my second finger in I moved my hand to the front grip on my rifle. We bobbed our heads in unison for the one count, moving on zero. I was first through the door, immediately moving to the right as I sighted on the male, Zemeck following through right behind me.

Days Of Perdition

The woman noticed us first, her fork clattering onto the stainless steel surface. The young man looked up, froze for a beat then went for a pistol that was holstered at his hip. I squeezed the trigger twice and he fell to the tile floor, dead. The woman looked down at him for a long moment then turned her gaze back to us and took a sharp breath.

Maybe she was going to scream, maybe not. Regardless, Zemeck and I both thought that was what she was about to do and the last thing we wanted was noise that would wake up the sleeping people. There were over fifty of them and I didn't want to have to fight them, nor did I feel the need to kill all of them. The thought flashed through my head in a fraction of a second and I pulled the trigger in tandem with Zemeck.

Both of us had gone for headshots and the woman pitched backwards off her stool, dead before she hit the floor next to the body I'd already put there. I was starting to turn to go to Katie but spun back at a noise of someone moving deeper in the kitchen. Zemeck and I looked at each other and spread apart as we started to move farther into the room.

45

Roach tried begging and pleading, but that didn't deter the man. When Jimmy dragged him into the room he drew him into a crushing embrace, lifting his feet clear of the floor as he planted his wet lips on Roach's face. Squirming and trying to bite his attacker only earned him a slap that left him seeing stars and a hard punch to the stomach.

Swaying on his feet and gasping for air, Roach tried to reach for the corkscrew but couldn't get his hand in his pocket before Jimmy stepped in and grabbed him by the wrists, forcing him to his knees. Hands numb from the pressure of Jimmy's grip, Roach began to cry as he pleaded for the man to stop but he was slapped again.

"This is going to happen, bitch." Jimmy said, fumbling his belt buckle with one hand as he held Roach's throat in his other. "If you bite me I will beat you so bad you'll wish you were dead, then when you heal I'll do it all over again."

Pants open, he pulled out his fully erect penis and pressed it against Roach's face. "Understand me, bitch?"

Roach nodded, tears streaming down his face as Jimmy forced himself into his mouth. When the reality of what was happening, and what was yet to come, hit him, Roach's mind shut down. He did what Jimmy told him to do, no longer crying or trying to resist. A few minutes later the big man stepped back and lifted Roach to his feet, violently stripping his pants off.

Roach neither resisted nor complained. As if he was a bystander, his body cooperated as Jimmy spun him around and pushed him over the edge of a table. When Jimmy grabbed his hips his mind suddenly screamed at him to fight, but before he could even react he was violently penetrated. He tried to turn away, tried to move, but the man was at least a hundred pounds heavier and kept him pinned as he savagely thrust into Roach.

Screaming and crying again, Roach reached out with a hand and felt his pants lying on the table where Jimmy had discarded them. Grasping the fabric he pulled them to him and frantically searched for the pocket with the corkscrew. Finally finding it he ripped it free as his attacker thrust deep inside him and shuddered with his release.

The corkscrew was a large tool that the wine stewards used to open bottles with a flourish.

Six inches of coiled, chrome steel ended in a needle sharp point, the other end firmly embedded in a thick, round wooden T handle. Roach gripped it in his right hand; the steel portion sticking out between his two middle fingers, holding it so tight his arm ached.

"That's a good little bitch." Jimmy said, sighing with contentment as he withdrew from Roach and stepped back.

He was leaning in to slap the bare ass in front of him when Roach suddenly spun and with every ounce of his being stabbed the entire length of the corkscrew into Jimmy's neck. The man's eye's went wide in shock as his hands flew upwards, but Roach was enraged and moving fast. Ripping the six inches of steel out of Jimmy's flesh he changed his target and stabbed into the man's groin, again burying the full length into his body.

Releasing the weapon he easily ducked Jimmy's clumsy attempt to wrap him up in one arm and stumbled across the room, putting the table between them. A thick jet of blood was pulsing out of his attacker's neck, more blood coursing from the wound to his crotch. Jimmy tried to step forward while holding a hand pressed to his throat, but stumbled and looked down at the tool still embedded in his body.

With his free hand he ripped it out, pulling a chunk of flesh and a fresh gout of blood with it. Looking up at Roach he took another step, then his knees buckled and he fell to the floor as his life continued to jet out of his neck. Roach stood there and watched as the man died, the fury inside of him growing.

This wouldn't have happened if Katie hadn't attacked him. Her attack had made him vulnerable when these people showed up. Rage blocking out the pain radiating from his anus, Roach pulled his pants on and stepped over Jimmy's corpse. The man had been carrying a small weapon that he'd laid on a chair when they'd entered the room.

Roach would normally have been happy to pick up a fully automatic Uzi pistol, but all he cared about was exacting his revenge on Katie. Stepping to the door he paused when he heard a gurgle from the man on the floor. Surprised Jimmy was still alive, he turned and looked down.

Jimmy's eyes were still open, staring up at him. Pleading for help. Roach looked around until he spotted the corkscrew and came back to stand over the dying man. With a smile he bent down and drove the steel into Jimmy's right eye until his knuckles came to a stop against his face. Still smiling, he stood up and headed for the door to finish his business with Katie.

46

Rachel and Dog dashed past the dead guard to the heavy glass door of the room as John and Zemeck disappeared into the kitchen. Pulling the door open carefully, she waved Dog inside, followed him and quietly closed the door. The six women were all asleep, and even though they all needed to be awakened she rushed to Katie first.

As soon as she touched her shoulder, Katie's eyes flew open and she turned to sit up.

"It's OK," Rachel said. "I'm here with John to get you out."

Katie's eyes went wide and shifted to the windows, looking for him.

"Rachel?" She asked when she didn't see her husband.

"How do you know my name?" Rachel was surprised.

"Roach told me about you," Katie said. "Said you and my husband were a couple."

"Don't believe anything that little shit told you. Here. Present from your husband," Rachel said in a rush, pressing the pistol John had given her into Katie's hand. "Help me wake everyone. We're leaving now."

Rachel didn't wait for an answer, dashing to the far side of the room and shaking two of the women awake. Katie was on her feet by now, pistol in her hand as she began waking the others. They quickly had all the women up and ready to move and Rachel went to the door, pausing before she pulled it open.

"No noise," she said, making sure everyone understood.

Exiting the room Katie was right behind her, Dog moving out ahead of them into the first row of slot machines. Rachel glanced around but John and Zemeck hadn't come out of the kitchen yet. Where the hell were they? Turning to the front she checked on Dog, then glanced over her shoulder to make sure the women were all still following.

Movement in her peripheral vision caught her eye and Rachel turned her head, expecting to see John. She froze for a heartbeat when she recognized Roach, walking towards her with a weapon in his right hand coming up to target them.

Katie looked to her left when the tall woman paused, her breath catching in her throat. Roach was walking directly towards them, raising a pistol. The woman was trying to bring an M4 rifle around but she could tell Roach had the drop on them and would start firing well before the rifle could come into the fight.

Reaching out, Katie shoved the woman in the middle of her back as she spun to bring her pistol up. Before she could raise the muzzle high enough to fire, Roach pulled the trigger and the small Uzi began spitting bullets. Time slowed and Katie heard two of them zip past her head before something slammed into her chest and she was falling.

Martinez cursed when she heard the burst of automatic weapon's fire. They'd been found and someone was in trouble. None of them were carrying an unsuppressed full auto weapon so she knew this was someone from the group occupying the casino.

Knowing what she had to do, she flipped the fire selector on her rifle to burst and aimed for the glass wall of the room to the right. Pulling the trigger twice she shifted aim and sent six more rounds into the windows on her left. The bullets shattered the heavy glass that crashed to the floor and left a wide opening into each space.

Dropping the rifle, Martinez picked up the first of four fragmentation grenades she had already lined up on the carpet. Pulling the pin she threw it hard at the right hand room, watching it sail through the opening she'd just created as she reached for the second one.

People in the two rooms were shouting and screaming now, struggling to get out of their sleeping bags. One enterprising soul didn't bother to do anything other than pick up his rifle and start firing blindly. Martinez ignored the bullets that were sailing wide around her location and threw the second grenade into the left room, quickly following with one more to each room.

Snatching her rifle off the floor she rolled behind a slot machine and onto her feet. A second later the four grenades detonated in sequence. The sound and concussion was ferocious, even with room in the massive space for it to spread out. All of the remaining glass shattered and was blown outwards, becoming thousands of pieces of razor sharp shrapnel that peppered the slot machines around her.

Glass screens cracked and imploded. Dust billowed and somewhere a loud bell began ringing as the blasts ruptured a sprinkler pipe and water began flowing through the fire suppression system. Five seconds after the final blast Martinez looked around the bank she was sheltering behind, rifle ready to engage anyone that was still wanting to fight.

There were no targets, but not everyone was dead. Screams of pain were coming from both rooms, and as the dust began to clear Martinez could tell there was no one on their feet. Stepping around she walked towards the carnage, rifle up just in case someone was still capable of aiming a weapon at her, but she stopped halfway when she got a look inside. Swallowing bile, she turned and ran towards Rachel's location when she heard screaming.

Rachel fell to her knees when Katie pushed her, cursing and rolling as she tried to get her rifle aimed at Roach. Then he fired and Rachel turned her head to see Katie fall backwards as a bullet struck her chest.

Screaming, Rachel finally got the rifle up and began pulling the trigger in burst mode. She kept pulling it until the magazine ran dry but didn't manage to hit Roach as far as she could tell. When she'd started firing he had turned and ran, heading into the maze of the casino floor.

"Oh my God, no! No, no, no, no…" Rachel dropped her rifle and dashed to Katie's side, Dog rushing up to stand guard next to her.

Katie had been shot in the upper right quadrant of her chest, the bullet entering just above her breast. Blood was welling out of the entrance wound and Rachel grabbed her shoulders and rolled her up to check for an exit wound. There was one just inside her right scapula. Putting her flat on her back she pressed both hands on Katie's chest and screamed for John as Martinez ran up and dropped to her knees on the other side of Katie.

Zemeck and I were pushing deeper into the kitchen, searching for whoever had made the noise when the sound of weapons fire reached us. We exchanged a quick glance and he tilted his head at the door, telling me to go. I shook my head, hesitant to leave him alone to clear the room. No matter how good you are, trying to find a potentially armed opponent in a cluttered area by yourself is extremely dangerous.

He shook his head and we continued, but had only covered a few more cautious yards when I heard Rachel scream my name. Looking at Zemeck I yanked a grenade out of my vest and pulled the pin, palm holding the spoon in place. He nodded, pulled one out and together we tossed them in the direction we thought the sound had come from, turned and ran.

Blasting through the swinging doors I had my rifle up and ready, Zemeck on my heels as I made the turn towards where I had left Rachel. The twin blasts from our grenades sounded behind and I involuntarily ducked but kept running. As I rounded the corner I could see Rachel and Martinez bent over someone on the floor, a small group of lingerie clad women clustered tightly together watching them.

"No, no, no…" I began repeating to myself as I let my rifle drop on its sling and ran as hard as I could.

Martinez moved aside and I fell to the floor beside Katie. She was awake and looked up at me and smiled.

"I waited for you. Where have you been?" She asked with a weak smile on her face.

"I'm sorry, babe." I said, leaning down and kissing her as tears began rolling down my face. "I got held up a little."

"What happened?" Zemeck was squatting behind me.

"Hi, Andre," Katie looked at him and tried to smile. She had always refused to call him Matt, preferring to poke him a little about his stature and call him Andre the Giant.

"Hi, pretty lady. Good to see you." He said, placing a big hand on my shoulder.

"It was Roach," Rachel said. "Came out of nowhere with a little machine pistol. She pushed me out of the way and took a round."

"How bad?" I asked, holding Katie's hand with one of mine and brushing a stray strand of hair off her face with the other.

"I don't know, but I need to get her back to Tinker. Now. I can work on her on the way." Rachel turned to Martinez. "Will that helicopter on the roof fly?"

"No," Martinez answered. "I checked it out when we were on the roof. But there's a field medic kit in it."

"Osprey is twenty minutes out," Zemeck said.

"Tell them to get the lead out," I said without taking my eyes off my wife.

"I'll take care of her," Rachel said to me. "You go get that fucking psychopath before he turns up again."

"He can wait," I started to say, but Rachel cut me off.

"No, he can't." She said. "Every time we think we're done with him, he shows up. This needs to end now. Trust me. I'll take care of her."

When I looked back down at Katie her eyes were closed. Leaning over her I kissed her lips, told her I loved her and stood up.

"Andre, pick her up," Rachel ordered, adopting Katie's nickname for Zemeck. "I'll need to walk next to you to keep pressure on the wound, so don't walk too fast."

I stepped back as my friend kneeled and scooped my wife up in his arms. Rachel never took her hands off Katie's chest and she looked back at me as they started to head for the stairs to the roof.

"You've got twenty," Zemeck shouted, adjusting her in his arms. "We're getting her back to Tinker as soon as our ride arrives. If we miss you, I'll come back."

"Kill that son of a bitch and cut his heart out so he can't come back!" Rachel said, turning and yelling for the women to follow her.

I stood watching them walk away and let the tears flow down my face until they dried up and turned to a ball of white-hot rage seething in my chest. Roach. I'd let too many opportunities to kill him pass me by. Not again. Time to end this.

47

I looked around the area, noticing for the first time that Dog had stayed with me. He sat next to my right leg, alert and patient, waiting to see what we were going to do next. We had to find Roach, but it was a big building and he could be almost anywhere in it by now. Well, that wasn't exactly true. He hadn't run past me into the kitchen areas. There was also access to the administrative offices just past the kitchen and I was confident he hadn't gone there either.

Where would I run if I were him? I looked around the large open space then remembered the sketch I'd been carrying with me. Pulling it out I stared at it for close to a minute. If I eliminated the service areas that I was currently standing next to as well as the VIP area where my group had gone...

Letting the paper fall to the floor I started running. The VIP area. That had to be how Roach had gotten in and it made sense he would head there in his attempt to escape. He had a head start and could be hiding in either the lounge or up on the roof. Zemeck's arms were full, carrying Katie, and Rachel was using both hands to keep pressure on her wound. That meant only Martinez had the freedom to fight and defend them from a surprise attack and she was rushing to get to the Pave Hawk's med-kit and might get caught unprepared.

Fear for my wife and friends leant wings to my feet as I charged across the length of the casino, Dog running beside me. I had covered perhaps fifty yards when I remembered the radio and began shouting into it as I ran, but Zemeck wasn't answering. I ran harder, rage supplanting the fear and coursing through my limbs. There would be no hesitation, no holding back. Roach would die the instant I had an opportunity.

It seemed to take forever but I'm pretty sure I broke my own speed records as I ran. Finally I could see the velvet ropes guarding the leather upholstered entrance to the VIP lounge. The door was closed, which didn't mean anything. There was most likely a pneumatic closer on it to ensure the privacy and comfort of the people who were granted access.

The ropes were hooked to portable stanchions and created a large buffer zone between the door and the main floor of the casino. Without slowing I vaulted over the barrier, Dog running underneath it, then pulled to a stop at the entrance to the lounge. I reached out to yank the door open but paused and forced myself to take two deep breaths to get my respiration and heart rate under control.

Rifle gripped in my right hand I raised it to the ready position as I turned the oversized knob with my left and slowly pushed the door open. I could immediately hear voices and Dog slipped through as soon as the opening was wide enough for him. I followed a second later, softly closing the door behind me.

There was a small vestibule, no more than a dozen feet across, then an archway on the right that opened into the lounge. Dog had moved to the corner and stopped, waiting for me. I joined him and listened a moment before peeking around the edge after recognizing Roach's voice.

He was ranting, the madness clear in his tone. Rachel was trying to talk him down. She was pleading with him to let them get to the roof but he was growing more agitated by the moment. Rifle ready I leaned my head out enough to see farther into the room. The first thing I saw was Martinez on the floor, blood soaking into the carpet underneath her. She had been shot and I couldn't tell if she was still alive or not.

Zemeck was standing, still cradling Katie in his arms, body turned to shield her from Roach. Rachel was facing him, both hands pressing on Katie's chest, her head turned to look at Roach as she begged for him to let them by. The other women we'd rescued were huddled together at the far edge of the room and Roach stood with his back to the door that led to the roof, facing my side of the room. He held a small Uzi at arm's length, aimed directly at Zemeck, Rachel and Katie. His finger was on the trigger.

The only way to take him was to step fully into the room so I could acquire my target and fire. Several problems with that. Friendlies were standing directly in my line of fire, which also meant they were in Roach's line of fire if he got a shot off when he saw me. He also already had his weapon up and aimed, his finger on the trigger. Something like five pounds of pressure was all that was needed for him to start firing. Could I do it?

Could I step out, target his head and put him down before he could fire? I didn't like the odds. I needed him to go down like someone had turned off a switch. That meant a shot to the brain stem at the back of the skull. That would be instant death with no possibility of a dying nerve impulse causing his finger to contract and fire the Uzi. I was confident I could take him out, but I wasn't comfortable enough that I could do it without getting my friends shot that I was willing to take the risk. That left one option.

"You want me. Not them." I said, stepping into the open with my hands at my side. I had already told Dog to stay back and he remained hidden around the corner.

"You!" Roach's eyes widened and he screamed, spittle flying from his lips. "You're the cause of all of this! Everything was fine until you showed up."

"That's right," I said, slowly moving forward. "It is my fault, and here I am. Let them go and we can settle this."

I had moved fully into the lounge and was now standing next to Zemeck. Roach glared at me, eyes wild as he swiveled the Uzi to point at my face. Slowly reaching out I put my hand on Matt's shoulder and pushed. He took a step to the side, opening a little space between us.

"You and me, Roach." I said, locking eyes with the madman. "They don't matter. Put the gun down and let's all walk away."

From the corner of my eye I could see Zemeck still edging away. I needed to keep Roach's attention on me so I slowly raised my hands and worked my rifle's sling over my head, gently placing the weapon on the floor opposite of where Matt stood. Roach's eyes followed my movements, which was exactly what I wanted.

Next I removed my vest, careful to lay it on the floor beside the rifle without blocking my access in case an opportunity arose for me to grab it. Finally, I carefully drew my pistol from its thigh holster, bending slightly to place it on top of the vest. Completely disarmed except for a couple of blades, I straightened, glad to note that Zemeck had opened up a few more feet while I was distracting Roach.

"Now I'm unarmed. I can't hurt you. Just walk away. No one will come after you. No one will be hunting you. I don't care. I just want to get my wife to a doctor."

I took a slow half step so that I was standing directly over the pistol. It was slightly above floor level, resting on my vest, and I knew I could get to it fast. When I'd pulled it out of the holster I'd clicked the safety off. There was already a round in the chamber and the hammer was cocked. All I had to do was drop, grab it, aim and pull the trigger. Sounds easy, and it is if there's not a psycho staring at you over the sights of a machine pistol.

Roach's eyes flicked down to my weapons, then back up to my face. He was sweating but seemed to be bringing himself under control. For a brief moment I actually thought he might turn and run, but he smiled a frightening smile.

"I've wanted to do this since the first time we met." He said and pulled the trigger.

I've always heard the expression 'my life flashed before my eyes', but had never experienced it until that moment. My mind sped up and a whole series of memories played out in a fraction of a second. Going quail hunting with my dad. My first beer. My first car accident. The death of every teammate I'd ever lost. The first time I ever saw Katie. Katie lying in our bed, smiling up at me.

Then the Uzi's hammer clicked, loud in the quiet room. I stood there waiting for the bullet that would be racing down the weapon's barrel, starting its spin as the rifling caused it to twist as it approached the muzzle. Then the flame from the burning gun powder that escaped just ahead of the projectile that would cross the thirty feet of open space in far less time than it would take me to blink. The impact of the round wouldn't hurt at first, pain coming later, or maybe not at all if it struck my head and tore through my brain.

But none of that happened. There was just the click when Roach pulled the trigger, then nothing. I stood there for a heartbeat, my mind at first not understanding why I was still alive. He was out of ammo, or the round in the chamber had failed to fire, or the weapon had malfunctioned. I processed all of these thoughts in an instant, then my body kicked in and I dove for the pistol.

Roach's reaction was faster than I expected as he dropped the Uzi, turned to slam through the door and run up the stairs to the roof. The door was already closing by the time I had the pistol up and even though I didn't have a clear target I put several rounds into the stairwell hoping for a lucky shot.

Running forward I blasted through the door in time to see Roach disappear through the opening onto the roof. Charging up after him I couldn't tell if there was any blood on the red carpet so I had no idea if he was wounded or not.

Not slowing at the top, I stumbled onto the roof and barely had time to register the attack coming from my right side before a vent pipe smashed into my right arm, knocking the pistol out of my grip to skid several feet away.

Roach lunged for the weapon, falling on it. I was on his back before he could pick it up, pinning his arms and rolling us away. He flailed and kicked as we rolled, his strength fueled by madness and panic and I was surprised when he was able to tear an arm free and reach for the pistol.

I still had one of his arms locked back and when he tried for the weapon I brought the heel of my free hand forward and snapped his elbow. The joint gave with a wet snap, Roach howling in pain a moment later. Not releasing the arm I dragged him twenty feet across the roof and rolled him over, intending to wrap him up and break his neck, but he slithered out of my arms and scrambled away from me.

Getting my feet under me I twisted and launched, driving my shoulder into his chest and up into his chin. He flopped back from the impact, but I had a grip on him now that he couldn't break, pinning his throat with my left hand. Swiveling, I went to a knee with my left shoulder in the middle of his back and my hand still locked around the front of his neck. He struggled, trying to break free, but I wasn't letting go.

Reaching up with my right hand I interlaced the fingers of both hands and jerked down with all the power in my arms and shoulders as I lifted up with my legs. I both felt and heard Roach's spine snap where it contacted my left shoulder, all movement from him immediately ceasing. Releasing him I pushed his body off of me where it flopped to the roof with a dull thud. Standing, I looked down and met his eyes.

They were no longer filled with madness, only fear and pain. Without a word I bent over and grabbed the front of his shirt, lifting his upper body off the roof as I dragged him to the edge. Looking over I could see the large group of infected Zemeck told me had arrived. Dozens of females looked up, several of them screaming when they saw me.

Wrapping my hands in the front of Roach's shirt I lifted him onto his useless legs, supporting his weight with his face inches from mine.

"God, please. No." He said, unable to turn his head to see the infected, but able to clearly hear them.

"God's not here. Only me." I said, shoving him out over the edge and releasing his shirt.

Roach started to cartwheel as he fell, screaming all the way down where he landed on the infected waiting with raised arms. His screams seemed to go on a long time as they tore into him with tooth and nail.

48

Commander McFadden stood in the missile spaces of the Alaska, looking at the boat's complement of Trident missiles. The team was working on the final missile, and once they were done he would order the submarine to launch depth. He wasn't as confident as Admiral Packard that this would work. When he'd pressed the issue and demanded to know exactly how they were bypassing the built in safeguards he wasn't happy with the answer.

They weren't using the logic built into the warheads, they were installing newly written code that would supposedly fire the nuclear trigger at a predetermined time after launch. Basically the engineer had written a virus that *could* cause a detonation. His navigator and XO had stared aghast at this bit of information, voicing their concerns before locking themselves away and calculating the time to use for each missile.

They had completed their work before the engineering team had finished loading the code into all the warheads; having two other officers double-check their calculations. They'd been accurate on their first attempt and now stood watching as the time to detonation was programmed into the last Trident.

"We're ready, skipper." The weapons officer said after double-checking the entry against a copy of the calculations.

"Very good," McFadden said, turning and picking up the handset of a sound powered phone that connected directly to the control room, telling the duty officer to ascend to launch depth.

Moments later the deck tilted slightly as the boat began to rise in the ocean, McFadden and his XO heading for the control room. Once there the CO listened briefly as reports flooded in. Nothing was on sonar. Nothing within detection range of the Alaska's sophisticated electronic suite of listening gear.

"Boat's at launch depth, Captain. Sonar is still clear. Ready to open doors on your order." The XO said a few minutes later.

"Open missile doors," McFadden said without hesitation.

"Open missile doors, aye, sir." The XO repeated the order back, then turned and passed it on to a Petty Officer seated at a panel that controlled the Alaska's missiles.

"Doors are open, Captain. We're green across the board." The XO reported a few moments later.

"Very good, XO. Commence firing." McFadden ordered.

The order was repeated and a few moments later the first Trident missile was forcefully ejected from its tube out of the top of the Alaska's hull by a powerful gas generator. When the missile broke the surface of the water its rocket motor fired and at the nose an aerodynamic spike was deployed to reduce atmospheric drag. Roaring skyward, the missile continued to gain speed and altitude as it headed for a spot over the central United States. If the Alaska's calculations had been correct it would detonate just above the Earth's atmosphere.

"Torpedos!" The shouted alarm came from the Alaska's young sonar operator.

"Close missile doors! Flank speed, emergency dive current bearing!" McFadden barked.

The crew in the control room responded immediately, the big submarine vibrating as the propeller spun up to its max speed.

"Sonar, where are those fish?" The XO shouted as he checked on the angle of their descent.

There wasn't an answer and both he and the Captain rushed to the small room where the sonar operators worked. They stopped as one when they saw the waterfall display a sailor was staring at in horror. Four seconds later two Russian Shkval, rocket assisted torpedos detonated on either side of the Alaska.

Less than a second later the sub's pressure hull was crushed between the twin concussions, rupturing and letting cold seawater flood in. The officers and crew were all killed by the overpressure inside the steel cylinder before the Alaska began its descent to the bottom of the north Pacific. They had only gotten one missile away.

Five years earlier the SVR had co-opted an American software engineer who worked for the Navy contractor that provided sonar systems. After several payments totaling five million dollars to an offshore account, he had inserted a few lines of code into a scheduled software patch that made the Navy's sonar deaf to specific acoustic signatures. The Russian Akula class attack submarine that had been shadowing the Alaska for over a month, undetected, closed its torpedo tube doors and disappeared into the cold, dark depths.

49

After finishing with Roach I had turned to see Zemeck and Rachel standing on the roof watching me. Matt was still cradling Katie in his arms and I was glad to see she was awake. Rushing to them I was about to stop next to her when Rachel reminded me that Martinez was still in the lounge. Changing direction, I ran through the door and pounded down the steps.

Martinez was still lying where I'd last seen her, but she was awake. She didn't look good, but then I've never seen anyone that had been shot that did look good. I took a second to pull my vest on and sling my rifle as I bent over her.

"You forgot to duck," I said. She smiled a weak smile and told me to kiss her ass in Spanish.

"You just hang in there and make it through this and I'll kiss your ass at noon in front of the flag pole." I said as I slipped my arms under her body.

She groaned in pain as I lifted her off the floor. I couldn't tell where she'd been shot, but there was a lot of blood that began soaking into my clothing as soon as I pulled her to me. Carrying her up the stairs I rushed over to the Pave Hawk where Rachel was working on Katie. Zemeck had laid her inside the back of the aircraft and I placed Martinez down next to her.

"You've got some explaining to do, buddy." Katie said, grimacing as Rachel probed the wound in her chest. "Running around with two women that look like these two."

"Thought I'd start a harem." I said, holding her hand. "Got an opening if you're interested."

"I'll give it some thought and get back to you," she started to smile then caught her breath and closed her eyes when Rachel pressed an instrument deeper into the bullet hole.

While Rachel worked on first Katie then Martinez, the Osprey came into view. Zemeck was in radio contact with them and before they picked us up he directed them to where we'd left Stephanie and the kids. Once they were safely on board the Osprey swooped down over the roof for us.

The helipad was occupied with the disabled Pave Hawk and the Marine pilot didn't want to trust the casino roof with the weight of his aircraft so he did an extremely admirable job of holding the

Osprey in a stable hover less than a foot above the roof. He held it there long enough for us all to get loaded, raising the rear ramp and gaining altitude as soon as Dog, bringing up the rear, leapt aboard.

The two Marines Zemeck had originally brought with him, as well as the five soldiers they had gone to pick up, made room for us. They pulled seats loose and created plenty of floor space for Katie and Martinez to lie flat, then squeezed against the walls with the captive women we'd brought out of the casino. I settled down between the two women, holding each of their hands as Rachel worked.

Katie was stable for the moment, but Martinez was in worse shape. She'd taken two rounds, one in the leg and one in the abdomen. Rachel still wasn't sure how bad she was, but assured me that if Martinez had lasted this long the odds were good that we'd get her to the hospital at Tinker in time.

The Trident missile flew perfectly, following its preprogrammed trajectory, which was intended to place it 50 miles directly above the Kansas/Oklahoma border when the timer program added to the nuclear trigger reached zero.

Everything worked as intended, the warhead firing when the computer code sent the command.

Without the Earth's atmosphere a nuclear blast expands dramatically faster and farther. The fireball grew to immense size, clearly visible from everywhere in North America. Massive amounts of gamma rays shot out in all directions. Dozens of orbiting satellites were destroyed in that initial EMP or Electromagnetic Pulse by the rays that headed away from the Earth.

The gamma rays that didn't shoot into space came in contact with the atmosphere and collided with air molecules, depositing their energy in the form of huge quantities of ions and recoil electrons which were then aligned and accelerated by the Earth's magnetic field. As they traveled along the invisible magnetic highways they began to lose energy, but any electronic device within a 1,500 mile radius of the initial pulse was susceptible to damage. The closer to the source, the stronger the energy and the greater the damage.

There isn't much on a modern aircraft that isn't controlled by electronics. The military requires that all of its equipment is "hardened" against an EMP, but the feasibility of protecting every sensitive electronic circuit on an Osprey against a High Altitude EMP is poor. Even more so when the EMP source is massive and less than 200 miles away.

We were flying south and didn't see the fireball directly, but the dark landscape beneath us lit up at the same time the aircraft's engines shut down. There were panicked looks all around and Katie squeezed my hand, pulling me down to wrap her in my arms.

"We're going down!" The pilot shouted. "Brace for crash!"

Dirk Patton

ALSO BY DIRK PATTON

Unleashed: V Plague Book One

Crucifixion: V Plague Book Two

Rolling Thunder: V Plague Book Three

Red Hammer: V Plague Book Four

Transmission: V Plague Book Five

Indestructible: V Plague Book Seven

Rules Of Engagement: A John Chase Short Story

Afterword

Wow, Book 6 already. Seems like just yesterday that I was working on the first V Plague, which by the way was mostly written in hotels and airport waiting areas. It's been an incredible year, and I'm looking forward to seeing what the future holds for my little band of survivors.

As always, a sincere thank you to everyone who has taken the time to email me or leave a post or message on Facebook. I love hearing from you, and appreciate the wonderful comments as well as the constructive criticism. I really do take it all in and it has affected both the story line and my writing style.

To Katie, thank you for your unwavering faith and support, as well as your input. For those of you who follow me on Facebook, you know where the idea for the casino came from. For those who don't...

A few months ago I was up early and sitting on the patio with Dog, enjoying my first coffee of the day. Katie walked outside and immediately called me an asshole.

"What?" I asked, putting on my best innocent look.

"I had a nightmare that I was trapped in a casino, being attacked by survivors and infected, and it's all your fault." She answered, and that's when I knew there was an abandoned casino scene coming.

So… Roach is gone. Finally. It was time, and oh so satisfying to write his demise. Yes, I couldn't resist a little poetic justice for the asshole, but in a strange way I'll miss him. I had thought about maybe doing something with him where he has a change of heart and saves the day. Kind of like the Grinch or Gollum, but in the end decided it was more fun to send him out with his ass in a sling (yes – pun intended).

Also, you can always correspond with me via email at voodooplague@gmail.com and on the internet at www.voodooplague.com and if you're on Facebook, please like my page at www.facebook.com/FearThePlague

I enjoy interacting with my fans on Facebook and I answer all of my email… eventually.

Thanks again for reading!

Days Of Perdition

Dirk Patton

January 2015

DATE DUE

BRODART, CO.   Cat. No. 23-221

Made in the USA
Lexington, KY
21 April 2016

51384023R00257